THE VIRGIN SPY

KRISTA BRIDGE

stories

THE
VIRGIN
spy

Douglas & McIntyre
Vancouver/Toronto

Douglas & McIntyre Ltd.
2323 Quebec Street, Suite 201
Vancouver, British Columbia
Canada v5T 4S7
www.douglas-mcintyre.com

Library and Archives Canada Cataloguing in Publication
Bridge, Krista, 1975–
The virgin spy : stories / Krista Bridge.

ISBN-13: 978-1-55365-162-8 · ISBN-10: 1-55365-162-6
I. Title.
PS8603.R53V57 2006   C813'.6   C2005-907419-1

Editing by Jennifer Glossop
Cover and text design by Jessica Sullivan
Cover photograph by © Images.com/CORBIS
Printed and bound in Canada by Friesens
Printed on acid-free paper that is forest friendly (100% post-consumer
recycled paper) and has been processed chlorine free

Credit for lyrics quoted in "What You Said You Wanted":
From "Black Dog" by John Paul Jones, Jimmy Page and Robert Plant on
Led Zeppelin IV by Led Zeppelin (Atlantic, 1971, SuperHype Music Inc. ASCAP)

We gratefully acknowledge the financial support of the Canada
Council for the Arts, the British Columbia Arts Council, and the Government
of Canada through the Book Publishing Industry Development
Program (BPIDP) for our publishing activities.

Versions of some stories have been published in the following periodicals
and anthologies: "Crusade": *Toronto Life*; "A Matter of Firsts": *Descant*,
Journey Prize Stories, and *05: Best Canadian Stories*; "Cockney Sunday": *Prairie Fire*;
"Retention with Afterflow": *PRISM international*.

For my mother

contents

stories

THE *virgin*
SPY

As a girl, I was a spy. The virgin spy, my brother called me. To me, a window was something begging to be looked through, from the outside in. Where I lived with my mother and my brother, Jamie, all the houses were wide, flat bungalows, and I prowled their perimeters, through the prickly hedges and small, fussy gardens, the well-swept stone paths, through the deadlock of lawns and low rusting fences and those minor, hopeful flares of personality (the stone dog by a front door here, the red door there), looking for secrets. A secret, to me, was just about anything one chose to do in private. Although I lacked specific malice, I was unrelenting, as well as malignantly curious, and when I came upon something, I was absolutely euphoric; these qualities, combined, made me dangerous.

Early in summer, I had stood on my toes and watched as my friend Trudy spoke intimately to our last year's class picture while sitting cross-legged on the edge of her bed. She cradled the photograph in her hands and spoke lovingly, at times emphatically, to it, then delicately placed it on her night table and spent the following twenty minutes writing into what I presumed was a diary. I had seen the mouthy private-school boy from across the street argue with his mother over a bag of new clothes, then cry and hug a large stuffed dog when she slammed the door and left. I witnessed a younger girl treating the curtain rod in her bathroom like the monkey bars in the playground, while she was naked and the bath was running. Another girl I caught twirling in front of the mirror in a long red velvet dress, a fraying, oversized dress of her mother's or grandmother's. Other girls I had seen simply trying on lipsticks, boys putting gel in their hair. It was exhilarating and appalling how much people did in their bedrooms, and with the curtains wide open.

What was wrong, really, with playing dress-up in front of the mirror, or putting on lipstick? I was twelve, and the people I spied on were not much younger or much older. Weren't these the things we were supposed to be doing? I had done these things myself, countless times. I had done things far less suitable for my age. No doubt, that was part of it. My closet was full of old dolls, which I pretended to have discarded, and I played with them on the far side of my bed with a book nearby, so that if someone came into my room, I could shove them quickly away and pick up my reading. My own keen sense of guilt made me ruthless—and undiscriminating. Whatever I saw, I meant to use.

The first-floor windows of several houses were too high for me to see into on my own. Sometimes, I persuaded my brother, Jamie, who was two years older than me, to come along on my hunts. On these days, I headed straight for the high windows. Jamie had a greater sense of politeness than I had, but his politeness also made him accommodating, and although I was burdened by his reservations, I could get a better view with him there. Hoisted up on his shoulders, I could see through the windows that otherwise eluded me.

"I think I hear something," I would say to him. "Crying or yelling. Get me up there."

More often, we didn't hear anything from outside, and the still face of a window made me only more certain that behind it was taking place something so glittering and obscene that the good of the entire neighbourhood was at stake. I stood facing that window, temptingly close and still impossibly out of reach, my stomach in somersaults and a nagging tickle spreading downwards and inwards, as a girl might stand in an alleyway facing a flasher who is taking far too long to whip open his trench coat.

On days when Jamie refused to lift me onto his shoulders, I tried to get leverage on a jutting brick and climb up to the window myself. And he did sometimes refuse. (Why had he come along? I would ask accusingly. Simply to torture me?) Eventually, though, my struggles to get up the brick wall would become undignified enough that he relented. This would be the last summer I thought of Jamie as someone unskilled at sticking with refusals.

The secrets I gathered while spying didn't stay secrets for long. I would gather the neighbourhood children on our lawn for an impromptu assembly. There, I would expose Trudy's conversation with the class picture, Kelly's gymnastics on the curtain rod, Ben's sampling of hair products. My skill was in making any act committed in privacy seem the dark secret of one's soul, the shameful exploits of a twisted mind. I was shrill and lordly, parading back and forth on our front porch, filled with delight so deep and strenuous that it couldn't even manifest itself as glee. Like many guilty people, I was puritanical. While I trotted out secrets from my perch, Jamie stood by looking embarrassed, but also guarded and alert, like my bodyguard. But never was I faulted for spying in the first place, too reduced were my victims, too certain that I had indeed identified something vile in them. Nor did it ever occur to my friends (none of whom stopped speaking to me) to shut their curtains when they played.

I was always one to be on the inside of injustice.

Jamie called me a peeping Tom, but the name failed to capture the seriousness of my curiosity, the extent to which I was driven and exultant. I didn't become the Virgin Spy until August, when spying started to be about something else. When it started to be about sex.

Next door to us lived an older girl named Celia. On the few occasions when our mother went out, Celia babysat for Jamie and me. Even on a Saturday night, she would sit at our kitchen table doing homework while we watched the TVOntario movies hosted by Elwy Yost, and sometimes, long after we were in bed, but still awake, her boyfriend, Graham, would arrive with snacks, and they would sit in our living room reading aloud to each other from children's books like *The Hobbit* and *The Lion, the Witch, and the Wardrobe.* Jamie and I called her the librarian because she wore owl glasses with frames that reached halfway down her cheeks, spoke just decibels above a whisper, and had dull flat hair whose mousy hue served only to further blanch her pale face.

For three years, Celia and Graham, a white-blond, rickety-legged, soft-spoken display of androgyny, presented an assault of blandness on our street. Never did they kiss or hug or make a public fuss over each other, which at that point in my life I understood to be the principal point of dating. Even when I eavesdropped as they read to each other in the living room, there were no sounds to indicate that anything other than reading was happening—no break in the rhythm of words, no sly laughter. The only sign of their romantic involvement was chronic hand-holding. As they walked here and there, holding hands, their faces and bodies seemed to have no association with what was going on at the end of their arms. It was a utilitarian grip, as if they were brother and sister ordered by their parents to stick together while crossing the street. But he never let go. He would raise his hand to point out birds in the sky, a child who had fallen across the street, a flowering bush in someone's garden, a spot on his own shirt, and with his hand went hers, never dropped. The closest they ever came to a full-bodied amorous show was sitting on a park bench, reading, hands held and knees touching.

One night Jamie and I were on our way back from a friend's house, cutting through backyards, when we heard noises coming from the shed behind Celia's. The noises were not immediately suggestive of sex. They lacked the painful edge I expected, the warring notes of terror and rhapsody, and that solitary pierce like nails drawn down a chalkboard. It sounded more like last breaths were being taken, and for years after that I thought that to engage in sex would be to teeter on the edge of a heart attack, that a carnal invasion would be enough to finish you off if you were not strong. But I knew what the sounds were. We crept over and looked in the cloudy window of the shed. I caught a flash of bare male bottom, even though they had covered themselves with an old afghan. At one point, they changed positions and I saw Graham's face, the serious, almost angry, expression on it. During the act itself, he didn't look as if he felt any affection for her, although when it was over, they lay side by side and he kissed her hands and nuzzled his face into her neck and they laughed. I had never seen anything resembling sex itself on television or in life, but still there was nothing in any of the motions that surprised me. What did get me was what looked like the sheer work of it. The brute, panting physicality. The librarian and her boyfriend were transformed by it, flushed and glistening and disoriented. But it didn't look like a pastime.

Jamie and I walked home in silence. Desire wasn't something you could have a friendly laugh about. From then on, we regarded the librarian with a new repulsion and respect. And I looked for sex when I went out to spy. Jamie sometimes came too. It was around this time that he began to call me the Virgin Spy. I liked the name and thought it sounded dignified and mysterious; it wrapped me up in a way that made sense. Years later, when I was leaving home to go to university, I decided that there had been mocking in it, as if Jamie had been somehow alluding to my lack of desirability, which was so great that I needed to spy on others, but by then I was in the process of re-evaluating everything about Jamie, everything about our childhood together, by then I was sorting through the muddled patchwork of my life with considerable paranoia.

After several weeks of creeping together, quietly, around the streets as late as we were allowed, Jamie was invaded by misgivings about me and came to my bedroom one night after I had gone to bed and made me promise not to tell anyone about the librarian, about looking for sex. I did have a big mouth, I was known for it, so it wasn't surprising that he was worried. But my brother was the one person whose secrets I did keep. My other friends would extract from me a promise on my life or the life of my mother, but Jamie did not press me for a contract. He was the kind of person who began with trust.

In the end, a contract wouldn't have changed what happened anyway. The librarian would make her way so placidly around the neighbourhood reading books on benches, eating carrots with her boyfriend, and her composure provoked me. I ended up telling my friend Trudy about what we had seen and about what I was looking for. Eventually a boy named Dean instigated an official spying mission. A group of eight or nine boys and girls began to meet at dusk in our backyard and from there we made the rounds of houses where the neighbourhood teenagers lived. Sex hunts. When it came out that I had told, Jamie didn't accuse me of betrayal, or even treat me coolly, and I was relieved to find out that he must not have been angry.

All I thought of at the time was that my revealing of our sex-spying was its own punishment. When Jamie and I had watched Celia and Graham alone, I had felt something quiet, a caving-in of my stomach. I sensed that there was something more authentic about the experience of watching something happen than there was in being involved. Something truer and grittier about standing on the outside, seeing the whole from a remove. And when I eventually had sex as a teenager, I realized this was true. You couldn't see the cavorting indignity of sex, the gymnastics of it, when you were the one doing it. When the neighbour kids joined us, we lost something. They giggled and poked each other. Their voyeurism wasn't reverent, like mine. They just wanted to be daring. And, in the end, we saw very little. Two or three older brothers and sisters gearing up for the start or lying in each other's arms in what could have been the aftermath. Nothing like what Jamie and I had seen in the shed that night. The twists and turns, the flourishes, the grizzly affection. Eventually, the group dissolved, and I left off spying.

Marginal activities lose their edge when they become public and official.

THAT FALL WHEN JAMIE and I got home after school, our mother would often be in our living room with her group, seven or eight middle-aged women from our neighbourhood who had bonded through their common desire to renounce men and enjoy middle age as the time of their lives. Our mother had become their unofficial leader, though she was not middle-aged and preferred to stay young-looking. She was, however, the one woman who had no husband and she possessed the calm demeanour of someone not burdened by sex drive. The women met once, sometimes twice a week, usually at our house because there they would not be interrupted by prying husbands (although they had renounced men to some degree, they planned on continuing to be married). They applauded our mother's long-term singleness, something that always struck me as odd, considering that our mother's state was neither chosen nor desired.

Our father had died when I was four, Jamie six. It was a car accident, big enough to be in the papers: on his way home from work late one night in heavy rain, my father's car skidded through the guardrail on the Gardiner Expressway and dropped thirty feet to Fort York Boulevard, where it landed on its roof. Our mother had told us about the accident with composure, scientifically, as if she were telling an item of interest about someone else's life. She believed that withholding unpleasant facts was false protection, a failure to arm your children with the journalistic objectivity necessary to navigate the world. Several weeks passed before Jamie and I were able to connect the event with its consequences. We were used to hearing stories of loss. My mother liked to talk about disaster; it put a look of bleak contentment on her face. She pointed out the houses of people who had come down with cancer or experienced financial distress. There was no malice in her voice, simply the recognition that such information was relevant to our lives, that we could not know our own place without understanding the position of others.

Our mother, I felt, was not the least bit pleased to have been relieved of her husband, but when she was around the women, she spoke contemptuously of the time when she had been enamoured of our father—her contempt was not for the man himself, but for herself, the weak-willed, lustful girl she had been. Sex and grief were part of the same weakness. She was determined to be unaffected by either.

Although the group's mandate was to extol the pleasures of aging and co-author a book about how to age gracefully, mostly all the women talked about were creams and home remedies and muscle exercises that would reverse the aging process. They installed an inspection station in the centre of our living room, and at every meeting, my mother would ceremoniously close the curtains while another woman turned off the lamps and flooded the room with the brightness of the unforgiving overhead light. Standing with their faces craned to the area where the light fell most harshly, they asked each other to judge whether their facial lines had deepened. "Break it to me gently," they said, or "Tell me the damage," their eyes closed. My mother brought down our bathroom scale and they stood in a line, stepping gingerly onto the scale one by one and recording their weights on a chalkboard mounted on the wall.

"I'm not sure *they* should be listening," a woman named Agatha said once, pointing to Jamie and me. We usually loitered around the edges of the living room eating the baked treats the women had brought, or we sat on the steps that led to the bedrooms, passing a bag of chips back and forth.

Linda, one of the women, had just started talking about her husband. I vaguely caught the word *position* and I made my way over to her side of the living room, but my mother, at Agatha's prodding, told us to go away. We went and sat on the steps in the darkness of the hallway, where our mother was able to tell herself we were out of sight, and therefore outside her jurisdiction. Linda often had tales of woe about her marriage, and this time, with some overeager encouragement from the women, she got to what was really bothering her. Her husband, Larry, made her engage in wild, distressing sex. Sex full of rabid need and reassurance. He insisted they engage in question and answer during the act itself. He would yell and she was expected to yell back.

Are these my tits?

Yes!

Is this your dick?

Yes!

Am I your baby?

Yes!

If she didn't yell loudly enough, Larry would repeat the question until he got the necessary zeal and volume. Linda was also worried that his interest in certain positions to the exclusion of all others indicated latent homosexuality. Inconsistently, she was also afraid that he was having an affair with another woman. She spoke of his possible lies with gusto, a strange mix of horror and hope. It seemed as though she believed, in spite of her professed agony, that her life would be terribly dreary without something to complain about. I had a sense that she eagerly anticipated her own betrayal.

(Jamie and I sang to each other, later, Are these my tits? Yes! Is this your dick? Yes! Am I your baby? Yes! Yes!)

Linda's concerns brought the women back around to a gleeful reiteration of their philosophy, that men should be renounced, if not in fact then at least in their hearts.

"Shelley came crawling back the other day," said Agatha, referring to a woman who had left the group. "She tells me she wants to help write the aging book. I said to her, 'Well, you're inactive now. It doesn't matter how much you contributed before, you're inactive now and our arms aren't necessarily open.' I told her that and I could tell she didn't like it one bit, but she knew I was right. She knows there have to be standards."

"I expect she wants to come back because she's bored now," my mother said. "Her husband left her after her tummy tuck, you know. Went off with another woman with big flaps of skin hanging from her arms."

"I wonder if there's a TV movie on tonight," said Karen, a woman whom our mother sometimes disliked. "I saw one last week about a young retarded boy who went into a normal high school and became class president."

"My friend's daughter had a baby just like that," Agatha offered. "She's only thirty, so how could she ever had been prepared? She's been on antidepressants for a year now. Imagine that. She has a whole life ahead with that child. I met one once and I could barely understand a word out of his mouth. I was truly mortified."

"She might enjoy her baby," my mother said. "People usually do, once they adjust."

"They were sent to institutions when I was a girl." This was Karen. "They were called Mongolian idiots. You could never get away with saying that now."

"Lord," said Agatha, "my friend's daughter has aged a good five years since having that baby. And now she and her husband aren't getting along and they're talking divorce. They've only been married for two years, but it's since the baby."

My mother stood up and rearranged the books on the coffee table.

"I expect that it's because of this woman's attitude more than the baby. She needs to get herself to a therapist and sort things out. Life will teach her that you can't plan everything." She made a noise here, a kind of punctuating snort that meant the conversation was finished.

When the meetings were ending, one of the women usually made a rousing speech about the wisdom and freedom that come with age. This person was usually Agatha, who once told me it was important for a woman to walk as if she was hearing applause.

"When I was a girl, I used to have a party for my girlfriends every Friday night. Saturday night was for the boys, even then." She rolled her eyes in pitying recollection of her youthful self.

"Back when we were around eight and ten, even eleven and twelve years old, we would have burping contests when ten or eleven o'clock rolled around and we were high on Coca-Cola and chocolate."

My mother, as well as several other women, looked down in embarrassment at the mention of flatulence, and Agatha revved herself up, encouraged.

"Well, we would have these burping contests. My brother Ted had a microphone and speaker set and I would set it up in a corner of the basement and we'd each get up there one by one and do our best to pull off a belch while someone held a microphone to our mouths. Cecile was the best. She could do it on cue, and did she ever have staying power. Of course, the parties changed as we got older and the burping was no longer the climax. Some of us wanted to smoke. And then others still wanted to burp, so I had to stand up on the couch and say, 'Listen, we can have it both ways.

Those who want to smoke, gather over by the door. Those who want to burp, gather by the couch.' And they appreciated that. We divided ourselves up pretty peacefully after that."

The women were quiet as they waited for the rousing part, which they knew was coming. Agatha specialized in stories of adolescent silliness giving way to the discernment of middle age.

"The point is, then boys started to crash our parties and you'd find people necking in the closet. Girls started fighting over a boy who wasn't much in the first place. We were all of us ruined. And it took us years to come back to the pure friendship with our fellow women that we'd once had. Some women are still out there and they haven't come back. They're getting up at five o'clock in the morning to make turkey and tomato sandwiches for His Highness's lunch. Ladies, I wouldn't go back to those days for all the tea in China. The intelligence I have now, the brains we share as a female unit, that is what our life journeys have been about. The power to be able to say, I'm fifty-two years old and I don't need anything but myself at the beginning and end of each day. A team of wild horses couldn't drag me back!"

Agatha shook her hips and hands and wrestled with the air as if a team of wild horses was in the process of trying to drag her back. The women hugged and departed in a tide of good will. And I went to my room, feeling discouraged. As I thought about how there was nothing preferable about becoming middle-aged and disdaining things like burping contests, clearly the delights of a much freer and more desirable time, I went through my mother's closet, pulled out her most glamorous old dresses, and slipped each one on slowly. It wasn't just my altered appearance in each dress that moved me. It was the foreign fabrics gliding over my shoulders, lapping at my wrists, not only the silks and rayons but also the scratchy wool that prickled me everywhere. I pinned my messy hair up in a pile on top of my head and dabbed on my mouth and cheeks the red lipsticks

my mother had accumulated but never used. Then I stood in front
of her cloudy old mirror and imagined myself older, but living in
a distant past, the early nineteen hundreds. The last thing I would
put on was an antique cameo that hung on a long, thin gold chain.
It was one of the few objects my mother regarded with reverence.
My father had given it to her; it had belonged to his grandmother.
The word *heirloom*, to me, was heavy with honour and admiration,
with a holiness both dreary and inspiring. The cameo was sacred
and unusable. I was allowed to try it on, but never did anyone, even
my mother, wear it out. Often, I tried to get my mother to wear it,
but she said it was too valuable to be worn outdoors on any but
the most special occasions. There was a sense of waiting about the
heirloom, as if we could only guard it so that people in the future
were able to enjoy its worth.

Like my continuing play with dolls, dressing up was not something I took lightly. I could not imagine outgrowing these games.
Although I was always pestering Jamie to play soccer or Frisbee
with me in the summer, to go tobogganing with me in the winter,
I was blocked, in his presence, from accessing the serious hopefulness, the private and thorough happiness, I felt when I was alone.

Once when I was standing there in a long, forest green silk
dress my mother had designed and sewn when she was just twenty,
the cameo resting in the imagined presence of breasts, Jamie
opened the door. In my house, we were usually respectful about
closed doors and I felt a surge of irritation at his interruption, followed by embarrassment about the state I was in. Then he bowed,
gallantly, theatrically, and came forward and took my hand. We
danced around the room and he dipped me far back, until my hair
brushed the ground.

Although we did play together, I had never thought that Jamie
would be someone who could enter into transformation with me. I
assumed that being a boy, and older, Jamie had no such endeavours,

no childish joys he clung to, nothing like an heirloom that could stir all his dreams so severely. His face was athletic and serious, and sometimes insolent, a quiet insolence you had to look closely to detect. But I felt reassured in that moment that there was some part of him that was like me, and that we were safer for it.

ONE COLD OCTOBER day after school, Jamie and I were out in the ravine behind our house collecting leaves for an arrangement our mother planned to make for Thanksgiving. I resented the chore and trudged around in silence. She wanted only red, orange, yellow leaves, intact, and she had given us brown wicker baskets in which to carry them. Although neither of us followed her instructions happily, Jamie snapped at me when I started complaining. (He was thirteen, but he was that way. He would wander the ravine with a basket to make our mother happy.)

I followed him, in part because I felt he was trying to get away from me. He kept touching his shirt pocket, and when I got closer, I saw a piece of paper folded inside it.

"What's that?" I asked.

"Nothing to you."

"I'm not asking what it is to me. I'm asking what it is to you," I said.

"It's just a list of things I need for the science fair project."

"So show it to me."

"I would, but you need to learn when something isn't your business," he said.

I supposed this was meant to sting me, but it didn't because Jamie said it so acidly that I knew the paper must contain supremely important information. I kicked his basket out of his hand, and while he was still registering what had happened, I snatched the paper.

It was not a list, but a note, which I had suspected. Curling over the page, in large flowery letters, were these words: "I know. Mrs.

Greyson is the worst. Algebra is going to be brutal! Don't you think she looks like a basset hound? Save me a seat in French if you're there first? Luv, Heidi."

"Who's Heidi," I asked, although I thought I knew just who Heidi was.

"Just a new girl," he said. "She needs my help with math. She lives on Birchmount."

This was what I had thought. Late that summer, a family had moved onto the street that curved into ours. Talk of the girl, Heidi, with the long blonde hair and black velvet headbands and the miniature schnauzer, had overtaken our neighbourhood all through August.

"She's not even pretty," I said, wishing I hadn't let that out. "Do you actually think she's pretty?"

"I guess she looks the way a girl is supposed to look," he answered, then took back his note and stuffed it messily into his back pocket, as if the note no longer mattered now that I had read it. He went back to collecting leaves.

I felt what would become a familiar feeling in future years: immediate dislike of a girl I had never spoken to.

Often, when Jamie and I were younger, we would play dead. I usually woke up early, but rather than getting up, I would lie in bed thinking. It gave me a sense of freedom and safety, as well something like premature nostalgia for my childhood life, a pleasing and gloomy sense of its brittleness, to think of my mother and Jamie sound asleep in their rooms. I also felt power over the whole street, to think that I alone was awake at six o'clock. So when Jamie came into my room on Saturday and Sunday mornings to wake me up, I was well prepared. I would pretend to be dead. After several weeks, this was no surprise to him; it was understood that I would be dead each morning. The key to the game was in his manipulation of my body, my attempts to maintain the appearance of death while he tried to expose that I was alive. He would creak open the door and tiptoe over to my bed, hope to startle me with a loud yell. This part was ordinary, and I prepared myself by thinking of the black spider that lived behind our laundry tub, or the taste of soggy cauliflower, anything unpleasant, so I could keep my composure. Then he would tickle me, twist my arms and legs up and around. I was allowed to hold no tension in my body. He would put a hand under my nose, and if he felt breath, he had won. But I could sense when his hand was approaching, and I was good at holding my breath, had done so in the YMCA swimming pool for as long as a minute. Then he shoved my entire body and I had to stay limp. The game usually ended with his win, when he jumped on me. He was careful never to come down too hard.

Jamie was collecting leaves with a meticulousness that bordered on parody. He picked up a leaf, held it up to the sun, inspecting, then put it in his basket if he deemed it satisfactory. I thought he was putting on a show, proving to me how far I was, and how far Heidi was, from his mind. I got an idea. Along a short, steep hill down in the ravine, there was a long flight of wooden steps that were in need of repair. Usually, we ran up and down the hill next to these stairs, but this time I raced down them and threw myself off the last step. As I fell, I screamed, and then I lay in the mound of leaves at the bottom of the stairs. My eyes were closed, and I heard loud rustling, pounding steps and Jamie shouting my name. His voice had never sounded so sharp and nervy, like a row of pins sticking straight up.

He ran down the hill, not saying a word, as if he already suspected I was unconscious or gravely wounded, incapable of speech. I went with this. He knelt beside me and touched my arm cautiously.

"Claire?" he said. "Wake up, Claire."

I could feel him hovering over me and it was difficult not to laugh.

"Oh," he said. "Oh, God."

I knew that his hand was on its way to my nose, so I held my breath. I loved the feeling of holding my breath. I often did so at night before I fell asleep to see if I could capture what the moment just before death might feel like.

"Wake up, Claire. Open your eyes. Claire."

He never used my name so much. I was about to sit up and tell him I was fine when he jumped up and ran back to the house. When he was out of sight, I got up and made my way home, gathering more leaves as I walked. I took my time. My plan was to walk into the kitchen as if nothing had happened, with an armful of leaves, which I would dump cheerfully on the kitchen table. I would go about my business without a word to Jamie, pour a glass of water, and take a long draught. I would say, in the British accent we often used with each other, "Fancy meeting you here."

Through the back screen door, however, I could heard hiccupping.

"Ta-da," I said, bursting into the kitchen and throwing the leaves up in the air. I spun around with my arms out as they fell to the ground and said, "All alive."

Jamie's face was blotchy. His chin was so red it looked as if someone had punched him. My mother was trying to calm him down. She was not in a panic. In spite of our father's accident, she was not overprotective. Indeed, she was quite permissive, as if letting us live freely were a testament to her strength. Believing that accidents were just that—accidental and uncommon—was a matter of pride with her. She was also not in a panic because she always suspected me of subterfuge. However, she did glare at me. Jamie didn't much look at me at all. After enduring my mother's lecture over dinner about how not knowing when to stop was about the most unlikable quality a person could have, I thought it was over.

Just a week later, I was dressing up in my mother's bedroom, and Jamie walked past the half-open door. I had adorned myself with my mother's pearl necklace, the cameo necklace, and strings and strings of gaudy plastic baubles, as well as clip-on rhinestone earrings. I was wearing my mother's flashiest dress, a gift she had never worn, a fiery red dress with a deep V-neck bordered with shimmery beads. I was also wearing my favourite of her high-heeled shoes, a black patent-leather pair she had deemed tasteless an hour after buying them.

"Care for a dance?" I said in a high, artificial voice as he passed.

He paused at the door and took me in. What I saw in his face was like nothing I had ever seen in anyone, even a friend or class-mate I'd had a nasty fight with. It was a look that shrivelled me, so that I no longer felt wild and unpredictable, beautiful. I saw that dressing up had not gilded me, bestowed a momentary glory. To him, at least, it degraded me.

"You're too old for that," he said, and walked away.

MY WORLD WAS FULL of women I was determined to be nothing like: my mother, who had told me once that she had lost all the sex-ual feeling in her body, as in an epidural; the group women, with their custard stomachs and their wide shelves of breast; a single mother whose children I babysat once a week, who came home from blind dates and flopped down on her sagging grey couch with a tall bag of rice cakes. She liked to give me advice. "Keep all the mementos given by lovers," she said. "You never know if you're going to have another." Her children were eight and four and she hadn't met a man worth a moment of her time since her husband left when her youngest child was six months old. Love letters, pictures, tacky presents like gold-plated necklaces with intertwined hearts, even notes scribbled in a rush and passed during class, all the evi-dence that someone, somewhere, had cared once. "Never throw it all out in a rage," she said. "There might not be a next time."

The idea I got from women was that once you got a taste of

men, you were likely never to be the same, as content and self-willed, captivating, captivated. Whereas before you might have been curious about oil painting, or the lives of the Romantic poets, once you had a man you would never again be interested in anything other than having a man. Your life would be unspeakably changed, as with a drug addiction. It would be less opulent and satisfying, bereft of wonder, but you would think it improved, you would think yourself grateful to be saved. I decided that when I eventually had my first boyfriend, I would never let him get away. Alternately, and improbably, considering my fascination with sex, I planned to engage in a life of antiquated spinsterhood. Not for me the independent women who simply never chose to marry, but the glorious spinsters of the early nineteen hundreds, austere and disapproving, sexless rather than sex-deprived, eyes dancing with teacherly criticism and self-satisfaction.

I often recalled the vision of my recently widowed mother. With her large, wide-set eyes, her simple clothes and pale pink lipstick, she looked almost like our much older sister. Shock and melancholy did not age her. Rather, there was a pale light in her face, a sadness that was unexpectedly sultry. For her children, she had to believe that life was not ruined. Solitude made her dreamy looking, as if she had recaptured something of her youth now that she had to go on pure hopefulness as she re-envisioned her life. In the week that followed our father's death, our dining room table was covered in varieties of desserts I'd never heard of. Black Forest cake, strawberry shortcake, chocolate raspberry truffles, fluffy white meringues with blueberries nested inside. Our house was always full of visitors, and Jamie and I would take a lemon meringue pie out to the backyard and sit under the old maple tree and eat the whole thing, passing the fork back and forth. Our mother told us that our father had not gone through pain, that car accidents could be rapid and strong and erase life instantly. This seemed almost magical to me, that our father could be alive one minute and dead the next. It seemed like a trick: the ultimate, coveted transformation.

In secret, I was proud that we were the victims of disaster. Misfortune seemed glamorous in some enviable way; those marked by adversity seemed superior. A year or two after my father's death, I began to wish that calamity would occur again. I imagined my mother's young beauty, alternately burning and docile, vehement and wispy, how it would simmer and explode if I were done away with. I dreamed of falling into a nameless country river and being swept away before crowds of people, standing aghast on an unknown bridge. I imagined slipping on a patch of slush and falling down the stairs at school. The renown I would receive, the nostalgic accolades, the write-ups.

My mother told me only one story about the early days of her marriage, when Jamie was a baby, but this story she told again and again.

"It was July," she would say, "and the heat was so bad that people were dying. I've forgotten now what that heat felt like, the way you forget things like that, but I know your dad and I couldn't bear to touch each other. We were driving from a holiday with your dad's parents in the Laurentians back to Toronto. It hadn't been a fun trip, and we were trying to get back as quickly as we could. So there we were, driving through a small town near Montreal at two o'clock in the morning. Our car had no air conditioning so we drove at night to keep as cool as possible. Jamie was in the back seat crying and your dad and I had sweat trickling down our necks. It was a cheap car, and our legs stuck to those vinyl seats. Your dad turned to me and said, 'I'd like to go swimming. Let's go find a house with a pool.' And I said yes, just like that. I didn't think twice about it. Your dad drove us into a quiet neighbourhood with lots of trees and we got out of our car to walk around. We had to climb over a fence to get to the pool. Your dad carried Jamie—he was about six months old—and I had to climb over the fence while your dad held him. Then he passed him to me and climbed over himself. We set Jamie on a patch of grass by the side of the pool and took off all our clothes and dove in. It was like we forgot we were in someone else's backyard, we were making so much noise, your dad was diving and splashing and dunking me under and such. At one point, I decided to get out, and your dad snuck up behind me and threw me back in. Jamie started laughing. It was a full moon that night, and up through the water I could see Jamie jerking his arms and laughing."

These were the essentials of the story, the only important parts in her mind: the driving around, the swimming, the laughing. I wanted more. Listening to the story made me feel displaced from my life—because the experience was happy and seminal to my mother's life, but I did not figure in it—but it also made me nosy and interested. My mother referred to my father as my dad, but I couldn't connect to this title. He had died when I was so young that his death had not left a present absence. Hearing him called my dad made me greedy. I wanted to know how cold the water had been, what they had done after. Was it uncomfortable sitting in the car half-wet? Why had they gone in naked instead of in their underwear?

"What town were you in? Was it pretty?"

"I don't remember."

"What if they had come out, the family who lived in the house?"

"It was unlikely; it was very late."

"But you were naked. What would you have done if they had come out?"

"I never thought it would happen."

"But what if?"

I wanted her to address the danger, the possibility of exposure, calls made to the police. I wanted her to show some understanding of risk and damage. I got none of this. Jamie would cut me off.

"Let her alone. She's told you enough already. Move on."

He was protective of our mother. Even when he was six, just after our father died, he watched over her. In the morning before school, he would climb up on the high stool and get the cereal box, then pour each of us a bowl. He even put our bowls in the sink when we were finished. When he told me to move on, I could see that he had fit me into a certain category; I was a person who sucks the life energy of others. I always wanted more than they gave, both of them. I felt this made me inferior to them in a way I couldn't identify and had no power to correct. I would swear to myself that I would say no the next time Jamie asked if I wanted to play. I pledged to indicate no preferences, to seem awash in indifference. I couldn't do it, though. I was always the one asking.

A change came the summer of my spying, when I was twelve. I heard my mother telling the pool story to the group one evening, and I never wanted to hear it again. I swore I would never be like them. I would never have a man who was the single happiness, or the single despair, of my life. I would never sit on the couch with rice cakes, trying to keep my weight down so someone might want me. I would never have one story I would milk for years, for all it was worth.

Of course, I was worse, far worse.

ONE AFTERNOON WHEN I came home from school, I thought the house was empty—it had that dim, uninhabited feel about it—but then I heard voices in Jamie's room. Our mother was at her job; three days a week she worked at the Clarke Institute leading meetings for young people with eating disorders, something she'd been doing for two years because the insurance money from our father's death was running low and because she believed that it was more important for children to learn independence than always to feel secure. The kitchen was in disarray, which wasn't usual. The women's group had met at our house the day before, and our mother had gone to bed early with a cold, so only half the dishes had been washed. For that same reason, she hadn't tidied up before work. It was Jamie's job, usually, to clean up our breakfast dishes when he got home from school. Although my mother wanted to cultivate competence in both her children, efficiency prevailed in this matter because Jamie would wash the dishes regularly and thoroughly whereas I would forget the task entirely half the time and the other half would leave bits of food encrusted between fork prongs or on the underside of a seemingly shiny plate.

There were also, I noticed, two knapsacks lying by the back door, Jamie's black one and a purple one covered in decorative buttons.

Standing in front of the open refrigerator, I ate the rest of a plate of brownies left over from the women's group. I could hear myself chewing, and I was irritated by it. The faint noises of laughter and music on the other side of the house made the silence in the kitchen that much more unsettling. I was sure I heard malice in the laughter. Then I knew better. What I was hearing was not that mirthless laughter of exclusion, the ill will in showy, confidential delight. They were not intentionally battering me with their fun. No, what I heard as malice was simply privacy. I was being assaulted by their seclusion, and by my own.

The week before, Jamie had stopped walking home with me. We used to meet at the edge of the playground, by the long rusty rack of bicycles, and make our way home by the longest route—by the house with the small, expressive gnomes milling around the front lawn, the house with the three dogs, two Dobermans and one miniature poodle, by the corner store where we would buy strings of licorice, red for him, black for me. I usually saw his long thin neck, his profusion of sandy hair, those shoulders slightly rounded under his heavy knapsack as soon as I stepped foot outside, but one afternoon he was not there, and he was never there again. "You don't wait anymore," I finally said to him in the kitchen one afternoon. I'd just got home, but already he was almost finished washing the breakfast dishes.

"It doesn't work," he answered. "I get sick of hanging around."

I tried to start many fights, but he wouldn't fight with me. I tipped his childhood Winnie the Pooh bowl, quite deliberately, off the counter. But he pretended to think it was an accident and called me a klutz. It was my mother who spent an hour trying to glue it back together. The summer, with its spying, seemed far away.

For a time, I sat at the kitchen table doing my homework. But I felt restless and unable to concentrate, and trapped. Also, I felt I was being too respectful of their privacy. I wanted them to be as restricted by my presence as I was by theirs. So I got up and started doing the dishes, loudly. Every now and then, my arms dripping soapy water onto the floor, I would stop and go stand in the doorway of the kitchen, listening for a change in the voices, a rise or lowering, some acknowledgement that they knew they were no longer alone. I got nothing. Finally, I slapped the dishrag down on the table and crossed the living room and dining room to the hallway that led to our bedrooms. The voices were now coming from my mother's bedroom, so I tiptoed down the hall and decided that, if caught, I would pretend I was on my way to the bathroom. Her bedroom door was wide open and inside were Jamie and Heidi. At first I couldn't tell what they were doing. What I fixed on was her long blonde hair, straight like threads of silk. The way a girl should look, Jamie had said. My own hair was coarse, plain brown and uneven, curly in places, straight in others. Along the side near my ear was a single, out-of-place ringlet. She was tall, with long skinny legs and bony knees, decidedly unathletic. My legs were short and stocky—capable, shamefully capable. I had beat the boys at races (ashamed of winning, unable to lose falsely). There was no part of this girl, Heidi, that could be laughed at. Even her clothes, a second-hand green private school blazer over a frilly cream blouse and a short denim skirt, an outfit that on anyone else would have been foolish, overreaching and therefore pathetic, made her worldly and confident, impossibly sexy.

Jamie was standing behind her with his hands on her shoulders, and the radio was on a low volume, those murmuring, voluptuous voices. Then I saw. Jamie was fastening something around her neck. She was wearing the cameo.

He was looking at her proudly, as if one day it would be hers.

I DID SOMETHING vulgar after that. I didn't plan it, but poor taste came naturally to me.

The women's group was over several evenings later to celebrate Agatha's birthday, and because Agatha had gained seven pounds, the assembled treats were bowls of Jell-O and a plate full of celery sticks and apple quarters. Jamie was at a basketball tryout. He and Heidi didn't know that I had seen them in my mother's room, and I didn't know what to do with what I had seen. I had accepted my feeling of violation quietly, and for once I didn't feel like embarrassing them publicly. I was also unsure how to make their actions, in looking at the cameo, seem more guilty than mine, in spying.

After wandering around my bedroom for some time, I went into my mother's room and put on the cameo necklace. I tucked it inside the thick cable-knit sweater I was wearing, wrapped a soft blue scarf around my neck, and headed out into the unseasonably cold late October evening. The necklace, initially cool, warmed against my skin, and I was aware, every moment, of it resting against my chest.

To school and back, I walked, keeping to the long route Jamie and I took when we were delaying getting home. At school, all the lights were on, and when I walked past the gym, I could hear the shouts and cheering of the tryout. I considered waiting for Jamie, but I knew he wouldn't be happy to see me. When I got back to our house, I stood on the sidewalk looking in the wide picture window. Agatha was standing in the middle of our living room with a carrot stick in one hand, and it looked as if she was stepping onto the scale; a moment later, she threw her hand against her forehead and gaped in the direction of the floor. I didn't want to go inside.

As I wandered around the streets, my hands grew rigid with cold and I pulled my sweater sleeves down over them. When I passed Heidi's house, my foot stepped straightaway onto the lawn, catching that old impulse before my mind got there. The house, which was smaller than ours and made of fresh grey stucco, was well lit, though the wooden shutters in what I assumed was the living room were closed. I circled the house and on the far right side located what seemed to be the bedrooms. At each window, I stood on my toes and craned up my neck (the windows were just high enough to make comfortable spying impossible). Two of the bedrooms were empty, though the lights were on—showing, I thought, an irresponsible, and indeed unintelligent, disregard for the cost of hydro. I felt briefly gratified to have discovered a weakness in her family, although it occurred to me a minute later that such a weakness was a luxury, indicating her family's greater wealth. I found Heidi in the last bedroom, which was painted pale blue and had a big brass bed, crisp white linens, and a number of small lamps with colourfully beaded shades. She was sitting at a small mahogany desk doing her homework. She looked far more absorbed than I ever looked when I was doing my homework. I watched her for several minutes, but nothing changed, so I left.

I sat on the cold concrete of the curb, on the corner of her street and ours, and thought about what to do next. When I remember this night, I often linger in this moment before anything happened. I linger here to search for some intention on my part, anything that allows me to feel that what I did was, at least in some fraction of my mind, what I meant to do. Even the most skewed logic would satisfy me—anything but the blankness, the almost complete absence of memory that attends my recollection of these moments. But I can't recall even the most stumbling, intoxicated progression towards a desired outcome. The workings of my mind in these brief moments are closed to me, just as, minutes before I did what I did, I looked at my chilled hands, and in the gradual numbing that was overtaking them, felt as unconnected to them as if they belonged to someone else.

I loosened my scarf and unhooked the cameo. I draped it over my hand and looked at it there in my palm. As I was doing this, Celia and Graham walked past, hand in hand. When they were out of sight, I held the cameo over the sewer grate and let it drop, slowly, from the end of the chain. Then I let the chain slither along after it. After determining that the necklace was gone, that not even a glint of gold flashed up at me, I got up and looked to the sky. My mother had told me that the space station would be visible for the entire week, that you could see it moving across the night sky. I couldn't see anything, but then, I was in the city. Not much could be seen from where I stood.

DROPPING THE CAMEO was only part of the vulgar thing I did. I also told Jamie and my mother that Heidi had stolen the cameo.

The following day, my mother came home from work late, just before dinner, and when we sat down to eat the meal Jamie had reheated in the oven, I told them that I had gone to her bedroom to dress up after school, since Jamie was staying late for the second round of tryouts and I had the house to myself. I had looked everywhere for my favourite necklace, the heirloom I loved dearly and wore with a swell of pride. Frustrated and worried, I went back to school to meet Jamie and enlist his help in the search, but he was still in the gym. On my way home, I had stopped at Heidi's house and fell into that old bad habit of mine, the spying, but for once caught someone who needed catching. Heidi was lying on her bed, wearing the cameo necklace, twirling the long chain around her finger. Here, I admitted, feigning reluctance, that I had accidentally seen Jamie and Heidi earlier that week, in my mother's bedroom, and that Jamie was showing off this family heirloom to the girl he hardly knew.

"She must have pocketed it on her way out," I finished off, and then sat back, looking unhappy about the whole situation, which I truly was, but not for the right reasons.

"Liar," Jamie said, pushing back his chair. "I don't believe you. This is such a lie. Look at her face."

We all trooped into my mother's room, and I stood in the doorway, watching, my arms primly crossed, as they searched for the cameo and found themselves unable to turn it up. After a silent dinner of macaroni and cheese, my mother grudgingly called Heidi's parents and told them what was going on. They spoke to Heidi, who denied it, crying inconsolably (she was the most honest, moral girl they'd ever met, her parents ventured apologetically). Against their better judgement—for to teach their children that they doubted them was to teach them that a promise or denial could be falsely given in the first place, and this sorry lesson would certainly smash their children's belief in the basic integrity of the world—they searched her room, her knapsack, the pockets of all her clothes. Heidi's mother told mine that she had vomited after doing this, and come down with a terrible headache, which put her in bed but rendered her unable to sleep. My mother was polite and understanding, but did suggest to Jamie and me that the parents were perhaps engaging in unnecessary histrionics.

"I wish I'd never seen it," I said earnestly. "Sometimes it's better not to know the truth about someone."

Jamie turned on me. "You think you know so much about people," he shouted. "It's a joke. What you know is nothing."

Now that Jamie was fighting with me, I sat at the kitchen table
looking sombre and contented.

Word of what had happened went around our neighbourhood
quite quickly. Even though I had been known to do many dishonest things, I benefited from Heidi's newness to our neighbourhood.
Besides, everyone agreed, I had no reason to lie. The heirloom
belonged to me anyway.

Two days later, Celia—and Graham, standing meekly behind
her—came knocking at our door.

"I thought and thought about what to do," she said to my
mother. "I don't like to get involved in other people's matters. And
then, when there are so many stories going around, you doubt
yourself, what you've seen."

Then she said that she and Graham had seen me with the
cameo the night before Heidi was supposedly caught with it in
her room. Did this contradict my account of things, she wanted
to know. Oh, yes, it did, my mother replied in a hard voice. It certainly did. According to this timeline, the girl, Heidi, would have
had no opportunity to steal the necklace, she told Celia.

It didn't take long to break me. My dishonesty didn't run that
deep. I was forced to call Heidi's family and apologize. I was
also forced to write a card of apology, to emphasize my remorse.
Agatha suggested that my mother contact the city to see if we could
get men down in the sewer.

Through her two-year relationship with Jamie, Heidi never
once came to our house when I was there.

My mother bought a new jewellery box with a lock on it. She
put all her old clothes in a trunk, also with a lock. In the absence of
my ability to answer for what I had done, she seemed to have connected what happened with my imagination, my inability to have

respect for the solid and ordinary in life, and she was newly restrictive. She insisted that the women's group meet at Linda's house or Agatha's because she feared the adult conversations were having a harmful effect on my mind.

Jamie barely spoke to me for four years, at which time he left home for good.

AN OVERREACTION, people said, when, as an adult, I told them about Jamie's response to my lie. Far, far out of proportion with my sin, or sins. I'm not sure even Jamie intended so much.

Jamie wasn't home often, so it was easy for him to ignore me at first. He made it onto the basketball team, so he spent two or three evenings a week at school practising. When he was home, he kept to his bedroom. Never did he even eat breakfast at home. I found out later that Heidi would meet him at the corner with a homemade muffin and a banana. On weekends, he spent almost all day at her house. Jamie passed me sometimes in the hallway or the kitchen. If I asked him a question, about the basketball team or a television show, or whether he'd like a cookie, he answered me in a callous monotone, almost barbarically repetitive, so far was it from his true, soft way of talking. He could make me feel, with the way he positioned his body in relation to mine, as though we were not even in the same room. Jamie knew how to ignore—his was not a pose that emphasized your abandoned status, but one that suggested you were not there at all. My mother told me to give him time.

I often looked at myself in the mirror, to see if I could spot my contamination, physically. I couldn't. How could you know what made you repulsive when, looking in the mirror or listening to yourself speak, you could only encounter something too familiar to be repulsive?

The summer Jamie left the house, for a year of living downtown with our uncle and working at his bookstore before going off to university, I caught a glimpse of him on Harbord Street. There were many people on the sidewalk, but I was sure it was him. I was standing in the doorway of a card store, and he was walking with a woman. Immediately my mind went to the things that were unattractive about her. Her face was too round and she had a slight double chin. The roundness of her face contrasted unpleasantly with her long, rather pointed nose. Her lips were thin. I made an inventory of these flaws in my head as I watched them. I thought I saw him mouth to her, "That's my sister," in a cool, informative way. He might not have said that at all. There was no recognition in his face.

Again, I hated the woman immediately, and with intensity.

Sometimes, I think I waited all my life for a moment that would stick with me so unpleasantly. Misfortune no longer seemed glamorous, but I did confront it with a satisfied defeatism. I was like Linda, hoping Larry was having an affair, or that he was a latent homosexual. I had eagerly anticipated my own betrayal.

WE CANNOT believe we have lost things. Even when we bring about the losing ourselves, we can't believe things are gone. We rail against it. We write pleading letters. We invent lives we haven't had.

I tried to be a keeper.

My mother liked to tell me the story my grade four teacher related at a parent-teacher interview. The teacher had asked us what things we collected as a hobby. She had gone around the room, starting at the back and I was at the front. The other kids spoke of stamp collections and doll collections, book collections, stickers, and when my turn came I said, "I collect memories." The teacher had been enchanted by this, and my mother had too, in turn. They spoke glowingly of my originality, the depth and sensitivity of my collection when the other students simply amassed objects.

I remember this day only vaguely. I had not been trying to say anything special, but I panicked as the teacher neared me. I collected nothing and felt envious of all the hobbying going on in the room, the foreign currencies, the Barbie dolls, the model cars. I said I collected memories to cover up the fact that I collected nothing at all.

My mother often paraded this story around, and she brought it out one day in September soon after I had started grade seven, after our summer of spying, when we had invited for dinner the young English teacher who had moved in next door. They laughed together and agreed that it was not every day that nine-year-olds possessed such magical, sad-eyed wisdom, such delicate sensibilities. Afterwards, I confessed the truth to my brother.

"Ever the fraud," he said.

EXPECTING

It isn't until three hours after the beginning of labour that you learn that somewhere at a hospital in downtown Toronto, your baby is being born. When the call comes, you are out jogging along the cold beach, and by the time you return, your husband has already left to find a crib that can be delivered in a day. A brief informative note is taped to the front door. Your husband's efficiency, his ability to circulate rapidly through possibilities and arrive at action, always seems a close relative of an optimism you deeply admire, and deeply revile.

So while he drives the green rental minivan all over the suburbs, through the flat grey mall landscapes of Richmond Hill and Brampton and Mississauga trying to find an in-stock crib, you sit on the couch and paint your toenails red.

You have not allowed preparation because you believe that preparation leads to failure. Wiping the excess polish from the brush, you rethink the moment: somewhere at a hospital in downtown Toronto, a baby is being born. Such revisions are often necessary when you are someone who is always ready not to have.

Your heart rate is 100 beats per minute. Somewhere in your mind, in snapshots that linger like fantasy and grip you like memory, a baby is taking to a nipple. These flashes have been coming at you for days. Yours is not an ordinary kind of waiting, for the heralding cramps, a cervical shifting. Occasionally, you do think you feel your uterus contract, but you know this is just the clench of absence, the tightness of a responsibility displaced, uncredited. You ease yourself off the couch and walk like a penguin so you don't smudge your toenails and you turn on the old air conditioner full blast even though it is the beginning of March. For a week, you have been too hot. You hold up your nylon running shirt and let the air cool the moist underside of your breasts. The living room still smells faintly of latex paint, and you worry that you have made the first in a long line of bad choices.

When a year ago you first saw this small house down near the beach, a white house with one and a half floors and chipping grey shutters and stained glass along the top of the living room window, you called your husband at work and told him you would never forgive him if he didn't love the place as much as you did. The two of you had spent all your weekend mornings for half a year combing the real estate pages of the *Globe and Mail*, but it was only when you took a wrong turn on Queen Street on your way to the doctor that you came across the right house in the corner of a dead-end street. All of your savings went into the down payment, your parents joined with his to buy you a new roof, and that was the end of the money. You didn't want to change anything anyway. You didn't want to peel the paint off the shutters and repaint. You didn't want to flood the lawn with herbicides to get rid of the weeds. Whatever was decrepit about the house made it seem romantic, like a country cottage with whitewashed walls and family antiques at the end of a long dirt road.

So in love were you already with the outside of the house, with its tucked-away charm, that promise of a sweet new life, that you were able to ignore the neglected interior. Instead of old plaster walls painted a fresh, warm white, you faced cheap drywall like dented cardboard and an ill-considered dark, dirty pink everywhere. Not the place of your country fantasies, not worn and well-loved, with hardwood floors rubbed pale by years of children and dogs padding in and out, walls dotted with holes where pictures had been hung—none of what you pictured when you were

imagining bright rooms piled high with books and whimsical dec-
orations, the laughter and calm of a summer house. On all the bedroom doors were locks, and in the wall of the master bedroom was
a small hole the size of a fist punched in. You and your husband
made minor changes—artwork on the walls, sheer curtains to let
in the light—but you consented to live here, for a time, in this pink
bloated place, this intestinal cage. After the realtors and lawyers,
the roof, and growing concerns about an unstable foundation, you
and your husband had no energy for painting. And your sister had
said that you needed to live in a house for a time before you knew
what you really wanted.

Lying in bed one mid-winter Saturday morning, your husband
had sat up suddenly and said, "I can't live with these pink walls
anymore. This place needs some personality. Don't you think
some warm, rich colours would be just the thing?"

He is able to live with things endlessly, your husband, never
complaining, until he is suddenly no longer able to tolerate them
for a second. He surprises you often with his gift for momentum.

"You feel like painting?" you asked. "Really?"

"We've put all our money here. We've put on a new roof. This
is where we are now. We're not in transition. It's time we made a
full investment in our emotional future."

You looked around at the pink walls and up at the ceiling, where
someone had stuck glow-in-the-dark stars. You get used to things.

"I don't know about all that work."

"How about dark red in here?" he said.

He pulled the sheet tight under you and flipped you out of bed.
"No excuses. I'm tired of living in someone else's house."

When he went out to the paint store that afternoon, you called
your friend—the friend your husband doesn't know about—who
said, "What are you doing this afternoon?"

"I'm busy making an investment in my emotional future," you
replied.

And when your husband came back that afternoon, he stacked ten cans of paint in the kitchen and pulled you close. "Let's be daring."

You had said, "I can do that."

The plan was for a quick turnover, sorcery of a kind. In the end, you were no help. You moved so slowly with the roller that he said it would be easier to paint by himself. Seven days later, your kitchen was a bursting yellow, your dining room an inky blue, your bedroom the deep red of a library.

"What do you think?" he asked, a smear of green across his cheek.

You and your husband have a pact that you are not allowed to criticize that which you have refused to become involved in.

"At least we're not living in a stomach anymore." You smiled and accepted his high-five.

You made phone calls from the orange bathroom.

"You're living in a fun fair," said your friend.

You agreed and told your friend about something that had been getting on your nerves for a while: that your husband gets bored in bookstores.

"I correct myself then," your friend answered. "It's Disney-world you're living in. A world of animation and songs. Words not welcome here."

A vision of your husband stretching the orange roller up to the ceiling with a tired grunt presented itself before you, and you were newly defensive.

"You're wrong, you don't get it," you said. "Who else would do all that work without any help? And he doesn't even hold it over my head."

You wish you could form an opinion and stick to it. You wish you could blame your hormones.

A week ago, you walked in the front door just as the afternoon sun was spilling into your lime green living room. You went straight back out to the hardware store and bought gallons of white paint and wondered how you had ever slept or breathed in a house with so much colour, so smirking and carnivalesque. Your husband was away on a business trip, and you called in sick to work, you painted from morning to night. When he returned, he nodded and said nothing. He thought it was your version of pregnancy cravings and aversions. It was understandable. He didn't say this, but you could tell he thought it, with the fatherly dismissiveness that sometimes makes you want to throw kitchen appliances at him. Now you're worried the latex fumes will give the baby brain damage. Your husband nods at this too. For the first time in your life, you have permission to be irrational, as if fluctuating hormones can be relocated from one body to another.

In the beginning, before the doctors and consultants and social workers, you wandered around baby stores on your lunch hour. You took Polaroids of mahogany sleigh cribs and canopied white cribs and stood in the spare room holding the images up to the empty wall, trying to predict which one would look best. You bought newborn sleepers in pink and blue and spread them on the bed between you and your husband. You measured their length against your hand. When your husband suggested vacations, you started sentences with, When we have a baby. After a while, you threw out the ovulation predictor kit. You burned the crib pictures in the fireplace. You learned not to start sentences with assumptions. After a while, you remembered not to expect.

YOUR HEART RATE holds steady at 100 beats per minute. You wonder how long the heart can sustain such stress.

To calm yourself, you think of the refrigerator, of all the fruit and vegetables that have gone to waste because you have been eating only cereal and yogurt. You think of the shrubs that need trimming in the backyard. You think of waterfalls. On your way to work one morning, you heard on the radio a biofeedback expert who recommended that patients calm their bodies not by focusing hard on a happy place, but by letting their minds graze over something that moves softly, with the tempo of a lullaby, such as palm trees swaying in the breeze. You chose mountainside waterfalls, even though you realized that they moved rapidly, not a languid lullaby but the grand flurry of a symphony's climax. It seemed to you that you could stand under that sparkling rush and have some good sense washed into you.

Your visions of waterfalls are based mainly on what you have seen on the Discovery channel or in *National Geographic*. It was not until your honeymoon in Jamaica that you saw a real waterfall. Your hotel organized a day trip to Dunn's River Falls, which turned out to be not steep and fast, like your fantasy waterfalls, but long and intricate, meandering, made up of many smaller, dome-shaped waterfalls. Visitors were allowed to climb, but only as a group, and were instructed to hold hands all the way up. As the chain of tourists wound its way ploddingly up the falls, you turned to the person next to you—a pasty woman who had informed you at the beginning of the hike that she was not an American—and said, "Don't you think we're much more likely to fall this way?" She looked at you as if you had just threatened to pitch her over the falls and aimed her words at your hand, gripped in hers, "In situations like this, you must always follow instructions."

Your husband was at the end of the chain, at least twenty people removed from you, intentionally. As the bus had rattled down the unpaved highway that morning, your husband sat next to you holding your hand—he had been doing this with an almost maniacal resolve since the wedding—and whispering, Almost there, Almost there. Because you were too busy trying not to throw up, you couldn't tell him that his efforts to alleviate your queasiness, a sweaty hand engorging yours, hot breath smelling faintly of pancakes, were even less helpful than the potholes in the road and the spirit of song your fellow hotel tourists had fallen into in spite of their discovery that "One Love" wasn't working as a round. He was even less helpful than the bus driver, a retired insurance salesman from Kansas who abruptly pulled the bus over to the side of the road to put a stop to the new song, "Ninety-nine Bottles of Beer," as the first few voices rose predictably in the back of the bus. You were actually grateful for the momentary reprieve from motion as the bus driver stood in the aisle and shouted, "Cut," slicing his hand quickly across his neck. "No songs about drinking on a moving vehicle," a declaration that put everyone, including your husband, even more feverishly in the spirit of song, as if they were schoolchildren again, left to this meagre rebellion. Less helpful than all of those things was how your husband managed to stop singing five times in the course of "American Pie" to stroke your hand and reassure you, Almost there, Almost there.

You weren't almost there, though. As a fleet of buses from other hotels joined yours along the way, your pace slowed and by the time you reached the parking lot near the waterfall, you and your husband had participated in a lengthy fight in your head about all-inclusive resorts. He debarked the bus first, saying, "I'm going to ask around if anyone has some Gravol."

The silence when he left was blissful and disorienting, something that wouldn't make it into his itinerary, and it seemed your own private rebellion. Solitude is not something committed people are supposed to want on their honeymoons. Your husband speaks often and fondly of committed people. A word with many conjugations, promises of future jailing. "I am being committed," you said to your mother the morning of your wedding as she looked on approvingly, securing an antique platinum bracelet around your wrist. You knew it was true that in order to enjoy this honeymoon fully, you would need to be committed. You were having your best moment alone on the bus, but you were supposed to be making friends. You were supposed to be getting into the spirit of things.

Looking through the windshield of the bus, you saw your husband making his way back to you. Farther in the distance, you saw the comradely busload talking to the locals who had set up booths to sell sarongs and sun hats and wooden figurines with movable barrels over well-equipped groins. Your husband had his hands in his pockets and was walking unhurriedly, whistling. His head was cocked to one side, his chin lifted, and he seemed to be looking at the windshield of the bus, right at you, but there was no connection between his eyes and yours.

There was a moment in which he was not yours. And while that should have pulled you to him—before marrying, you had worried that his looks would be marred by familiarity, that you would never be able to conjure desperation without detachment—it did not. What you wanted to be dark about him was light, and what ought to have been light was dark. You had imagined your future husband dark-haired, the blackest brown, with pale blue eyes, but your true husband, the whistling man, has sandy hair and chocolate eyes. You had wanted pale thin lips, held tightly, almost primly, in perpetual reserve because to you such a mouth suggested a tense, discerning mind, a debilitating contempt for stupidity from which you, and few others, would be spared. Your true husband has full red lips, a gentle and sympathetic mouth, undiscerning, a mouth for the masses, its offerings appreciated by many women before you. You could hear him whistling as he approached, that strong whistle capable of carrying difficult tunes.

You noticed then what he was wearing—a chocolate brown T-shirt and shorts of a colour between mustard and brown. Two browns, absolutely wrong together. He ran a hand through his hair, another wrong shade of brown.

"No Gravol," he said, climbing on the bus. "This is a sturdy group."

"Have you seen what you're wearing?" you asked.

"Well, yes, I'm wearing it, after all."

"So it's your opinion that you've made a decent choice, with those browns, mustard and chocolate, waging a war on your body." You knew your voice was too cutting.

You had surprised him with this. He was in a good mood.

"It's my opinion that we're going to climb a waterfall, which will presumably make us wet, and it's also my opinion that no one gives a shit what I'm wearing, except, perhaps, the woman I just married."

"So now that we're married, you've decided just to let it all hang out."

He didn't fight. He never did, but he left the bus and stopped speaking to you.

Every now and then, holding the hands of the woman and man on either side of you, you peered over the waterfall and saw him several levels down, bringing up the rear.

At the top, your hotel guide arranged your group of fifty tourists into several rows in a waist-high pool of water at the base of one of the mini waterfalls. He instructed everyone to jump up in the water at once and shout, "Irie, mon!" on the count of three. In the picture, which your husband bought a copy of, everyone is jumping at a different time, and the word "Irie" has turned out smiles that look more like grimaces. Your husband is lost in the picture, eclipsed by a crowd of German vacationers. You are standing on a plane of rock at the top of the waterfall, one level above the other tourists, with your hands on your hips.

This is not one of the pictures you sent to the girl who chose you.

YOUR FRIEND LESLIE was the first to have a baby. Leslie was lost now, good and gone.

She used to be a stand-up comedian. She used to live in an old unrenovated Victorian house in Parkdale and ride her bike everywhere. She used to say that her ideal marriage would be full of affairs on her side and impotence on his. She used to have long curly red hair. She told you, quite seriously, that she sang "Amazing Grace" while her hairdresser cut it off.

"Not for me, those blubbering babes," she told you. "'I can't watch, I don't think I can go through with it. Please make it quick, Hold my hand.' Nope. I made him take his time. I wanted to savour it. I actually felt myself becoming lighter. 'I once was lost, but now I'm found.' He said, 'Why can't all women be like you?'"

Now Leslie is married to a man named Pat, and they live in Mississauga on a treeless street where all the houses are identical. Leslie believes joking confuses children and has concerned conversations about diaper content with her husband. Leslie will drive an extra hour to avoid going through Parkdale because she is afraid of getting shot. Leslie says to you, staring at her son in her lap, "Who cares about sex once you've finally met the true love of your life?" Leslie leaves a trail of used-to-bes.

Leslie named her baby Stan because that was both her father's name and Pat's grandfather's name. "We're interested in maintaining these family connections," she said to you. "That's all that matters now."

You and your husband invited Leslie, Pat, and Stan to your house for a barbecue shortly after you moved in. Leslie looked around sympathetically at the dim pink walls and even more sympathetically at your tiny plot of sparse grass and weeds in the back. It had been raining for a week, and the yard was full of little muddy swamps.

"This is why we bought in Mississauga," Pat said. "We thought it was important for kids to grow up with a big backyard and a neighbourhood full of kids to play with. All our decisions are about Stan now. You'll see one day. My bet is you'll sell this place within six months of having your first baby. We can put out real estate feelers in our neighbourhood if you like."

"Look at all these weeds!" Leslie exclaimed.

"I think they're pretty," you said.

Leslie stepped off the porch and her sandaled foot sunk into a patch of mud.

"Ooh, oh, no," she squealed.

Pat looked at you accusingly. "She just had a pedicure yesterday."

Later, while your husband and Pat sat on the porch in the cooling night, you and Leslie went inside to the kitchen because Leslie was afraid of exposing Stan to the possibility of mosquito bites. She sat on the floor with the baby and tickled his stomach while he lay on his back. When he let out half a cry, she picked him up and started breastfeeding him while she gazed down into his eyes.

"Your mom gave me great advice when I started breastfeeding," she said. "She gave me all the literature. She was so ahead of her time."

"I don't think I could breastfeed," you said. Your mother breastfed you for two and a half years. You avoid telling people this, but your mother considers her proudest moment to be the time you overturned a glass of milk at a crowded restaurant and climbed up onto her lap, screaming, "I don't want cow's milk, I want Mommy's milk," while you clawed at her blouse.

Leslie looked at you in horror. "You can't be serious. These nine months have been the most fulfilling of my life."

Stan reached his pudgy hands up towards her hair.

"No, no, my lovebug," she said. "I've outwitted you."

She looked up and said to you, "The worst agony of breastfeeding was not at the beginning, but when he developed enough motor control to reach up and pull my hair while I fed him."

She lowered her head again, that fiery halo.

When you first met Leslie in university, she wore big black horn-rimmed glasses and heavy black motorcycle boots, and she celebrated everything she found ugly and impractical, but now she wears contact lenses so Stan can make closer eye contact with her.

When she was finished feeding him, she carried him around the kitchen, pointing out various objects and carefully enunciating their names, then explaining their functions.

"Blender," she said. "Blen-Der. That's what Mama uses in the morning to mash your carrots and your peas and your sweet potatoes and your apples and all that good stuff that's making you a healthy boy. Blender."

She held up the lid of the coffee tin and said, "Circle. This is a circle, Stan."

She held the lid close to his face. "Can you say circle? Try to say it. Circle."

The baby looked at her and spat out a word resembling badass.

"Yes, good. Good work, Stan. What else is a circle? Point out the circles to Mommy."

She drew her finger around the rim of her water glass. "Circle."

"What else is a circle?"

The baby pointed at the refrigerator, and Leslie walked excitedly over to it and searched the door. Her eyes zeroed in on a magnet of a seal balancing a ball on its nose.

"Good boy, Stan," she said, pointing to the ball. "Yes, this is a circle."

Sitting at the kitchen table, you asked Leslie, "Don't you ever miss comedy?"

"You're kidding me."

"You used to love it. You thrived on that feeling of being in front of an audience. Sometimes you were on a high for a week after a good show."

Leslie shook her head definitively. "Being a comedian was about having my heart closed. It made me cynical and I had to be cynical to do it properly. My heart is open now. I can't do it any more. I don't want to do it any more."

She took Stan over to the kitchen window and held him up, "Look, Stan, it's Daddy."

"I couldn't even be faithful before," she said. "Now all that matters is the family. The only Other Man in my life now is Stan."

Watching Leslie, you could see how the life people have chosen and found contentment in, learning how to make homemade soup with less salt, feeding children snacks of peanut butter and honey on crackers, reading long novels in twenty-page snatches before bedtime, becomes the thing they have to get out of.

She sat down across from you at the table and said, "I pity my old self. I can't tell you what a relief it is to be rid of my libido."

This was before you knew that there is a hierarchy of women, those who can and those who can't. This was back when you thought it was just a matter of choosing.

Later that night, you said to your husband, "Leslie is completely faithful now. No more other men. Can you believe that? She's changed so much. It's tragic."

"You're going to have to explain to me how this is a bad thing, that Leslie no longer wants other men."

Your husband is less flexible on these issues than you are. To him, there is no such thing as degrees of fidelity.

In the beginning, you agreed with him, but lately you have thought that it isn't so wrong to have a friend who is allowed to feel up your leg once in a while. Not when there are so many ways of being so much more wrong.

YOU MET YOUR FRIEND when you were in the process of being regularly serviced by your husband. Once a month for a year, you had been mired in what your husband called the Proceedings. Still intact were the romantic formalities, the ceremony and reverence that both of you considered essential to the conjuring of life. You lit scented candles and turned off the lights, drenched yourself in sugary bath gels and body lotions and draped yourself in lilac lingerie. Your husband kissed your neck gently and drew a finger along your cheek. You felt you were coaxing the spirit of the baby to enter your body. See how well behaved we are? We will attend to your life with the same care. The Proceedings were always long and ardent in a polite sort of way, in defiance of the merely functional, which you felt would be an insult to the miracle you were asking to attend you. Afterwards, you lay in bed and your husband sat next you on the side of the bed, as if hovering over an invalid, and he stroked your arms and your forehead.

You were a year into this when you met your friend, and you were getting over lighting candles and eating yams and soy milk. Doctors were involved.

You were jogging on the beach one Saturday after rushed morning Proceedings—no tub-soaking, no lotions or candles, but special doctor-prescribed vitamins served with your temperature-taking before, a quick cool shower together after—and that was how you met your friend. You were thinking about how you couldn't believe your husband's bottom would be yours forever, how you would know all its incarnations, the flattening and drooping, its gradual merging with the top of his thigh, how you would know it, better than your own, and see it on his every journey out of bed, his standing in the shower, his nightly teeth-brushing before the sink. You would see its genial slackness many more times, as you had seen it that morning when he jumped back out of bed to fetch a coaster after you placed your water glass directly on the unprotected night table. As you jogged along the beach, you thought about how you were locked with that ass in an animosity surprisingly like solidarity.

Someone called out behind you, "Awesome calves."

You turned and said, "Excuse me?"

"You have incredible calves. I've been jogging behind you watching them. What exercises do you do?"

You watched him warily, searching for malice, casually disrobing. How slowly let go, that girlish cowering, the fear of being duped, duped and taunted. You have always hated your calves.

"They're amazing," he said. "No matter how hard I exercise, I can't get calf definition."

"They're just that way naturally," you said, still on guard. "I would never actually try for this."

"Are you kidding me? People would pay for calves like that if they could. There's nothing worse than piano legs."

"Piano legs?"

"Legs that go straight down with no muscle definition. Just straight into the ankles."

He had wavy brown hair that fell across his dark eyes when he jogged, and he barely sweated as you finished your run together. You sprinted for the last stretch, and you thought you almost beat him, but then you realized as you walked home how much he'd been hanging back, how obviously he wasn't working his hardest. He was showing you the power of your calves.

"I don't know many women who can run like that," he had said.

You thought he probably knew many women.

You jogged with him the following day, then the following weekend, and the following. You started jogging on weekday evenings so you would be in better shape.

One evening when you were walking home from the subway, a black Jeep turned onto the side street ahead of you and pulled over. The window lowered slowly, and your friend was sitting there in a grey suit, one hand raised in salute.

"Your carriage awaits," he said.

You got in and held your purse in your lap.

"So, in order not to seem creepy, I guess this is the part where I pretend not to know where you live," he said.

"That's probably the best idea."

You worried that if he touched you, he would feel how damp your hands were. Not truly, though. You weren't hoping something would happen, not truly.

He kept looking from the road to you, then back to the road.

"I have to confess I've become a little sweet on you," he said.

He spoke with false shyness, pretending to be a little bit afraid of you as part of the seduction. Your husband isn't this suave. On your third date, he stood at your front door looking at you nervously for twenty minutes and finally kissed you lightly after saying, "Firsts make me nervous."

The Jeep was cool and clean.

"Sweet on me," you said, rolling your eyes. "How sweet."

It is important to you that he doesn't think you fall for things.

You didn't think about betrayal, not even as you let your new friend's hand creep up your leg. What you thought was, I wonder if his sperm is strong.

"You know I have to get home to my husband," you said.

Before you got out of the car, you agreed to give him your phone number, but you made a pact that if your husband answered the phone, he would pretend to be a telemarketer, the only people to whom your husband is dependably rude.

When you walked in the front door, your husband was standing there with a glass of chocolate milk for you. He had prepared dinner: baby peas, baby corn, baby carrots.

"Tonight's the night," he said. "I think it is."

It was your husband who first suggested having a baby. Although he was your partner in life—you had married, obviously, with longevity in mind—you were startled to think that anyone would look at you and see the possibility of competence. You stalled, initially, evaded baby talk and worked longer hours. You didn't know if you could handle the conversations motherhood required.

What colour is this, sweet pea?

Yes, blue.

What else is blue?

Your mother swore to you that it would be different with your own child—that every mangled word, every fussy cry, every boring moment of absolute anxious devotion, would leave you starstruck, clamouring for the baby book so you could write it all down, that every banality would become as grimly precious as things are when you know they won't last. She pleaded with you to give motherhood a chance.

"I'm not saying I don't want to," you said. "I just can't picture it."

"A baby will complete you," she replied. "A baby will make you happy. If you don't listen to me about anything else, listen to me about this."

A year and a half later, after your first doctor's appointment, you told her about all the trying. You were on the phone, and in the background you could hear your father playing *Clair de lune* on their new baby grand piano.

"I'm your mother," she said. "Couldn't you have told me sooner?"

"I didn't want to jinx anything."

"You're becoming so secretive."

You told her what the doctor said, the testing he wanted to do, the procedures and drugs that would likely be necessary.

"So now you want to be a mother," your mother said. "You see? It's not always so easy. It's not always a matter of, Okay, I want it now, Let's get this show on the road. God, give me what I want."

"God has nothing to do with it."

Before she hung up, she said, "I hope you learned something."

What is it? you yelled at the silent phone. What is it that I'm supposed to learn?

YOUR HEART RATE stays at 112 and you try to do biofeedback, thinking of waterfalls. When your phone rings, you will know you have come to the end of waiting. You also know that you will begin a different kind of waiting.

You do not think of the baby who is being born at a hospital in downtown Toronto. You do not think of the crib that might be on its way. You do not think of diapers or sleepers or receiving blankets, as you rest on the couch with one hand on your pulse.

It has become your habit, for the past week, to take your pulse every ten minutes. It is possible, you think, that you are exhibiting signs of an undiagnosed heart condition. Every night, you feel your heart pounding against the hard mattress, kicking madly, with lawless hysteria. You have begun to sleep, half sitting up, on a chair in the living room. Last night, you went to *Swan Lake* with your sister, and the woman sitting next to you had bad breath, like the pages of an old book, with a vein of stale garlic running through it. This smell and the overheated congestion of the theatre combined to make you terrified, halfway through the second act, that someone had planted a bomb in the basement of the Hummingbird Centre. As the swan dancers in their white sequinned tutus flooded the stage, aligning themselves with delicate precision as their paper-thin arms disappeared into the backlights, you mapped out the exit signs, you imagined grabbing your sister's hand and guiding her through the screaming masses, through the hazards of fire and smoke. When you were on your way to the car after the ballet, stepping over deep puddles on the sidewalk, you wondered when neurosis stopped being occasional and started being necessary—no longer reckless and arbitrary, something you couldn't get rid of, but a ritual you relied on, as essential to you as a child's anticipation of her coming birthday.

In the letter you wrote to the agency, you and your husband described yourselves as a fun-loving couple whose idea of a perfect Saturday night was a barbecue, a few friends, and a display of fireworks.

"But I hate fireworks," you said to your husband when he read you his draft. "So do you."

"I'm trying to paint a picture of an all-American life. She's a teenage girl. I'm sure that's the kind of home she'll want for her child. She doesn't want to hear that you won't let me talk to you on Saturday morning until you've read for an hour. She doesn't want to hear that you think it's sad that Leslie no longer takes lovers."

"But who are these impossibly perky people?"

There's nothing we like better than to take a walk with our dog Steve and go window-shopping on Queen Street, then finish off the morning with a picnic on the beach. We love to spend time in the kitchen experimenting with new recipes and inventing gourmet meals from visions culled in the furthest reaches of our imaginations. Have you ever tried Dal Makhani, a lentil delicacy from India, or Feijoada, Brazilian black bean and pork stew? Neither have we, but with our adventurous spirits, there's nothing we won't test once.

The letter began, "Dear Birthmother," two words joined as one in the lexicon of adoption.

"It's not accurate," you told your husband. "You've tweaked everything so much that the whole thing feels like a lie."

"Well, what would you have me say?"

What would you have him say? You should probably not describe yourself as someone who likes to feel she is always about to lose something.

You wanted to send the picture of your husband dangling you by your legs over the edge of the high deck at his parents' cottage. Your husband wouldn't allow it. He assembled an array of pictures, all thoughtfully posed but designed to look natural, selected to back up the letter's view of you and your husband as the parents-next-door, the fun-loving, mutually respectful admirers of fireworks. Paddling in a canoe on Lake Kioshkokwi on a camping trip with friends in Algonquin Park. Jumping off a cliff hand-in-hand into the lake at a friend's cottage. Sitting on your back deck under pots of hanging flowers with the dog at your feet. We are adventurous homebodies, these pictures said. Try to find more well-rounded people, they challenged. Your husband also included some playful choices, to show the kind of kidding around the baby would be lucky enough to be part of if you were chosen: your husband pretending to eat your wedding bouquet, you giving your husband a piggyback ride at a black-tie fundraiser. Each of these pictures, at the moment of its taking, was perfectly staged, and you barely recognize yourself in them. It is only in candid pictures that you look remotely like yourself. Your husband didn't think it appropriate to send the kind of pictures where someone calls your name, and when you turn around, a camera flash pops.

"Why are you trying so hard to be subversive?" he said. "Can't you just grow up?"

You acknowledged that it was a decent question. Since you were a little girl, you have felt that admitting how much you want something is the best way of ensuring that you don't get it. It is with some satisfaction that you consider how right you were.

You don't pray. Instead, you look up at a far point in the sky and say, Good job. You sure showed me.

YOUR HEART RATE is 107 beats per minute.

When it climbs to 115, you decide to take a cool shower. As you lather up the shampoo and massage it through your scalp, your hair starts coming out in small clumps of five or six hairs at a time. Long strands swirl around the drain. Your husband has bought you a Lact-Aid system and two herbal supplements, Fenugreek and Blessed Thistle, because he is hoping your body can learn to produce breast milk for the baby. Your mother encourages this. Even though you know that the antibodies in breast milk are good for a baby's health, you do not feel entitled to put your breast in the mouth of a child who did not come from your body. It seems the ultimate perversion, a rank deception at its core: you as an earth mother. As you rub the water over your breasts, you look at the centre of your nipple. Both your mother and your husband have informed you that the milk comes from the whole nipple, like a sponge, not from a pinprick hole at the centre, as you had thought. Before you turn off the water, you use a thick white shower cream to moisturize because your skin is so dry it has started peeling. You do not ask what causes your hair and skin to shed. Your body cannot hold onto things. After two years of trying to have a baby, this is what you have come to understand.

It was at Stan's first birthday party that you stopped finding new ways of saying no. You and your husband arrived early because you overestimated the amount of time it would take to get to Mississauga. Leslie was holding Stan, naked, in her arms when she opened the door. She held him up to you and your husband.

"Look," she said. "His birthday suit."

Pat came out from the kitchen and offered your husband a beer, and they went to the basement to watch a basketball game while you went upstairs with Leslie to get the baby dressed. You kept apologizing for being early and told Leslie that you would have gone to a coffee shop if you'd known the area better. Leslie was happy to have you, though, and all you could think about was how adaptable they were, and how privately irritated you would have been if someone had shown up early to a party at your house, how capable you would have been of maintaining that irritation all afternoon. The old Leslie would have been irritated too. She would have acted grandly put out and asked you to wait in the living room with a magazine until the designated time. But here was Leslie, showing you the mural she painted in Stan's bedroom, an overgrown old tree inhabited by elves and chipmunks, a sky of bright birds overhead, fluffy white rabbits conversing in a blooming garden. Here was Leslie, asking you to choose Stan's birthday clothes. Here she was, handing you her baby. As you held him, he looked up at you with his pale blue watery eyes and laughed as he touched your long twinkly earrings. You kissed the top of his soft bald head because Leslie was watching and you thought something was expected, and then kissed it again when she turned away. You asked yourself, What if?

Then Leslie came and took him so she could put his clothes on. You saw how his face changed when he looked at her, as though everything had just come together. He reached up both his hands and put them on her cheeks. "Mamama," he said.

You do not think about this, as you wait for the phone to ring. You do not think of your husband out buying a crib, or your mother, who you know has secretly bought baby clothes even though you have forbidden preparation. You do not think of your husband's body and how it curled itself around you when the news came about how poorly yours operated.

You thought you wanted interesting conversations forever.

Now all you want is to hear yourself say, Yes, blue. What else is blue?

THE PHONE RINGS and you leap to answer it.

It is your friend. He doesn't call you much now that he knows you are interested in babies.

"I got your message. Congratulations in a way."

"In a way?"

"In a way, meaning when you know you're happy for someone but you're not quite happy for them yet."

You are silent.

"You'll be so busy, who knows when I'll see you again."

"We will," you say. "We'll make time."

You say this without conviction. It has had its time. Your husband may drink the milk left over in his bowl of cereal, he may get bored in bookstores, but you are still fascinated too. Your friend doesn't understand this. He thinks that he is the one you think about. He doesn't understand that it's not really about him. Small deceits keep you feeling that you still belong to yourself.

"How will we make time?" he asks. "Soon you'll be a mother. In a way."

You hang up on him.

YOU DO NOT THINK of your friend after you have hung up the phone. You do not think of your heart rate, its solo race in your chest. You do not think of the supplies your husband has been smuggling into the basement.

What you do think of, often, is the girl. The sandy-haired fifteen-year-old who is in labour in downtown Toronto, this girl who chose you based on a picture. Another picture from the Jamaican vacation, a picture where you are standing next to your husband against a background of deep-green ferns and wild ginger lilies and orchids, holding hands while your hair flashes with beaded braids you agreed to out of respect for the principle of getting into the spirit of things—the only picture where you look at all like yourself, in spite of the braids, because you seem to have forgotten, finally, that someone is looking at you. You do think of this girl, with lips so full they make you want to cry. You think about this world she knows intimately, a world of obstetrical wonder, a world you will never know, although you do sometimes classify your husband's stare as gynecological as he leans in to kiss your forehead at night. You do think of her body, ripping open for you.

Your friends ask when you are bringing your baby home. You cringe at the word *your*. You feel you have no right, that this baby will lie with unresolved tenancy in your arms. For the past two years, you have not taken your eyes off women with strollers, women with fat stomachs, women who say "my daughter" and "my son" with heartbreaking carelessness, as if they are rhyming off brands of cereal. It has seemed to you that the world is filled with children who could be yours. And you've tried to ignore how the opposite is much more true: the world is filled with children who will never be yours. You do not know how to be one of these women, a woman who expects and claims, a woman who complains about lack of sleep and babies crying, a woman who knows the tenderness of possession that is not possession at all, but something much closer to a constant giving away.

Your heart rate is 105 beats per minute as you climb the stairs to your bedroom. On your bed is a package your mother mailed to you yesterday. It contains a paperback book of baby names and a yellowing letter you wrote to God as a child. She found it in the back of an old photograph album. The letter is unfinished—you wrote it the summer you were eight, and you abandoned it so you could go swimming in the lake. On the back of the letter is a picture you drew of you consulting with God in his pink throne. The letter has always made your mother laugh, because of your assumption, even then, that you would fail to make it into heaven.

You hear your husband pull up in the minivan, and you look out the window. He is pulling a tall, narrow cardboard box out of the back. He yanks too aggressively, the box gets stuck, and he lands on his bottom on the snowy grass. You climb into bed and unfold the letter.

Dear God,
When I am long dead and my dear children die, I hope
you will let me visit my children in heaven. I will be 105.
My son will be 97 and my daughter will be 93. I hope you
will let me see them again so I can hug them. I will look
different, but they will know I am their mother. They will
be sitting on clouds and I will run when I see them.

A VERSION *of* LOVELINESS

My grandmother called me a God person, meaning that I believed. Calling me a Christian wouldn't have addressed the matter fully. Christians were people who applied themselves to tidy worship with a devotion that was respectful and appropriate, comfortingly institutionalized, driven by duty and habit and moderate affection. Their behaviour was in good taste. I was fifteen and thought that good taste was simply a lack of soulfulness. I had written a letter to the Pope professing that there was never a moment in which I did not spare a tender thought for him. I had read and reread Donne's holy sonnets and highlighted the sections I found most applicable to my own situation. I sympathized with persecuted religious groups and was disappointed that my own religion was not in any such danger. I went to confession almost every day and made up sins when I felt I hadn't committed enough to rouse the priest's full attention. Christianity couldn't cover what I wanted to get at. I was a God person; every moment of my day, every thought passing through my head, was bursting with hot piety, a fierce and panting awareness of God.

My grandmother was in most ways blasphemous. She outdid herself. She was quick to lay blame at God's feet when she stubbed a toe or mistakenly added the wrong ingredient to a dish. When the sky opened in unforeseen showers, she looked heavenward and inquired why it was that He couldn't resist the temptation to thwart her. Her tone was mild enough in these expressions of spiritual disappointment, but she did not hesitate to let Him know how she felt.

She did pray, though, so she resisted wholeheartedly my charge of sacrilege. Her prayers were diligent and orderly. Every morning, she prayed for her family's health and general well-being, and she let it be known that help was welcome as we strove to overcome our deficiencies. She placed extra emphasis on me, that I might learn to be less argumentative. At the end, she arrived at herself and confessed to her own shortcomings, then asked for the things she needed. She prayed aloud, so that she would hear her own requests—she did not want to lose track and be unreasonable. On the edge of her night table, she pasted yellow sticky notes to remind herself about who needed special prayers in any given week: her daughter, who had encountered an enemy at work; her sister, who was plagued by her sciatic nerve; her neighbour, who had given birth to an illegitimate child. All of us she prayed for with concern and enthusiasm. Later, she would check in on the status of our problems, monitor for improvements. When reports were positive, she said to me, "See? I told you he's listening. I can feel him all around me."

It was in these prayers where her blasphemy revealed itself most flagrantly. I threatened that she was on her way to purgatory, at best.

"They say that one day in purgatory feels like fifty, Nana," I said. "That can't be what you want."

"Who's this 'they'?" she asked.

I thought about that and told her the priests. (Although I thought about God nearly constantly, it was not then in my nature to think about what exactly it was that I believed, and where those beliefs came from.)

"How could they know?" she said.

My sister and I spent most afternoons after school at our grandparents' house that spring because our parents were divorcing. It was not fighting that drove us from our own house, but an eerie new peace. Our father was sleeping on a futon in the screened-in porch and working until ten o'clock every night. Our mother was at the beginning of a bitter love affair. They were rarely home, and when they were, their polite conversations about the contents of the refrigerator, the current events covered in the newspaper, the meeting with their lawyers—these people who, three months before, could yell for an hour over which of them had put the dishes in the dishwasher without first cleaning off the food—announced how fully they had disowned each other. Their terrible civility testified to what an irrelevant thing our family had become. So we went to our grandparents' house, where there was no shortage of noise.

My sister read novels inside while I helped in the garden. My grandmother liked a wild and overgrown garden, a haphazard country look that actually required much maintenance. When I arrived there from school, the garden tools would be neatly laid out for me on a tattered old quilt, and I went straight to work. For fifteen years, my grandmother had suffered from rheumatoid arthritis so severe that no movement was without pain. She loved a garden but could no longer have any part in its creation. Because her hands were swollen and creaky, and her bent fingers slanted diagonally away from her knuckles, she could not hold a spade, or exert any kind of force. As I worked, she sat on a yellow lawn chair, her legs elevated to reduce the pressure on her knees and feet, and she identified which were weeds and which were plants, for I could not tell the difference. She often seemed irritated by the slow rate at which I worked, but she was also used to having other people do physical work for her. Sometimes she looked restless, as if she might get up and take over, but she never did. I enjoyed the gardening. Unlike my sister, I had no interest in reading. I was often offended by what I felt was the lack of morality in novels. I liked a book with good moral examples, books populated by rigorous people who were not conflicted, who did not lie, and who were at least religiously inclined. I also liked a book to provide a moral at the end. As a result, I rarely read for pleasure. I pictured my sister inside, happily absorbed, and I pounded at the soil as hard as I could with the spade.

My grandmother was a tall woman with a neat silver bob and a frail elegance, and even then, at eighty, she was erratically fashionable. She might wear long, high-waisted white linen pants and a flowing violet blouse or a long dress covered in green apples. Because she had to protect herself from the sun, she covered herself with loose, bright fabrics, with the exception of her face, which was always shielded with a hat. And because it had rarely seen sun, her skin was remarkably pale and smooth. With her fair and pretty bearing, it was easy to think that all her life had been easy. She didn't look like someone who would be stoical, but she certainly was. Occasionally, she got up from her lawn chair and took a turn around the garden, inspecting its different corners for weeds, or leaning down to smell a flower. When she walked, she used a cane and had a slight limp that seemed not feeble, but graceful and aristocratic.

"Nana, don't you want to smell those flowers' true perfume? Don't you think life would be better if you could detect these fragrances in the way that God created them?" I asked.

This was a subject I never left for long. I often tried to convince people that my own godliness enabled me to better enjoy life. I insisted that foods tasted sweeter, flowers smelled more fragrant, and fruit was juicier when you recognized that these things were created by God. I almost convinced my sister, who was three years younger than I, that broccoli would taste like chocolate chip cookies if she believed. This was part of the contract we create with God, I explained. You scratch my back, I scratch yours.

"If I want something, I know who to ask," my grandmother said. "And anyway I'm happy enough with what I smell now."

I collected the weeds in a white wicker basket and pretended that the conversation was not about to take the turn I knew it was about to take.

"Pray to Beau that we get some rain today or tomorrow," she said. "These peonies are parched."

This was the crux of my grandmother's blasphemy, the problem I had tried, unsuccessfully, to make headway on. My grandmother prayed to her dead dog, Beau.

"I'm willing to pray to God for rain," I offered.

"Pray to God until you're blue in the face. I think he has more important things to worry about than whether our flowers get watered. But Beau loves me and I believe he'll see to it that we get a few drops."

"Beau doesn't make rain," I said. "God does."

"Well, neither of them makes rain if you want to be technical about it," she answered.

I tried to ignore her, and she tried to ignore me. She saw my refusal to pray to Beau as a direct affront to her. When the dog was alive, he had rivalled my grandfather in her affections. He was a beautiful dog, gentle and tolerant, a golden retriever with ringlets down his chest. When my sister and I were young, he let us dress him up in pink bonnets and frilly shirts and take photographs of him. When he came prancing into a room, my grandmother lit up.

"Is that my precious love?" she would croon. "Is that my boy, the love of my life?"

Although my grandmother rarely spoke of her pain, she tried everything that was rumoured to relieve it—Aspirin, gold treatment, acupuncture. Nothing worked. Then my grandfather came home one day with a dog from the Humane Society. Beau would lie next to her with his head in her lap, and every now and then, he would lift his head high to give her chin a small, dignified lick. He sniffed her hands and gently nuzzled them. He slept on the floor beside her bed and barked for my grandfather if she had to get up in the night. My grandmother swore the throbbing abated a little, she swore his breath on her skin had the warmth of a light anaesthetic. She produced articles as evidence that animal therapy was approved by medical experts. As a child, I thought that the rheumatoid arthritis was her misshapen hands, her distended knees and feet, that the results were the thing itself, and that pain was a distant corollary rather than the root, the pulse point of it all.

My grandmother was not generally a fanciful woman. She had lived for forty-five years with my grandfather, who was passionate, impulsive, and volatile, likely to waste large amounts of money in fits of gift-buying affection. As the manager of their lives, she was calm and thoughtful. It would not have occurred to her that praying to the dog was strange or laughable. Her prayers were organized and serious. They were like meditations, and quite without histrionic flair. When I think of it now, I realize that she was probably not praying, not really. She was gathering herself, quietly, in some expression of hopefulness towards the world.

It was only when I was much older that I realized what she had to live with. She never spoke of pain except to comment on its improvement.

THAT WAS THE LAST spring I saw my grandmother in her garden. She went into the hospital that summer. I was away at camp training to be a counsellor, although I had never been to camp as a camper and was sensitive to insects and drafts and public toilets. Weekly, I wrote letters home that were full of lies: I had strep throat but the nurse refused to treat it; a gash on my leg, sustained when I cut myself on a rusty nail, grew puffier by the day; a storm had brought a giant old tree down onto our cabin, narrowly grazing my bed. I also resented that chapel was held only once a week. In each letter, I suggested at length that home would be safer, but

refused to admit I was homesick. One day two weeks before I was
to return, my mother sent me a letter telling me that my grandfather had been helping my grandmother to the bathroom in the
middle of the night when he had a dizzy spell and let her fall. Her
hip was broken. Surgery was needed to repair the break, to restore
some fraction of her mobility, but the doctors didn't want to put
her under general anaesthetic. They had discovered congestive
heart failure.

"Down like a tonne of bricks," my grandfather said to me when
I returned from camp. He spoke with wonder, as if amazed and
impressed that my grandmother's body could contain that much
substance. I thought it sounded unflattering, and was indelicate,
considering the whole thing had been his fault.

My grandparents slept in separate bedrooms, and when their
dog Beau had been alive, he had roused my grandfather in the
night by trotting into his room and nudging him awake when my
grandmother needed help. Since Beau's death, my grandmother
had relied on a silver bell to alert my grandfather, and my mother
was intent on blaming my grandfather's midnight dizziness on
the demise of Beau and the birth of the bell. During my first visit
upon returning from camp, my whole family went to the hospital
together, and we milled around the visitors' sitting area talking
about how this would never have happened if Beau had still been
alive. It occurred to me that that wouldn't have changed anything
other than how quickly my grandfather woke up, but for once I
kept my mouth shut.

There was a constant hum of noise on the ward. As I walked
along the hallway to my grandmother's room, patients reached out
for me from their wheelchairs. One woman grabbed my hand and
asked if I had seen Earl. A man was walking sideways down the
hall holding onto the wall with both hands. He winked at me and
said, "Are we on for Saturday night, Stacey?" I didn't say anything

and he gazed past my shoulder. Then a change came over his face, and he looked at me again with watery eyes, servile eyes. "I'm wet," he said. "Can someone please change me?" This was just one walk down the hall. I was proud of my grandmother, that she lay there so quietly.

She was on a special bed, with an alternating pressure air mattress intended to relieve the weight on her broken hip. The nurses came in every hour to turn her, as she no longer could turn herself. While this was happening, my grandmother seemed able to behave as if it were not. She was in a semi-private room, but the bed next to hers was empty. Such was the compromised privacy of her new life. My mother had already handed me bus fare, kissed her mother on the forehead, and hurried off with my sister, whom she dropped at a friend's house.

"Chuck, Chuck," my grandmother said. "Her kingdom for half an hour with Chuck."

Chuck was my mother's married boyfriend, and he had presented my mother with a narrow window to see him that day, a window through which my mother clambered with ungainly eagerness. My family seemed somehow accustomed to the new hospital routine, as if there was an inevitability about my grandmother's injury that rendered it somehow inconsequential.

"God does not approve of adultery," I said.

"Ah, well. We are talking about Chuck here." There was a mock exasperation in her voice, even a kind of amused respect that suggested she was impressed by my mother's ability to surrender to inescapable disappointment.

"Have you done your exercises?" she asked.

My grandmother had the idea that young people are exuberant and eager to burn energy by means of calisthenics. Whenever my sister and I slept over as children, she had us do a series of jumping jacks in the morning on the back lawn. She chose jumping jacks because she thought they were my favourite single exercise, my way of expressing physically the abundant cheer inside me. There was a famous story about how I had broken out into jumping jacks at my first sight of an alligator at the Toronto Zoo when I was six.

"And camp. How was it?" she asked.

"The worst, most godless experience of my life," I said.

I told her all the stories I had already told through letters. I never got tired of rehashing the litany of my discomforts. Then I wanted to analyze why I had found camp so terrible, and why I had wanted to go in the first place, given my dislike of the outdoors. I wanted to analyze why my mother had allowed me to do something I was so clearly going to dislike, why I had stayed in spite of impediments to my safety, why I had so avidly pursued a summer of affliction.

"You used to enjoy camping in our backyard," my grandmother said. "You and your sister used to set up a tent and sleep outside and pretend that the back of the garden was a swamp full of frogs. So you made a mistake. You thought it would be fun."

I told her I found it more likely that I was trying in some fashion to atone for my sins.

"Perhaps, dear," she said, "though I don't know that you've done anything so very wrong."

In the beginning, I visited her often enough to allay any questions about the future. In the beginning. It did not occur to me then that something had been finalized.

MY GRANDMOTHER was not generally a storyteller. That was my grandfather. If you wanted stories about my grandmother's life, you usually had to get them from him. She was insular that way. She knew how to prevent you from feeling her absences.

While my grandfather talked about this woman, Nora, whom he'd met in a bakery shortly after she had immigrated to Toronto from England, my grandmother looked on, polite and indulgent but also slightly puzzled, as if she couldn't believe that anyone could want to hear so much about her early life. She wasn't troubled by self-fascination. My grandfather said that something about my grandmother made her highly visible. She was dressed plainly, in a grey wool dress and a long black coat, with a white silk scarf about her neck, and she was not decorated with makeup or jewellery, but everyone turned to look at her. And when she spoke, she had the most refined voice he had ever heard. He wanted to sit in a dusky, firelit room and listen to her read aloud. She bought a loaf of white bread and a dozen meringues and was gone. He followed her out, forgetting his wallet on the counter. The only comment my grandmother would volunteer was that it went against all her instincts and her upbringing to converse with a strange man on the street outside a bakery, let alone to agree to have tea with him the following day at a café on Yonge Street.

They married six months later. Both of them were older, thirty-five, which was unusual for their generation (and I never was able to gather a clear account of what they had been doing in the years since they'd finished school). Their wedding was not as small as they would have liked. My grandfather's many friends had come, and his many Scottish relatives had taken the train from Nova Scotia, and some of my grandmother's relatives had come the month before for an extended visit. And because they got married at a small church, their wedding felt twice as large as it actually was because their party filled the pews.

Though she was a woman whose looks invited attention, my grandmother disliked being stared at. She was happy to be marrying my grandfather, but as she stood at the back of the church in her slender white dress and her long lace veil, she couldn't just then imagine that walk down the aisle (firmly married, she confessed all doubt a week later). She didn't exactly think of leaving the church, but she hadn't agreed to so much preening fanfare for two ordinary people who had simply met in a bakery and taken a liking to each other. But the procession began and she was, necessarily, at the back of it. She stepped slowly, at that funereal wedding pace, and watched the enormous cross above the altar. No walk, she was sure, had ever been longer. When she was halfway to my grandfather, someone shouted, above the steady organ music, "Smile!"

It was not said maliciously, but certainly there was reproach there—an amusing comment had gone wrong somewhere and had come out as an indignant correction. People had travelled far for a show. Of course, upon hearing that command, she was less able to smile than ever. She and my grandfather had never been able to identify the guilty party. No one owned up. My grandfather wondered if the voice hadn't sounded remarkably like my grandmother's old Aunt Eva. Here, the comment my grandmother would add was that no relative of hers would have shouted such a thing.

At the reception, she had asked her new husband if he had heard. He said, "I heard something, but I didn't know what it was. I was too busy looking at you. You were a vision of loveliness."

There was a band playing, and people sitting at tables, talking and sipping champagne. She couldn't quite hear him. She thought he had said, "You were a version of loveliness." She thought he was saying that it didn't matter if she hadn't smiled, if she had looked sulky and disagreeable heading down the aisle, that he had made his choice and he was prepared to continue believing it was the right one, even if it wasn't the perfect one, but just a version of what he'd really wanted. She thought he was insulting her. For two days, she went around thinking that, trying to adjust to being the wife of this man who had insulted her on their wedding day. Finally, she brought it up. She let him know that they weren't off to a good start. (She had married that most vicious species of liar, she thought, one who pretends at happiness, one whose tact and solicitude are a form of hiding.) He corrected her, of course, and she tried to correct her memory of the day.

Except for this single lapse in hearing, my grandmother was an excellent listener. She listened to my grandfather tell stories about her. She listened to me tell stories about school and my friends, and when religion hit me, church and God. She listened to my mother tell stories about my father and Chuck, the shocks of her sexual awakening. And she would say just the thing to put all your thoughts in the right order.

One evening while my parents were still separating, while my grandmother still lived at home, my mother, my sister, and I, along with our dog, a thick-necked black Labrador retriever, went to my grandparents' house for dinner. Our dog, Pete, was not like our grandparents' dog Beau had been. Beau was the sort of dog who kept walking when other dogs barked and growled. My grandfather didn't even need to use a leash; Beau would simply heel at his side. Pete was strong and determinedly friendly, willing to pull my mother over at his first sight of a dog or cat or person he might like to greet. That evening when we arrived at my grandparents', their neighbour, who looked at us suspiciously whenever he saw us piling out of the car and had once commented to my grandmother that he was terribly sorry, though not terribly surprised, that my mother was divorcing, was out on his front lawn watering his petunias. Pete started barking when he saw him through the window, then, once out of the car, pulled my mother to the ground as he barrelled over to say hello. She was wearing a short stretchy black skirt—a gift from Chuck and a symbol of her emancipation from my sexually staid father—and she skinned her knee badly on the sidewalk.

"I'm going to murder you," she yelled at the dog. "You bad dog, Pete, you're a bad, bad dog."

She limped over to the neighbour's lawn, and as she collected the dog, she said to Pete again, "I really think I could murder you. I really could." Then to the neighbour, she apologized, "I'm sorry, but you know, of course, he's friendly."

The man set his hose on the grass. "I don't know what you're doing with that dog," he said. "Someone should take him away from you. Clearly, you can't handle him."

"I told you that he's friendly. He's just young and overexcited," my mother replied.

"That is not a friendly dog. That is not the kind of dog people like you should be owning."

"Why don't you mind your own business," my mother said.

"People like you shouldn't have dogs," he continued, even more emphatically. "I ought to call the Humane Society. That dog is a menace and you can't control him."

Hearing the commotion, my grandparents had come out of their house, just in time to hear my mother venture an observation, that he was nothing but a stupid old man, and to offer the following advice for his next course of action, that he go fuck himself. Then she turned around and stormed up to my grandparents' porch. Her hands were trembling, and I said to her angrily, "God is listening to you, Mother. You might go to hell."

"Well, if He doesn't like it, He can put in earplugs! *He* can go to hell," she shrieked at me.

My grandmother put on the kettle for a pot of herbal tea, and we sat at the kitchen table not eating dinner. As my mother's anger subsided, embarrassment set in. The man had been in the wrong, she affirmed, but perhaps she should have kept her mouth shut so that she could be even more in the right.

Finally, my grandmother, who had seemed amused the entire time, said, "You'll forget all about this. Isn't that reassuring? You'll remember the sense of what happened, but not the specifics. He might recall that you said he was a stupid old man, but you likely won't. It's much easier to remember the nasty things that have been done and said to you than it is to remember the nasty things you've done and said."

"But I want him to forget about it," my mother moaned.

"No," said my grandmother. "If you forget it, then it no longer exists."

My mother did calm down then. It seemed to comfort her that this incident probably wouldn't remain on her record of the things she'd done wrong in her life.

I said something once to my grandfather when my grandmother was in the hospital, to the effect that she had been an invalid for her entire life. In spite of everything I'd seen and lived through with her, I could hold this view. For me, somehow, the hospital blotted out everything that had come before it.

My grandfather said, "Don't forget that your grandmother had a long life before the one you knew her in."

I suppose I stopped giving her credit for having had a younger self. Biking through London on a fall afternoon. Tobogganing in Switzerland, playing tennis in long white dresses, siestas in the dusty summer afternoons of colonial Trinidad. These became matters of conjecture. A life lived in sickness was my view, the last years became the whole.

Once when I went to the hospital, my grandmother looked different. The student hairdressers had come. Her neat bob had been cut short and permed, the way older people are expected to wear their hair.

I was very upset and was not careful to conceal how much I disliked her haircut.

My grandmother had no mirrors in her room, and she couldn't have held a hand mirror even if she had one.

"What's the difference?" she said, smiling at me. "*I* can't see it."

MY GRANDMOTHER kept a picture of Beau at her bedside. She also kept a book there, a lifelong habit, though she could no longer hold books.

After several months in the Wellesley Hospital, she was moved to a chronic care facility, against her wishes. She wanted to go home.

One Sunday close to a year after she first went into the hospital, I arrived to find her sitting in a large orange geriatric chair, looking out the window. I hadn't seen her for two weeks because I'd had school exams and my mother had begun seeing someone new, having discovered that Chuck was the kind of man who looks at a woman and easily sees the flab on her stomach. Finally, I'd come alone in a taxi, intending to take her to mass in the basement. She refused. When the nurse came in, she also refused to return to bed.

It seemed that earlier that morning, after her breakfast tray was taken away, she had looked up and seen a fat brown spider on the ceiling. My grandmother had been terrified of spiders all her life, and she watched it as it sat directly above her head. She tried to remain calm; she felt embarrassed to disturb a nurse over a harmless spider. It meandered around and eventually began to lower itself slowly on an invisible string. She watched it as it swung lower and lower, and she told herself that any moment it would spring back up to the ceiling and be on its way. When it continued its way down, she buzzed for the nurse. She waited, but the nurse didn't come, so she rang again, but still the nurse didn't come. Finally, the spider lowered itself directly onto her knee. The room had been overheated at breakfast time and the nurse had pulled the covers back so my grandmother could feel a pleasant draft on her legs. This was why the nurse didn't respond now—she had tended to my grandmother not long before. The nurses were kind and attentive, but irritable sometimes because many of the patients rang them for no particular reason. The spider had deposited itself on my grandmother's bare skin.

She was trapped. Without help, she could move only minimally. Even her arms she could move only within a limited range, certainly not with enough force to locate and kill the spider. Her bed was positioned so that her upper half was more or less in a seated position, so she watched mutely, unable to bend, as the spider moved its legs thickly up her bare thigh.

"Why didn't you call out for the nurse?" I asked her.

This was a silly question. My grandmother regarded need, vocalized, as obscene. In the same way that she would never have asked you to repeat yourself, though she was hard of hearing, she would never have allowed herself to call out, even in the most dignified voice. She had heard too many patients cry out for help. She was determined never to be like them.

When the nurse finally came, the spider had made its way under her gown and had settled on her stomach. The nurse had to undo the hospital gown from behind and take it completely off in order to find the spider. My grandmother mentioned that while the nurse had looked around for the spider—it had by then scurried down to her other leg—she seemed skeptical, as if she suspected hallucinations were at play.

I understood only then the meaning of the word *chronic*, its highway stretch of sameness.

She saw me looking at her picture of Beau.

"I know what it is you think," she said sourly. "I've brought this on myself."

She had never let on before that moment that she thought less of me because of my vision of the world, my version of it.

There was a new sign over her bed, "This patient is deaf." I pretended not to notice.

WE HAD THE SAME name, my grandmother and I. My grandfather called us Big Nora and Little Nora. The rest of my family called me Hutby. It wasn't until I was around ten that I asked what Hutby meant.

My mother said, "Old woman. Like a gaffer is an old man, a hutby is an old woman."

I liked that. It seemed a reflection of my unlikely wisdom. It seemed an honour. They had started to call me Hutby when I was too young even to think about it, but I decided, at ten, that my naming had been unintentionally prophetic.

Only when I was a grown woman, married, a resolute atheist, did it occur to me to look up *hutby* in the dictionary. I discovered that it did not mean old woman, and was not even a word at all.

Then, my naming seemed unintentionally prophetic in an entirely different way: my family had known, when I was as young as three, that my grandmother and I should not have the same name.

THE FIRST TIME I set foot in a church was with my grandmother. I was three and a half, and my mother had called her in a panic. Several months before, my sister had been born, and my mother was breastfeeding, something she hadn't done when I was a baby because she had been afraid, but she was entirely different by the time my sister was born: educated about the health benefits of breast milk, sensible and determined in a way that seemed more competitive than maternal. On this Sunday morning, while my sister had been having her nap, my mother and I took a bath together. At first, all was uneventful. I played with my bath doll and my mother splashed me and pretended the rubber duck was a shark on its way to eat my foot. Out of nowhere (this part, later, was emphasized: we were having the loveliest time and this nastiness came *out of nowhere*), I leaned forward and bit my mother's nipple. Hard.

It is clear to me now what I was thinking. I was old enough to understand that my sister was being fed by my mother's breast, but what exactly was going on hadn't been explained to me. My mother's nipple brought food. I bit my food. I bit the nipple. My mother

refused to accept this interpretation, offered calmly by my grandmother. Instead, she saw it as the advent of a mean streak, the coming of a taste for violence too horrific to contemplate. As evidence
she produced the drops of blood on her white towel. She called on
my grandmother to remove me from her presence. This was in
the days when my grandmother still went to mass several times a
month, before she became bored with it and realized she felt less
spiritual in church than anywhere else. My mother requested that
something be done to stem my ugliness, so my grandmother took
me to church.

The singing is what stays with me. My grandmother was known
for her singing voice, for her clear soprano too pure and thin to
be opera, too interesting to be chorus. I sat on the hard wooden
pew while red, yellow, and blue light streamed through the stained
glass into the dark space as my grandmother sang hymns from
memory. She knew all the words and kept the pitch while others
faltered. Her voice was not ambitious. It did not trill showily or
hold notes too long so its song could outlive the others. But still it
came through beyond the rest. Hers was the voice your ear sought
out. She stopped halfway through "And Did Those Feet in Ancient
Time" and turned to me.

"Hum along, darling," she said. "Everyone wants to hear you
sing."

My grandmother had it in her head that I had a beautiful singing voice, which I did not, and she encouraged me to sing in the car,
at home, in the park. Even then, I sensed that I did not have a good
voice. Later, I knew I was not like my grandmother in many ways.

Years later, long after my grandmother had died, I was at the
National Gallery in Ottawa, standing next to a botanical exhibit,
outside the reconstructed nineteenth-century Rideau Chapel,
thinking of where to go for lunch, when I heard choral music inside
the chapel. It was a sound exhibit by Janet Cardiff called *Forty-Part*

Motet, a recording of the piece "Spem in Alium" by the sixteenth-century composer Thomas Tallis. Positioned all around the gilded chapel were tall black speakers. There were forty voices altogether, and each had been separately recorded and assigned to one of the speakers. When I stood in the middle of the room, the voices resonated as a choir, and when I walked a path next to the speakers, I felt I was next to each singer. The voices were like dominoes, one standing, the one behind it falling. I moved from the centre of the chapel to the sides, back and forth again and again, so I could hear the change from singer to chorus, the merging and the retreat, the one into many, many into one.

As I walked along the line of sopranos, I heard a voice just like my grandmother's. It was a fine voice, and full, more grave and intimate than the others. I wanted to claw through the speaker.

There was one story my grandmother did tell, of her childhood and youth in England. My grandmother was born in Port of Spain, Trinidad, but she and her five brothers and sisters attended boarding school in England. There is an old sepia picture, mounted on grey cardboard, of her and her sister, dressed identically in tweed car coats, woven wicker hats, their long braids tied with wide ribbons, about to board the boat to the other country where they lived out the school year. It was a privileged life, but a difficult one in many ways. A child away from her mother and father, my grandmother was forced to embrace independence and self-discipline. At night, she lay in her dormitory bed afraid that banshees were going to appear before her, wailing the death of someone she loved. She looked forward to her time away from the school, her days out in the real London air, and when she was old enough, she was allowed to go out on Saturdays without an adult. Freed from her school uniform, her favourite outfit was a crisp white dress with a pattern of large cherries. One spring afternoon, she was sweeping through the narrow streets on her bicycle when she heard a child call out excitedly in a Cockney accent, "Ow, look at the cherries!" When my grandmother told the story, she imitated the child's Cockney pitch perfectly. In that one exclamation, I saw it all: the fashionable dress, the old-fashioned bicycle, the cheery, ragged child with an accent so vulgar her life's possibilities must have been set from her first word. My grandmother loved to tell that one story, and I loved to hear it. There were many other things about her life then that she didn't remember—and I had tried, I had probed relentlessly, many times—but this single bicycle ride, this brief and delighted exclamation, had stuck with her through her whole life.

"Don't worry. It won't stay with you," my grandmother once said to me when an old man trailed me, crying for his childhood cat, into her room. Just two months after she died, I tried to recall the exact image of her thin porcelain body in her wheelchair by the window, and found that I could not. Forgetfulness is more efficient than memory: we do away with the details.

What remains is something less than memory, and something more: a wet nose nudging your hands; a bicycle, ridden in May; a dozen meringues; that sudden moment of glee; the long life of a voice.

RETENTION
with AFTERFLOW

It was the beginning of winter, when threadbare skies and naked trees still seemed romantic, and I decided that having sex too often was making me look dirty. Just after dawn, I looked in the bathroom mirror and noticed that my skin looked greasy and tired, my arms undernourished and sinewy. I turned back to the bedroom, where Stephen was still sleeping, and it smelled like breath, like mouths held open all night. I thought I might be tired of commitments.

This happened in the year I turned twenty-seven, just before I met my old friend Julie again—before I met her husband, Angus, and a jolt of something keen and sly went through me. It was the year I learned that reciprocation need have no part in love.

Each morning and night, I took a hot shower and scrubbed myself with potent antibacterial soap. I massaged my scalp with tingly green shampoo that smelled of men's cologne. In the dawn cool of our apartment one morning, I examined my hair, which hung in flat ropes, and my cheeks, which had no colour, and informed Stephen that we would no longer be having sex. All he did was raise his eyebrows. He was standing naked by the toaster. His body was wide and stocky, but his face had a prettiness about it—the sort of ordinary womanly prettiness that doesn't say anything. People sometimes thought we were brother and sister, and I would say, "No! We're not," too loudly, without managing, or even attempting, to hide my horror—not the horror, as they thought, of being mistaken for my lover's sibling, but of looking like someone I considered bland. When I got home, I would stare at my face in the mirror and think of how profoundly insulted I was. Other times, I was grateful and knew I was lucky to be connected to him; I hadn't had a real job since finishing grad school and he was a biotechnologist who supported me without a word of complaint. His apartment was bare and beautiful, with white walls and high ceilings and the conveniences of someone who appreciates technology, as he did.

Stephen dropped two slices of bread into the toaster after I suggested we attempt celibacy for a time. It was his habit not to respond to me. He considered exaggeration the sign of a fanciful character, and was skilled at refusing to indulge it. When he sat down at the table, he slapped thick wedges of cold butter on his toast and said, "You're perfectly clean, you know. I've never seen anyone so clean. So if you want to stop, we'll stop, but I'm not the one waking up the neighbours at two o'clock in the morning."

He was right. I did that. We didn't stop having sex, though. And, in fact, I initiated it at two o'clock in the morning. The more I hated sex, the more I became convinced that it was robbing me of something fine and pure, the more defiantly I took to proclaiming my love of it. When Stephen traced a hand along the side of my neck, I shuddered and moaned at a low, ripe pitch. When we moved from the kitchen to the bed, from the bathroom to the bed, from our desks to the bed, I panted meaningfully, as if I had never known such painful anticipation, such temptation. I shrieked as if sex were returning me to something essential, to a primordial kind of efficiency, as if only sex and breathing could be necessary. The more I wanted to push his body away, the more freely I screamed. Afterwards, I would lie in bed with a burning between my legs and a ringing in my ears. I often couldn't sleep until I had a bag of frozen vegetables hugged between my thighs.

This became typical. I realized later that we were waiting to fall in love. All that teasing made us feel that it might be on the verge of happening, but it never did. All through autumn, we had been waiting, but we couldn't have said what we were waiting for. It was nothing palpable, like news of an exciting job opportunity or a windfall of money. Nonetheless, our time together had that useless, meandering quality life has when you are waiting for something golden and idealized, something transformative. This is what made our patience so thin, what made us turn to the militant physicality of sex. We were waiting for something that should have happened long before.

ONE DAY ON Bloor Street near the start of December, I ran into my old friend Julie. We met as teenagers, a time when every day held the possibility of treachery, at a small Toronto girls' school where our powers of fault observation became attuned like the hearing of wolves. I hadn't spoken to her since grade twelve, when I decided I was tired of her and started scrupulously avoiding her. When I spotted her, she was on the far side of the street looking in the window of a store selling yoga gear. I crossed to get a closer look, but pretended not to see her until she saw me. Two days later, we were sitting in a small café, our table ringed with sunlight.

Julie had acquired glamour with age. The intervening years had made her look more appealing, more interesting. She still had that lightly freckled oval face, but her skin was fairly sun-damaged, with lines already deepening around her eyes, and the loss of baby fat made her chin rather pointy, perhaps too sharply defined. But her flaws, if indeed they were flaws, worked to her advantage. When we were fifteen, everyone had wished to look like Julie—to brush in the mornings such pale strawberry hair (now considerably darkened); to offer such small, tidy hands to a reaching boy; to own such round, dewy cheeks and such regular blue eyes; to be so naturally well-groomed, so innocuous. I had sometimes thought Julie too typical-looking, but the years had made her more pronounced, and she seemed to know the advantages of her looks because she wasn't wearing any makeup. Her clothes, too, were far better considered than my jeans and black sweater. She was wearing a thick white turtleneck and a short black pleated skirt, slightly schoolgirlish, but she had offset the plainness of the sweater, the adolescence of the skirt, by throwing a black cashmere shawl around her neck like a scarf.

We steeped our tea until it was almost as black as coffee and ate the crunchy winter pears she had smuggled in.

"Isn't this the week for running into people!" Julie said. "Last week I saw Ryan Little, this week you. Has he ever lost his looks. He thought I would give him my phone number, just like that. I mean, even if he weren't so ghastly looking. Your mother said he would be. He was so pretty back then, but your mom could tell he wouldn't stay that way."

"I never thought he was so pretty in the first place," I said.

"But you never thought anyone was. You never liked anyone! Your mom and I used to wonder."

"Wondered?"

"You know," she said. "Your mom told me to keep an eye out for signs."

Julie and I were unlikely friends. We became so only when I was designated to keep track of her homework and upcoming assignments because she was going to be out of school for two weeks for minor surgery. Our class was small, but we had barely known each other. There was a certain rowdiness about her I found off-putting. Always, when she laughed, I thought there was mockery in it; I thought she was noticing that my ponytail wasn't as smooth as hers, that my breath wasn't quite right, or that the pleats in the back of my kilt needed ironing. Our teacher had chosen me to take her work to her because we lived near each other. What made our friendship possible was that Julie's candour, so unexpected, immediately capsized all my opinions about her. The first time we sat down in her kitchen to make a schedule for when I would come by, she told me all about her surgery. She had a problem called retention with afterflow. It was a bladder problem, more common among older women. She would think she had emptied her bladder, then she would have to go a little more, sometimes even urinating a bit without feeling it.

"It's just that it doesn't all come out when you want it to," she had said. "And there it is a bit later, when you have no control."

Talking about bladder control: undoubtedly the beginning of something.

Her mother thought the problem was caused by the fact that Julie, as a child, had refused to urinate more than twice a day and had even gone away for the weekend to a friend's cottage and drank little and allowed herself to go only when everyone was outside, after she had already been there for almost twenty-four hours. She was mortified by the prospect of people hearing the revealing tinkle through the thin wooden walls. Of course, Julie's mother had no medical knowledge whatsoever, other than being married to a cardiologist and being impressed by all doctors. She was a shopgirl at Holt Renfrew and had long, thick red nails. She insisted that all their cars have vanity plates and believed that there was not a man alive who could fail to become besotted with Julie. When she talked about the reason for Julie's retention with after-flow, her voice became loud and nasal and she used words that were not words, like *lossage* and *drainery*.

My friendship with Julie lasted for as long as it did, not because we had such a special connection, but because I was fascinated by her, and I never stopped being honoured that she had told me the reason for her surgery so openly, given that she had the kind of mother who invented words to replace the words that corresponded to the real functions of the human body. Julie would always surprise me in this way. She would behave in a way that her behaviour a moment later would call into question—ashamed at the prospect of people hearing her urinate during a cottage weekend, but capa-

ble of telling me she had a bladder control problem. It is difficult
not to fall for unpredictability.

And several weeks later, at my house, Julie bonded with my
mother over their fondness for discussing sex. I came from looser
people than Julie did, but I had turned out much tighter. In my
house, the toilet was likely to be full of unflushed urine at any given
time. Julie had had sex, which her mother did not know, and she
and my mother were united through their sex-loving complacency.
Halfway through grade ten, Julie broke up with her first boyfriend,
and for six months in the wake of the breakup, he argued for her
love through daily letters. "He's obsessed," Julie told my mother
matter-of-factly and my mother nodded eagerly, beaming. The
three of us pored over his letters at my dining room table after
school. "You move through my head like some useless tune I have
unconsciously taken to," he wrote. "I whistle your cherry kiss,
your sweet honey voice all day. I hum your spirit!" Each paragraph
ended with an exclamation mark. He never signed his name to the
letters, and in one of them explained that he couldn't bring himself
to sign his name to Julie. He was afraid that the name would throw
her off, that she wouldn't be able to connect it to the person he was
in her head. "It is my label, but it is not my essence as you know it,"
he wrote. He spoke frequently of his essence. Instead of signing,
he trailed off each letter with a squiggly line.

My mother was immensely comforted by my affiliation with
Julie. She had been disturbed by my lack of sexual activity, and she
wanted to be reassured that I masturbated. She seemed to harbour
suspicions that I was not sufficiently sexual, and that I failed to
experience the degree of horniness that normal teenaged girls did.
When facing her inquiries, I often pretended that I did masturbate
regularly, although I did not, simply to ease her mind. Later, during my phase of furious sex with Stephen, my mother came to visit
and made it known to me before she left that she was delighted to
see three empty condom boxes in the garbage.

"I feel personally rewarded," she said. "Personally rewarded."

Julie was living with her husband, Angus, in Riverdale, but that day in the café all she wanted to talk about was her therapist, whom she had seen just that morning. At the beginning of the therapy, he had been a disappointment, short and unattractive with copper-coloured hair and a bald patch he attempted to conceal with highlights, but (no doubt through some devious psychological strategy, she said) he had gotten to her. She was having nightly dreams about him.

"I had a sexual nightmare," she said. "I went for my appointment and he wanted to take me somewhere else. I was afraid and didn't want to go, but felt I couldn't say no. So he drove me to a building, where he had this stark, empty apartment. We went in and he spread a blanket out on the floor, as if we were going to have a picnic, and he was staring at me in a gross way, kind of flirty and scolding. Then he started stroking my breast through my sweater in a slow, horrible way. He was sitting cross-legged and his penis was bulging out of his pants. I was afraid of him and wanted to get out, but I didn't want to be rude. I thought that it was best to go along with it and get it over with. I kept noticing this bare patch of skin above his black socks, and it made me hate him."

After that dream, at a mainly silent session during which he watched Julie while she sighed theatrically and contemplated the diplomas on his wall, she had suggested leaving. He shook his head apologetically and smiled as if at a small child pleading for candy. It was unthinkable, he explained, she wasn't nearly ready to be on her own. "You're being resistant," he said with a tender dip of his head. "But that's part of the process."

I told her that twice I had seen a female therapist who called me *doll* and assigned as homework a book entitled *Goodbye Mother, Hello Woman.*

"I know," said Julie. "They're all bullshit. I can see that, but I can't see that, if you know what I mean."

I did know what she meant, exactly.

Julie spoke to me as if we had never stopped speaking. She had never been one for slow introductions, for easing through beginnings that could be bypassed. Her voice was full of impetuous goodwill, a desire to abandon false reserve, and she made me feel I didn't have to work with her. Her voice had a regal breathiness that made you want to lean in and listen, and we talked with that rare mix of comfort and newness that occurs with girls quite young. Our conversation seemed expansive and mysterious, something not bound by consequence or expectation. While I was with her, I forgot all about Stephen. I forgot that I would have to go home to him. At one point, she took a long breath, looked at me and said, "I realize I've missed you." It was the only time I had been out of Stephen's and my apartment in three days, and I was hungry for the first time in a week. I thought, Finally, here is what I need: a warping and rechannelling of routine, unplanned alterations.

"I think I'm secretly in love with Dr. Stillman," Julie said. "But I'm not sure."

Looking back, I can see how what seemed so lovely was, in fact, the start of the problem. I wanted something of her life. It all seemed simple enough: Julie felt a kind of repelled love for her therapist, a pornographic undercurrent in every moment she spent with him. She hated her husband.

I suppose my need was such that I could not separate, then, what she told me from what I believed she had told me.

THE FIRST TIME I met Angus, Julie wasn't there. She had invited me to her house for breakfast, and when I arrived, there was only him, sitting in the back of the small, pretty house in Riverdale, in a greenhouse he'd built on the back of their kitchen. He was surrounded by glossy emerald plants and ink-stained paper. I remembered, even years later, exactly how he smelled, like tree roots and ravine air.

When I arrived, no one answered the door. After knocking and ringing the doorbell for five minutes, I finally went around to the backyard. I had it in my head that Julie might be gardening, that it was the kind of thing she might do, even though it was December and there was no garden to tend. I was calling Julie's name as I walked around to the back and saw the greenhouse. I knocked on its glass door and turned the knob, which was unlocked. When I went in, at the far end I saw a man sitting at a desk, facing the rear windows.

"Is Julie here?" I asked. I didn't usually walk right into people's houses unannounced, but I didn't feel in the least embarrassed that I had done so.

The man turned around. His black hair was beautifully unkempt, the kind of profusion that's ruined by grooming. All around him were plants, in handmade pots along shelves by the windows, on the floor in large, bright ceramic pots. The desk was covered in loose papers, and there was a portable heater churning loudly next to it. The man's eyes were green. They were half-open, but gave the impression of uncommon alertness.

"You're Julie's friend."

I nodded. "She invited me for breakfast."

"Julie's not here," he said. "She went to a medical doctor. Her therapist. But he is, in fact, a medical doctor."

I didn't know what to say to that.

"It was an emergency," he added. "I'm obviously Julie's husband."

Then he disappeared into the kitchen and returned dragging a chair. "Would you like to sit?" he asked.

"I can go," I said. "I don't want to interrupt."

He set the chair down definitively.

He was wearing a T-shirt that said, "I'M SURROUNDED BY ASSHOLES," and I noticed when he came close that all his fingernails were bitten. He was tall and had a flabby thinness, with a little belly that went around his waistline like a snake. Julie had told me about this T-shirt—one of her greatest struggles was his insistence on wearing it on teaching days. He was a psychology professor at the University of Toronto, and he neglected his teaching responsibilities but worked hard on his own research. This is what he talked about as we sat in the greenhouse. I imagined him lecturing a hall of first-year students, the kind of teenagers who ingratiate themselves with a well-timed compliment, then devastate you with a smirk of pure contempt.

"Drunks are surprisingly responsible," he said. "At least when it comes to sex. That's what we found, and of course it runs contrary to a popular belief."

He was writing an article on the psychological underpinnings of drunk and sober decision-making. I asked him about his research and he talked about it with jumpy gestures that periodically blew the papers off his desk. When this happened, he snatched them back up from the ground immediately and stashed them protectively under his arm.

"I promise I won't steal them," I said.

"There's so much people don't understand. There's so much we don't understand, even though we study this," he said. "People who are drunk—when informed about the dangers of unprotected sex—are actually less likely to have unprotected sex. Isn't that a surprise? It's very exciting."

He explained his research very clearly, and while he spoke, he looked at my stomach. There was a sweet asexuality about him. He was an odd mixture of jittery discomfort and academic composure. His entire body stayed perfectly still while his hands flapped nervously. I could see that he was probably often on the receiving end of that dirty adolescent laughter, the kind of laughter that wants you to know you're being laughed at. He had been married before,

Julie had told me. When he was twenty-five, he had married a red-head who was fifty but looked thirty. She was perpetually melan-choly, a closet poet. He came home one day to find that she had sloppily burned all her poems, which he hadn't even known existed, in the middle of the kitchen floor, and all her clothes were gone. Everywhere were little burned bits of paper with allusions to other poems, such as "The Grecian urn has cracked," and "We will not go then you and I until our blood has lit the morning sky."

Julie had said, "Being a poet says a lot about a person."

She had also said, in a satisfied sort of way, "When you marry a divorced man, you're getting another woman's baggage."

Angus stretched his spine over the back of his chair, and his T-shirt receded, exposing the lower part of his stomach. I noticed he had a scar the shape of a crescent moon over his navel.

"Julie showed me an old picture of you from a yearbook," he said. "I almost wouldn't have recognized you." He leaned forward. "Is there anything you need?"

I asked for a glass of water, although I didn't particularly want it, because I had the sense that he wanted to do something for me. The cordless phone on his desk rang, and he answered, listened for several moments, then cupped his hand over the receiver and told me that he'd be several minutes and that there was a Brita filter in the refrigerator.

I was sweating under my heavy sweater and winter coat, and the kitchen was cool like a rush of outdoor spring air. I do not know what I thought of Angus then. Certainly I was not aware of any romantic envy of Julie, any immediate fascination with his sexual self, or even the kind of person he was. What I felt most was the nosiness that had at one time been my most infamous character trait, that itchy longing to know other people's business that had led my sister to have a lock put on her door when she was fourteen.

I looked at the kitchen ceiling and imagined I could hear,

beyond the distant stir of old copper pipes, the paint chipping slowly, peeling away in smooth curls. The glasses were in the first cupboard I opened, but I kept going. I inched each cupboard door open, afraid that their creaky hinges would give me away. I wasn't looking for anything specific, just the usual. Something distasteful, something foreign and subversive. Things I would never buy. Teriyaki sauce. Gnocchi. Strawberry Pop-Tarts. Crystal Light drink mix. But Julie's cupboards were stacked just like mine. Rice Krispies. Peanut butter. Spaghetti noodles. It was all the same. I couldn't quite see to the top shelf, but I thought I glimpsed something familiar. I leaned around the corner and saw Angus, sitting motionless with his back to me, at his desk. Quickly, I pulled myself up onto the counter, determined to find out what was up there. I stooped on the counter so my head wouldn't hit the ceiling, and looked into the top shelf. In the corner was an egg cup in the shape of Humpty Dumpty, a birthday present I had given Julie when she turned fifteen, in the days when she was caught up in memorizing nursery rhymes. I put it down and started digging to the back of the highest shelf. It was mostly cobwebs and kitchen things no one ever used, like beer mugs and rusty whisks.

I was trying to figure out what Angus's favourite foods might be when he walked in. He stood for a minute quietly. My arm was extended into the back corner of the cupboard farthest from the door.

"What are you doing?" he asked. He sounded calm and curious, as if he had just caught me in the middle of a benign activity, like reading a geography book.

He came over to the counter and stood beneath me, looking up. He lifted his arms like a child, and I lowered myself into them. He set me on the ground delicately and looked at me. That was all it took. In his eyes, I saw the possibility that he had never harmed anyone.

Then he turned to the refrigerator and took out a pitcher of water.

I stood behind him and tried not to imagine myself touching the worn back of his T-shirt.

WHEN I WAS A teenager, I would lie in bed at night wondering what it was like to be on the receiving end of obsession. It seemed to me the most honourable gift you could bestow upon someone. I knew I would behave quite differently than Julie if someone were possessed by me, consumed to the point of superlatives and imperatives, the hyperbolic language of hope and defeat. Every afternoon when Julie arrived home from school for those six months after the breakup with that first boyfriend, she would find love letters in the mailbox. At first she found them flattering, but a change came after some months, and Julie no longer found the letters amusing. The boy told her that she never left his mind for a moment, and that he would always love her. "What a burden," Julie shouted, slamming the letter into the garbage. "I absolutely can't stand this following me around forever." And she meant it. Even in the first comic blush of the boy's obsession, Julie never felt these epistolary outbursts were anything she needed. She didn't feel adoration gave her anything extra; it didn't nourish her in some way she was not already nourished. And for this I sometimes hated her. I was desperate to be the victim of terrorizing, vicious affection, such persistent and dishevelled lust. At best, I thought, I would find a typical love.

It is the typical that often breaks you. After hours of fighting one night, I initiated sex with Stephen at two o'clock in the morning because I thought it would warm me to him again. Afterwards, I couldn't sleep. My whole body felt genital, rocking with a hot, queasy pulse. Stephen was already snoring beside me, and I got out of bed, making sure to slam the door when I left. I ran a shallow oatmeal bath to soak in. The water was cool and I was shivering, so I wrapped a towel around my shoulders and sat looking at my lumpy reflection in the faucets. It was one of those moments when the unpleasant becomes ritualized, the typical threatening. I felt the shift. It was the end of something, a movement away from that frenzied middle space we had been occupying.

Stephen finally came and stood in the doorway of the bathroom. "Is there anything I can do?" he asked.

"No," I said, thinking, You've done enough.

"Are you very sore?"

I didn't answer. I couldn't take my eyes off him, his body was so stocky and immovable. He had a bit of an erection, and I couldn't help thinking how different he was from Angus. There seemed something so childish and uncouth about having an erection while I was in the bath, something offensively predictable about that link between arousal and nudity. I felt that Angus's sexuality would be so much more dignified, somehow compartmentalized from the rest of him.

"We've been having a lot of problems like this lately," Stephen said.

He tended to overuse the word *we*.

"We should assess this logically. Maybe you have low estrogen. Or maybe you need a multivitamin."

"It's gone beyond everything," I said. "Can't you see it on me?"

I stepped out of the bath, and he came into the bathroom, pulling the door closed behind him, and we stood next to each other, looking in the mirror, the long oval mirror on the back of the door.

"Look at my skin," I said. "These dark circles, I can't get rid of them. It's not just the lighting. They're just as bad in all the mirrors."

Standing there with him, I noticed the changes even more. My problem had gone beyond dirty-looking skin. My breasts hung a little lower, a little more out to the side. There was a taint, a bluish pallor, on my skin that wouldn't wash off with good hard soap. My body looked as if it had aged, and my skin was covered in tiny, colourless bumps.

"Feel this," I said, placing his hand under my breast. "Doesn't it feel slack to you? Almost like it's detaching itself from my body?"

"It feels exactly the same," he said.

He was watching me with a gunman's gaze—wild yet exacting. We stood in silence looking at my body. The mirror was old, bought by my grandmother in the early days of her marriage, and there was a distortion—a cloudy long curve like a river—along its centre. This made the distance between our bodies seem even greater. In the reflection, my body looked like it was straining away from Stephen's body, leaning precariously in the other direction, as if rejecting proximity to other bodies, rejecting the fingers and tongues and penises that had been inside it over the years. I got into the bath again and leaned back.

"You're beautiful," Stephen said. "Your body is beautiful."

THE SHIFT FROM FRIEND to competitor was sudden and surprised even me. Julie was on my mind constantly. One morning, I awoke at dawn in the middle of a dream because a branch was scratching the window next to my cheek. I opened my eyes with a start because I imagined, in the lazy tension of half-sleep, that men with long fingernails were trying to climb into my apartment through the window. I could hear the pull and creak of streetcars outside. Stephen was not moving beside me.

I had dreamed that I was standing in the greenhouse with Angus. My hair was wet, and had frozen in the cold air. He went over to his desk and sat down, then opened the top, pulled out a piece of paper, and handed it to me. The writing was neat, in clear black ink: "Love is for others."

"You feel that way, don't you?" he asked. His voice sounded slender and relaxed, cigarette-tipped.

He undressed me slowly and held me. His body was nearly hairless, but it had the kind of masculinity that doesn't need to announce itself. Then my high school math teacher came to the door and said, "But you haven't done your homework," and I turned from Angus and noticed that the plants were actually car parts.

I wouldn't have called it longing, what I felt in the dream. It was more of a solemn, furtive feeling. At that time in my life, I thought there was something sort of obscene about longing anyway: it made me think of musty motel rooms and too many lit candles, of booming bass and cars with tinted windows, Stephen's hot breath in my face. It was not something you could feel with a quiet man in a greenhouse mid morning. It was not something you could feel as you rose slowly from the ground with that man, as he took off your coat with a pure sadness like the sadness of childhood, as he pulled your sweater over your head and unhooked your bra, as he unbuttoned your pants and let them drop around your ankles. It was not something you could feel when he reached out his hands, when your breasts felt firm in his grip.

But, oh, the longing did come later, when Julie called before breakfast and I heard Angus in the background asking her about strawberry jam. She wanted to make plans and I found that I was trying to contrive something that would require him to be there. The longing came when I lay in bed every night for a week, falling back into my dream every time I closed my eyes, wondering whether Julie and Angus were in their bedroom, talking in intimate spousal voices. It came with a smacking vengeance that made me vile to anyone who dared speak to me.

Does it matter whether we create these feelings or whether they have grounding in something substantial? No, I think not. I found ways to support my beliefs, as people often will when they are working from nothing.

One Saturday afternoon, Julie and I went for a walk. It was an unusually warm February day, and we walked by the river through the Rosedale golf course. Our jackets were open, and we were sipping tall coffees Julie had bought for us. There was relief in the air, the kind that comes with spring.

"Angus is in a depression," she said.

She said it just that way several times—in a depression—rather than saying that he was depressed. I pictured Angus sitting in a groove dug out of the ground, just sitting there calmly. I imagined his face the way it was when he found me going through the kitchen cupboards: bemused, allowing, detached in an affectionate way. I already imagined that his face often carried this expression to some degree, so he could conceal what he was truly thinking. And I believed that this was the face of someone I could finally love, someone who kept things hidden, unlike Stephen, who showed whatever he happened to be feeling.

"Again," she said. "He is in a depression again, I should say."

"This happens often?" I asked casually, sympathetically, not wanting to show how interested I was. I wanted to know everything about him, the worst things first.

"At least four times a year, maybe for a month at a time. You have no idea what it's like living with someone who's like that."

Abiding depression, submerging then surfacing, only made him more attractive to me. She told me that several years before, he had had a near-death experience and he had not fully recovered from its impact. He had gone into the hospital to have his gall bladder removed by laparoscopic surgery, and was allergic to the anaesthetic. His blood pressure dropped and he went into cardiac arrest. In the end, he was fine, but he told Julie afterwards that he had been dead for a moment. For the rest of his stay in the hospital, he had acted strange, quiet and punished. She attributed his behaviour to nerves. Then he told her when they got home that something had happened when he was hovering near death. Julie drew out these words with relish—hovering near death—as if she was proud of Angus for such an accomplishment, impressed by

his ability to almost die when the rest of us landed squarely in one
extreme or the other. He had announced in the middle of the kitchen
that almost dying was like having an extended orgasm.

"In the middle of the morning!" she said. "I was drinking
orange juice!"

He had encouraged Julie to imagine the most intense orgasm
she had ever had, one that went on and on, the kind that made you
feel, for a few minutes anyway, that everything in the world is fine,
anything could happen. He had never experienced bliss quite like
that, he said, and knew he wouldn't again, not until he really died.

"Imagine telling this to your new wife," she shrieked. "That
you've never felt happiness like almost dying."

Then she said that once, after he got out of the hospital, he took
too many Tylenols, a fraction of him hoping to die, a fraction hoping not to, just so he could have that feeling again, that ringing
physical bliss, even in his forehead and his fingertips.

"Dr. Stillman and I have analyzed it," she added. "It's why he
still gets depressed sometimes. It's a death wish mixed with guilt
and love. And he doesn't really want to die."

I didn't say much while she was talking. I was afraid that any
comment on my part would steer her off course, and I would get less
information. And Julie had always been someone who could talk
on and on and get no response. The more I heard about Angus, the
more I believed I was bound to him beyond all reason. When I was
three, I had run headfirst into a wide concrete pillar in a neighbour's
basement, and I had never forgotten the feeling I had at the exact
moment of impact. A wonderful numbing had come before the pain,
before I was carted upstairs and given a squeaky orange teddy bear,
before my forehead split from the swelling and bled down my nose,
long before the neighbour jarred me with her acrid breath and tried
to lull me to sleep (tempting death by concussion, my mother later
accused). I had never forgotten that moment of impact, my head
banged so hard that my entire body catapulted into a state of deep

relaxation. When something was quite close upon you, it felt like anything but the thing it was.

I believed that not only was Angus's sexuality concealed and resplendent, but in fact made more brilliant and forceful by its removal from the public view. You would not know his desire until it was upon you. He would stand by what did not make good sense, by a sensation that had occurred when he was too compromised to confirm it lucidly. Never would I have guessed such things about him at our first meeting. Stephen would roll his eyes at such musings. He would make jokes. "I went to the car wash today. It was like skydiving from a plane up in the clouds."

The more Julie spoke, the more I began to think it was only right that I should feel the way I did about Angus. I felt that, although she was his wife, she was clearly not an authority on his character and in fact knew nothing about him that really mattered. She might know his toothpaste brand and the colour of his underwear. She might know the sound of his breathing in the dark. But these things couldn't matter if they weren't attached to a more important, resonant knowledge, if they weren't attached to a silent connection of wills, to a cloistering of affection.

The language of obsession and reason are often alike: arguments are measured out carefully, with passion that restrains itself, with a bite of superiority.

To anyone looking at us, Julie and I would have looked like the same kind of woman: responsible and educated, domestic and well-groomed, pretty enough, wives, future mothers. In our black woolen coats, almost identical, we looked like women who would be friends. But there was a difference. It was as obvious to me as anything. Julie looked as though she had always been loved. I sat by the river, and swept my fingers through the current. Julie knelt beside and put her arm around me.

"Anyway," she said, "I just can't stand it when he gets this way. He's just black black black."

"Look on the bright side," I said. "If he were happy, you'd have nothing to complain about."

She didn't take her arm off my shoulder, and she showed no surprise, but I saw her face steady itself as she looked towards the ground. I could tell she was making her way back from me.

AS I LAY IN BED at night, two scenes came to me again and again. Not dreams exactly, but deliberate conjurings, my personal theatre. One scene was real, the other not, though they seemed to have switched places in my mind, with the real masquerading as fantasy, the fantasy posing as reality. The real scene loitered in my head in a lazy way, in the washed-out grey of distant imaginings, so that I had to remind myself that it had happened:

Stephen is at work on his computer when I get home from a walk, but he gets up energetically when I come in. I turn my back to him as I close the door and hang up my coat, and he comes up behind me and grabs me around the waist. He presses himself into me and rocks me from side to side in his arms.

"How was your walk?" He speaks directly into my ear and I can feel his breath deep in my ear canal. He smells of wet wool and apples. He keeps rocking me and I resist. "Come on. Won't you dance with me?"

I wrench his arms loose enough to turn around, and he bends his knees and slings me over his shoulder in a fireman's grip, laughing uproariously, as if we are two university students who have been drunkenly flirting and touching and sidling our way towards sex all night.

"Ouch," I say, pushing at his head. "Your shoulder is digging into my stomach."

He half-runs across the living room into the bedroom and throws me down on the bed. He descends on me quickly and straddles my legs so I can't move. He looks down into my face.

"Get off me," I say, squirming.

He holds his hand above my stomach, soaring it back and forth like an airplane. "This is the hand," he says with dramatic menace. "This is the hand that has come to discipline you."

He pulls up my shirt and starts tickling my stomach and underarms and the back of my neck. I bat him away until he grabs both of my wrists in one of his hands and holds them against the mattress above my head, all the while tickling me with his other hand. I try to move my legs, but he has me pinned firmly.

"Stop it."

"Oh, no," he laughs. "The discipline has just begun."

I squirm up enough to flip over onto my stomach, and I start to crawl away. I kick at him and he grabs my ankle. Then he catches hold of my waist and twists me again onto my back. He moves his hand up to the side of my cheek and kisses the length of my neck. Long wet kisses broken up by tiny nips at my ear.

"Ah ha," he whispers. "Submission at last."

Separating truth from imagining can be like devising a list of pros and cons. I had to puzzle things out, focus hard to determine which was which. The more I entertained my fantasies about Angus, the more real they became, while the truth of my moments with Stephen faded the more I considered them—with playing and replaying they became as tepid and irrelevant as childhood nightmares. I could not fathom that these dreams about Angus had not happened:

A gift arrives in a cardboard box wrapped in plain kraft paper. My name and address are printed across the top in black marker. I set it on the bed and begin to unwrap, carefully peeling back the tape so I won't rip the thick brown paper. Inside is a long flannel Victorian nightgown with yellowing antique lace trim. I hold it out in front of me, and the hem dangles to the ground. I glance back to the box and a handwritten note is lying at the bottom. I know it is Angus's handwriting. "Wear this sometimes, and think of me," is all it says. I slip the nightgown over my head, and it makes me feel generous and untroubled, like a woman from another era. A woman with a softened imperial dignity, an innate nobility that doesn't think itself noble. I feel this so strongly I can't conceive of it not being real.

Letters arriving under cover of night, sealed with a stamp of dark red wax. Being lifted as he lifted me that day from the counter in his kitchen, as if I weigh nothing. He holds me, as in my first dream about him, and the air in his greenhouse is so humid it coats us with dampness. He is always naked and never naked. Wherever we have been is a spasm of silence in the air, the silence of allowing. No laughter, sharp like the taste of scotch. No shrieks of abandon, promises and retractions.

For two weeks, I even checked my drawers for the nightgown.

WANTING ANGUS made me secretive and strong. It allowed me to escape from the dependence and irritation and lethargy that had been my everyday life for so long. I tried out different roles that kept me feeling light and powerful when I was with Julie. Concerned supporter, analyzer of therapeutic intentions. Deliverer of ribald stories about the mania of sex. Devotee of yoga and all secular spirituality. Long-suffering girlfriend, stoic while being taken for granted by the man to whom she gives everything. I told her about the fights with Stephen. I made them sound more dazzling and tragic than they were. I told her we yelled so loudly that the neighbours pounded on the walls. In truth, we hardly raised our voices. The fights had a kind of opacity to them, unfolding in gestures like the disgusted turning of a head. Gritty voices punctuated by long bouts of awkward silence. I told how he resented me for refusing to make eye contact, and how he forcefully turned my head to his and pushed my eyelids back. I made this moment sound desperate and dangerous, when it had actually made both of us laugh. Even in the thick of the fights, that pungent cauldron of accusations and door slamming, our hearts didn't seem to be in it. Our words and gestures had a certain spent quality, as if we knew we should be doing better but couldn't dredge up the energy.

All this allowed me to feel that I was on a level playing field with Julie. I served myself up as someone with a teeming and exotic life, a person worthy of shock and concern. By this time, I had noticed a trademark tone of voice when Julie spoke of Angus. She talked about everything from his desire to invest their money unwisely to the way he poured chocolate soy milk on his Cheerios. There was always a conceited contempt in her voice, as if she was gratified to have a husband about whom she could complain. I was careful to show nothing. I asked no questions when it came to him.

Later, I would rant to Stephen.

"This is why we couldn't stay friends in high school," I said. "Julie is a woman who has everything and thinks she has nothing."

"Is that why you couldn't stay friends?"

"Absolutely! I tried but it became too much."

He pointed out that I had never kept any friend for more than two years.

"Well, she's always been this great complainer. But an outward complainer only. I can assure you Julie doesn't cry herself to sleep at night."

"Maybe she's going through something. It's temporary."

"And she has this terrific husband," I said. "Terrific."

"Terrific?" he asked. *Terrific* was not a word I ever used.

"Terrific," I said again emphatically.

Stephen said something about how he was glad men weren't friends the way women were. He had known all his closest friends since high school, and they spoke an intimate code, full of nicknames and short forms, like lovers almost. He said female friendships were a process of dissection, but a dissection performed without a scalpel or a clear knowledge of what you were supposed to remove.

Julie printed out e-mails written to her by two close male friends and showed them to me. One had recently moved to New York; the other had retreated from her life after objections from Angus. Both professed feeling adrift in their lives, without the easy intimacy they had with Julie to sustain them through each day. One said that he could not see the interior of an almond without thinking of the colour of her skin.

Julie said, "This happens to me sometimes. People think I'm the person they connect with best."

Not me, I thought. I felt superior, a kind of calm bitter triumph that no one really knew me.

I SAW JULIE and Angus together only once. One evening I met Julie at their house before we went to a movie. We were in the kitchen. Julie was standing with her back to the greenhouse and I was sitting at the antique oak table, facing it. Angus came up behind her, put his arms around her waist, and swung her around, laughing.

I noticed that his gums showed as he laughed. This made him seem like an altogether different person than I had imagined, more eager and vulnerable.

He heaved her up and swung her around, let his head fall back. His gums looked hard and streaky, not a uniform pink.

I thought I detected that he was careful not to look at me.

Still laughing, walking with a dizzy clumsiness, Julie went down the front hall to get her purse. When she was halfway along the hall, she stopped and did a little jump with a sideways kick.

For a long time after that, I tried to replay what happened next, tried to rescue it from the canals of memory and set it before me like an artifact, so I could determine whether I saw what I thought

I saw. I had been drinking tea while Julie put on her makeup, and I had left my cup half-full on the counter. While I was watching Julie, I thought I saw, out of the corner of my eye, Angus pick up my teacup and hold it to his lips in a casual but lingering way, then take a long sip. By the time I turned to him, he had put the cup down and lowered his arms to his sides as if nothing had happened.

WHAT HAPPENED NEXT I am sure of.

I went to Julie's when no one was home and let myself in. Julie always left the back door, the greenhouse door, unlocked. I took a roll of quarters with me and stopped at a pay phone to call her house every ten minutes on my way to make sure no one was home. It was a cold, windy day, and as I stood in the phone booths, I imagined the wind would blow the glass in on me and I would have to go home to Stephen cut and bleeding, possibly disfigured and knowing I deserved it. I came up with a story about why I was cut in case this happened. My story was logical and I took care not to make it too dramatic. I had spent the past week being vigilant about nearly everything—it was not easy to be as watchful, as detail-conscious, as vigilance required but also to be so broad about it, noticing everything from the chipping paint on the windowsills to the fingerprints on the metal of the toaster to the background voices on Julie's answering machine.

It was two o'clock, and I knew from the e-mails Julie sent me from work that she didn't generally leave until four o'clock.

I knocked on the front door, then the back door to affirm again that no one was home. Then I eased the door open and went inside. I thought, What I'm doing is fine because I know it is not fine. I'm not a bad person if I think I'm a bad person. As I looked again through the cupboards and listened to her answering machine, I repeated to myself that as long as I understood my fundamental badness, everything I did remained in the realm of the acceptable.

I started up the stairs to look through their dresser drawers and their bathroom cabinet, then I doubled back to the kitchen and opened the door to the greenhouse. It was hot again inside, and the heaters were churning loudly. At the far end, Angus's desk had been cleared of papers. I went over and stared down at it before opening its top. It was an old-fashioned desk, a large version of a child's school desk. In high school, Julie and I had had desks like these, but they were connected, the seat of each moulded into the desk behind it. Sometimes we rocked aggressively in our chairs, trying to topple the whole row. This was a solid desk, an antique, and the top creaked loudly as I raised it. The inside was a mess. All the papers had been stuffed in and some pieces were half crumpled. It was one of these that I took, smoothed out, and read: "I will always remember the flat underside of your forearms, your sideways smile." This line was written over and over, at different angles all over the page. I put it back and pulled out another. The writing was cramped and difficult to read.

> She looks at me through the distance of waves.
> She tells me
> asking gets us less
> and less will never give to more.
>
> It's all liquid in memory:
> loving her too much
> is the swell through me.
> The sound that crests quietly on the surface,
> but resounds in the lapping wide deep
> far below.

I flipped the page over. On the back, the sentence "I would have allowed you anything" was crossed out and he had written above and below it, "Your long thick hair, your path-worn stare." I stuffed these papers back into the desk and tried to make it look as disorganized as when I started.

I sat on Angus's chair. This was my moment. The pile of evidence that confirmed the theories I had been amassing. Angus was a man with secrets. Julie did not really know him. He was the kind of man a woman could never really know, a man who holds his privacy as privilege. At this moment, I was certain he had drunk from my teacup. I was certain that he had held the tea on his tongue, turning it over like fine wine, possibly even hoping my saliva was in it. I ignored the real smile on his face when he had spun Julie around, the goofy splendour of it. There was nowhere my mind didn't go. I planned that we would have dinner parties when we were together. Although I hated cooking, I imagined that we would invite Julie; we would adopt her and feed her nourishing food as a break from the frozen dinners she would be addicted to. She would be gracious about our efforts and she would entertain us with stories of her hapless loves, the men who stuck around but failed to please. There would be a rich dark library in our house, books piled up against walls everywhere, and we would sit in leather armchairs while Julie cheerfully wallowed and we would pity her the fleeting joys she magnified to get herself through each day.

Did I think the poems were written for me? I do not know. Later, I allowed myself to acknowledge that there had been a framed black-and-white photograph of Julie on top of the desk, and that there was a difference in her smile, something lopsided and careless, and beautiful.

Then, though, walking home, I did not think that I wouldn't talk to Julie again. That I would be besieged by visions of Julie and Angus in bed, images of Angus laughing at me with his arm fixed around Julie's waist. Julie didn't call me for days, and I became convinced that they had a hidden camera in the greenhouse recording

all my actions and that they watched it at night in their den, whispering to each other words like *unbalanced*, congratulating themselves
for installing surveillance that rescued their marriage from me. I
heard the word *rescued*, its world of protection and companionship,
over and over until I crawled under the covers. When the phone did
start ringing, I let it ring and ring through the day. I did not know
as I walked home that I would feel so virulently that I had no choice
other than this course of action. That it would be months before I
could even regain enough sense to ask myself who I felt I had lost.

No, that day as I walked home, I felt euphoric. There was even
flight in my step. There was an energy in the trees that week, a
windiness that was caustic and rowdy. Branches scraped our windows while we slept. A truck tipped over on the highway. Sometimes the wind was loud, gusty, and we could hear it ripping
around outside, whistling like a kettle, banging up against buildings. Sometimes it was quiet, rolling evenly over the city. The
day before, Stephen had come home with a cut the length of his
cheek—when he was walking home, a branch had snapped off a
tree and flown into his face.

As teenagers, Julie and I had loved winds like this. On our way
home from school, we would toss aside our knapsacks and stand
facing the wind, letting our hair whip around until it was tangled
up in knots. It was the only ritual of our friendship, the only thing
I could look back on years later and know that we had shared in
invention. Leaning into the dusty currents, we would trudge uphill,
chins upright, like young women coaxing older lovers.

We always reached her house first, and I would leave her there,
waving, on the doorstep, then make the rest of my way home alone.
I would think of how the school day never seemed to be over, as I
gathered up its contents and examined them, mapping each hour's
grievances and victories, contracts broken, the sullen intimacies,
and my peculiar, unmendable mistakes.

A MATTER
of FIRSTS

Your father's New York mistress was the one you
met. The exotic one. She used to say, "'Balls,' said
the queen. 'If I had two, I'd be king.'" That was her expression,
whether something irritated her, like losing her keys, or whether
there was a pleasant surprise, like one last piece of birthday cake
in the refrigerator. Balls, said the queen. Your father tried to correct her usage. The phrase had exasperation in it, he claimed, and
was appropriate only as a response to something negative. She said,
"Perhaps you're right," and smiled, but you could tell she was not
the type to capitulate in action.

Of course, it was not open to you that she was your father's
mistress, although you clearly knew, and they knew it. Your father
often went to medical conferences in New York, and he couldn't
tolerate hotels, their bedsheets gave him a rash, so he stayed with
her—Ella, an old friend from medical school. This is what he
told you and your mother, although there was an impish smirk
about him when he said so, a conspiratorial wink, as if such pat-
ent untruths, and the acceptance of them, were in keeping with the
true spirit of family. Three times when you were thirteen he took
you with him to New York because your mother had to look after
your grandfather, who was in and out of the hospital. Around you,
they acted stiff and professional, no sly looks or illicit touches. Of
course, the minute you saw her, you knew she was no doctor. It was
the body that halted your gaze. Unexpected: its creamy fatness, so

graceful, so much itself, that it challenged thinness everywhere. A fatness impossible to reduce with euphemisms. A soothing romantic welcome. This body rolled out of itself. Said, I am the way to be.

She lived in the Bronx on a quiet dead-end street lined with trees in an old brick house with high ceilings and a rickety wooden porch in the back. The air smelled like freshly cut grass and homemade shepherd's pie. On the other streets in her neighbourhood, the air smelled like fried food and smoke, traces of cumin and paprika drifting by on the breeze. You could hardly see to the sky. Everywhere you looked were apartment buildings with fire escapes zigzagging down the crumbling brick. Groups of teenagers lounged on front stoops, yelling at each other in languages you didn't understand. Your father wouldn't even let you walk off Ella's street alone. Her house was big enough for a family of eight, but she lived there by herself. She had bought it with her first husband, who had left at her request two years later, gladly signing the house over to her because he hated the way it felt empty no matter how much furniture they bought, the way their voices echoed in the large square rooms. He said that people start off with a backyard vegetable garden, not an acreage of farm: a marriage needed a small, fertile space in which to grow.

"There is no such thing as being prepared for marriage," Ella said to you. "I was prepared. But not that prepared."

She told you that she had dated that husband for seven months, and then one night during a walk through the park, he got down on one knee and proposed. (This was an essential part of the story, the getting down on one knee. It exposed their romantic folly, the traditional gestures that failed to pan out into traditional emotions.) He had no ring at the time and insisted that a store-bought engagement ring wouldn't be good enough for her. He would fashion his own with the minimal help of a jeweller. For the next two months, he drew up sketches hour after hour in his tiny apartment.

He picked up pencils in restaurants and brainstormed designs on greasy napkins. Six months later, the ring still was not made or even in the works. The sketches had been abandoned and he said to her one day, "You don't really want an engagement ring, do you? It's such an extravagant expense." And she had said no, of course not, she was not an envier of diamonds.

They got married not long after, with plain gold wedding bands, and went on a honeymoon to Key West. It was on that honeymoon that she was reluctantly, forcibly, made aware of what the engagement ring incident just dimly foreshadowed. She and her husband went out to dinner one night to a restaurant that was dusty and poorly lit. It was on a narrow downtown street, a street with no other shops or restaurants, and there were flies on all the tables. Her husband was always on the lookout for the cheapest restaurant, always had an eye out for a deal. They ate the same dinner, the same food, crabs and black-eyed peas, but he was violently sick later and she was fine. They were sitting in the hotel room, and he was shivering, crouching on the bed with a blanket wrapped around his shoulders. Then he took off for the bathroom.

He was there for a long time while she sat on the bed reading *Sister Carrie*. After a while, she thought maybe she should check on him. What she saw, across the long, narrow bathroom, was her new husband, naked, on all fours, vomiting into the toilet. He had all his clothes in a neat pile at the door, and he was naked and heaving. On all fours. She had the back view. She told you it shook the foundation of her belief in what she was doing, this perspective like an aerial view of his penis hanging down, his scrotum tightening each time he heaved. An aerial view.

In every word he spoke after that, every touch of his hand, she saw the aerial view, and with it, the chipped affection, the shock of revulsion, the bitterness and fatigue—the detritus of a thirty-year marriage—piling at the door of their week-old union. She even made an unsuccessful attempt to book a plane ticket home. She saw the direction they were headed, the headiness, the glorification, the dependence, then the genital views, the aborted optimism. The triumph of the unflattering. Only twenty-two and married for three days, she already knew that one corner of her marriage was over, the corner in which she stored hopes of rescue and release, where she still believed ecstasy could be a daily event. Before she had left, her mother told her, "There are things that scare women on their honeymoons. No matter how long you've known him, there are things that will scare you and make you want to come home. You can't come home." Ella was prepared. But not that prepared.

This story, combined with her favourite expression, caused you to see her as a woman eminently concerned with balls. In those days, vulgarity and glamour were inextricable in your mind, bound together in all things attractive. There was nothing in these early exchanges about genitalia that troubled you. Already you had separated your relationship with her from her relationship with your father. The story about her honeymoon helped you understand why she liked your father, why being with a man as remote as him was freeing to her when it was only oppressive to you. But everything else about them was separate. To you, she said, "Love is a euphemism for lying. Falling in love is lying to yourself. You think you're falling in love with someone, but really you're falling in love with someone wanting you. Bear this in mind." And you did, for years and years.

The other thing you bore in mind for years and years was that first day you met her, Ella standing on the front lawn of her house under the shade of a willow tree, looking exactly the opposite of what you had imagined. As you sat next to your father on the plane to New York, you pictured a woman who always wore red pumps and silk dresses. You hoped for a cool elegance, a high-heeled woman rarely affected by heat. Shiny straight hair. A doctor's air of presumption, that New York woman's mix of candour and detachment, deserving. It was July, and in fact the mistress was sweating so profusely that she looked as if she had just stepped out of the shower. When she looked at you, you could not help but smile. Married men do not introduce their children to their mistresses. You knew this. There is a wrongness about it—a cheeky, bald-faced wrongness—but somehow the mistress's fatness made it right.

"The gap between your front teeth is about the width of a cracker," the mistress said. Just like that, even before her name. She extended her hand palm down, as if waiting for a kiss.

The name "Ella" made you think of a beachy calm, sustenance and refreshment.

You could not stop smiling.

Leaning against the willow, she stared at you with mellow concentration, as if she were holding a ruler up to that gap, approving of these places you broke off more than the places you stayed together. A look that transformed your plainness into something less neutral. You tried to imagine how she might be seeing you, but you could not settle on something reliable. Whenever you heard a recording of your own voice, you thought it sounded juicy and plump, like the voice of an ugly person. When you saw yourself in the mirror, you looked much wider and lumpier than you expected. This always disturbed you, not because you were less attractive than you hoped, but because of the constant misleading of self, the inaccurate cataloguing of your own value, the predictable return to foolishness. While Ella looked at you, you tried to stand erect and forthcoming, like someone open-hearted, yet discriminating. You worried she might just see a sogginess, a frizzing that wouldn't be tamed.

"Lovely," she said. "Just lovely."

On that perfect hot day in the honeyed laziness of air that doesn't move, at the age of thirteen, you learned what it might feel like to be memorized.

ON ONE OF THE New York visits, you heard them in Ella's bed-room at two o'clock in the morning. It was the only time you ever heard them together. They didn't say much, but each sound was lined with erotic urgency, a moody pulse. The tender coercions of love. The mistress was a woman who knew how to say *baby*. As if she had thought things over, and it was the only word she could come up with.

You always thought of her as the exotic one. But why? It was more than the New York accent, which made you think of chipped teeth and long, black hair. It was more than the way she looked, the skin stretched to excess and the mop of sandy curls. She rode her bicycle, with its wicker basket on the front, everywhere she went, and despite her weight looked as nimble as a child, almost as if her weight helped her achieve balance, that Southern lady's sense of unhurried pace. These things you admired. They made her watch-able. But the exoticism came from somewhere else. It seemed to you that she'd had so many lives before the one you knew her in.

On your first morning in New York, as you ate breakfast, she told you about the honeymoon with her first husband, about the aerial view.

"Men can do such things to you," she said. "You have to be so careful, careful not to let yourself go too much. Sex espe-cially, honey, watch out. You're so young; your emotions will get involved. It's a matter of firsts. That's all."

She told you about how, as a child, she would lie behind the living room couch all day. The sun shone down just so through the front window, and she lay there. Her sisters would fight over dolls and sweaters while demanding sandwiches and forming accu-sations, and her mother would come up with activities to keep the fighting to a minimum, arts and crafts activities like painting their own stained glass. Ella stayed away. She was that contented behind the couch. Only when communication was absolutely necessary did she send out word. She delivered notes through the dog. *I vote hamburgers for dinner. Would someone be so kind as to send a glass of water? It is not true that I got my math test back last week and failed.*

"I called him my own personal Purolator courier," she said. "He would take the notes in his mouth and drop them at my mother's feet."

Her second husband had been a photographer for *National Geographic*. He had been to Africa and had flown his own small plane over Kenya. You thought that she probably had no use, ultimately, for your father and you greatly respected her for this.

You asked what it was like, living in the house where she had planned a future with her first husband.

"The first week after he left, my furnace went out and I couldn't get a man in to fix it for a week. It was so cold that frost flowers were forming on the windows, and none of my blankets did the trick. I discovered when I was cleaning that my husband had forgotten just one belonging, his red sleeping bag in the back of the closet. So for all that week I had no heat, I wrapped it around my shoulders day and night. And I moaned and wondered if I'd made a mistake and I cozied up under that sleeping bag as if it were the man himself. After the furnace man came, I cranked up the heat and sweated it all out. I put the sleeping bag back where I found it and haven't looked at it since."

She filled the copper kettle with water and set it loudly on the hissing burner, as if that was the only end her story needed. "I'd rather be trampled by a horse than ground up slowly by nostalgia."

In the sunny kitchen, she was naked under a lace nightgown and you could see everything. You hadn't seen your own mother naked since you were four or five, but it took you no time to adjust to Ella's failure to cover up. There was your father's mistress in the kitchen cooking, and there was her entire body. Your father had once said about her, after an argument, "She's in fine form." And this hadn't made you think of debates at all, of feisty opinions and an unwillingness to back down. It seemed to refer to her body. Such fine form. She walked around, smiling at you from time to time as if she had no idea her nightgown could be seen right through. The rolls of fat, like bread dough. You wanted to squish your hands in and feel the warmth. Your father had already gone off to his conference and he was gone all day. She made you an omelette, with Brie, portobello mushrooms, tomatoes, and spinach.

"We need to fatten you up," she said.

You felt she was taking responsibility for you, tending to you. Normally, you picked at your food, and your father talked about how all the women in his family had no fat on them, they were as thin as could be. He said this with a bit of mocking, as if you were all silly for being thin, but it was clear that he was proud too, proud to be affiliated with this clan of rigorous, thin women. But you stuffed the omelette in your mouth quickly and asked for more. You wanted her to see that you were not like most people: you approved of fat, curbs of skin folding, one onto the next.

Ella's face was round and lineless. Your mother was bony and gaunt. You did not want to be associated with her murky demands. She held her past tightly, refused to distribute childhood stories as entertainment. Although you made these comparisons, sitting in Ella's kitchen as she talked in her lace nightgown, they did not mean you saw Ella as a more desirable mother. That was not how you saw her.

A man knocked on the front door, and she reached into a closet in the kitchen and pulled out a bathrobe, wrapped it tightly around her before answering. So she must have been aware then, she must have been aware of all that could be seen.

You were just a child. How can it grip you even now, after all the men, the men and the years?

Later that first day, she took you to a local outdoor swimming pool. She wore a wide-brimmed straw hat and didn't swim, but sat on a lawn chair waving to you when you looked her way. She was wearing another lace top, but this time she had a shirt on underneath. The pool was full of people, so you couldn't swim properly, but you tried your best to look as if you were cavorting around, having a good time. The sun was hot, beating down on the water so that it felt like a bath. There were no trees around, just a parking lot on one side of the pool, an apartment building on the other. You snuck looks at Ella and hoped she wouldn't notice. You took water into your mouth and streamed it out through the gap in your teeth.

You wanted to call out, "Come swim with me," but you hadn't the courage. She looked so serene in her straw hat.

When you were ready to get out, she wrapped a fluffy pink towel around your shoulders, then followed you into the change room, which was a large concrete area with no private, curtained areas. You tried to change from your bathing suit into your clothes without showing your body and without looking as if you were hiding it from her. By accident, you dropped the towel when you went to put on your bra. It was your first bra, and you were not an expert at getting it on and off. So surprised were you to find yourself standing before her, watching calmly, that you simply stood there topless, exposing breasts you were barely familiar with yourself.

Ella said nothing at first. It occurred to you that all you would ever want from love was someone to call you baby, to say it at the lowest pitch of longing and regret.

Finally, looking at your stomach, she said, "You have a scar."

The year before, you had had your appendix out. The scar seemed new, still pinkish-purple. She leaned in and traced an index finger over the thin raised dash, still tender in the way that scars with a history never quite stop feeling tender. You hadn't let your stomach be seen since the nurse held your hand in the recovery room as you cried with anaesthetic nausea and unanticipated soreness, the awareness that something had been removed that could never be replaced.

But you stood there with Ella as her finger skimmed over your scar. You closed your eyes and held your wet bathing suit against your leg so that the water trickled down your thigh.

THE FINGERS HAVE a memory far longer than the mind's.

After dinner, your father wanted you to give a recital of your grade eight Royal Conservatory pieces. In her living room, Ella had an old Steinway grand piano, barely in tune, with heavy ivory keys. Your father always organized concerts of this kind, after elaborate family dinners on Christmas and Easter, mobilizing aunts and uncles and cousins and grandparents into the living room for an impromptu piano recital. For days before, he would hound you into extra practice, then on event day would find himself at the dinner table folding his cranberry sauce–stained napkin, the thought occurring to him just then that they might all enjoy a musical interlude. You would play your pieces from List A through to List D, then the two studies, waiting after each for your family to clap obediently like a symphony audience, waiting, after the second study's final note, overdramatized with a pedal sustained too long, for the lone "Bravo" to issue from your father, standing in the doorway.

The same you did for Ella. Only she didn't clap and even your father seemed embarrassed by his "Bravo" in an audience of two, as you kept your foot on the pedal and the sound of the final, off tune A flat of Study No. 3 hummed in the air.

"I'll teach you a real piece," she said. "Something worth knowing."

She nudged you off the piano bench and pulled from inside it the yellowing pages of Debussy's *La fille aux cheveux de lin* and set them before you.

"But it's grade nine," you objected.

"It's slow. You can learn it."

The following morning, after your father left, she went through it with you, telling you where to pedal and where to create the *legato* with just your fingers. She corrected you at the end, when you played the reprisal of the primary melody too loudly.

"Softly," she said. "As if contemplating."

You played it every hour on the hour twice, and when you performed it for your father on the last day of the visit, you let the music fall from the stand because your fingers held the tune.

ON THE SECOND VISIT, you got the flu. You lay in bed sweating and shivering, and Ella took your temperature and murmured in concern. She blotted your forehead with a soft flannel blanket. Your temperature went up to 102, and Ella called your father at the conference hotel and got him out of one of his seminars. Over the phone, he suggested a cool bath. She came into the guest room and put a hand on your cheek. You opened your eyes but could barely see her because the window was at her back. There was just her silhouette, the sheer white curtains rippling around her.

"You need a cool bath," she said.

You stood and allowed yourself to be led to the bathroom. So weak you felt, so glad to be weak. She held your hand as if she was initiating you into something.

The bathtub was a large, claw-footed tub and the water in it looked clear except for specks of rust, barely visible. Dust floated in the stream of sun through the window. She undressed you then. You leaned against her as she pulled your nightgown over your head, as you stepped out of your underwear. You rested against her arm as she helped lower you into the tub.

You were sweating, and she turned on a fan and set it in the doorway.

"You'll have hot and cold on your skin now," she says. "You'll like it. I know your skin."

Ella kneeled and leaned against the white porcelain, wet her hands. She held you forward gently, your chest against her forearm, while she spooned cool water up over your back. Then she reached for the soap and held it gently while it glided over your back, as if it were soaping you itself. Lifting your foot, she rubbed her thumb along its bottom, and she worked the soap between her hands and made hills of lather along your arm. She hummed.

"I could wash your parts all day," she said.

She did everything for you. Soaping you with conjugal diligence, she held a wet washcloth against your forehead and made sure each part got as clean as the others. She cupped your foot as if measuring its exact weight. Then she rinsed you, making waves in the tub and letting the water lap against your breasts before she scooped it into a small wooden bowl and poured it over your head, shielding your eyes with her hand.

"There you go, baby," Ella said. "Clean as clean."

That evening you spent on the couch covered in an old afghan, afraid to be alone in your room because every time you closed your eyes, you could see, through the dark inside of your eyelids, enormous black birds with long, trailing wings gliding over your head. Ella made you chicken noodle soup from scratch, and you hoped that your father wouldn't arrive and make a fuss that you were spreading germs in the communal areas of the house. On the coffee table was an old photograph of a balding man with a younger, black-haired woman looking formal and legitimate in a wedding photograph beneath an overgrown oak tree.

"Who are they?" you asked Ella when she brought you a bowl of soup.

"My parents."

"They have a grumpy look about them," you said. "Like someone's forcing them to apologize."

"I suppose they do, don't they?" she said, looking at the picture curiously, as if she had just spotted in a crowd the person she was searching for.

Her mother was Canadian and had grown up in Windsor, she told you, and her father was an American living in Detroit, and they met when he was visiting relatives in Windsor for the summer. For their first date, they arranged to go see a matinee of *Guys and Dolls* across the river in Detroit. She had suggested meeting him at the drugstore on the corner of his street. She was liberated before women were liberated, Ella said. Also, she knew that making an impressive entrance meant more than just sweeping down the stairs while your date stood at the front door under the eyes of your father. She was a woman who knew her entrance. She did not go to the trouble of hot rollers and her bangs taped to her forehead all night for the sake of one mere boy. She dressed for her larger public. An entrance meant a bevy of turned heads; it meant all eyes, male and female, compelled to take her in; it meant the odd reverential whisper passed between strangers. And so she swung open the door of the drugstore and stepped inside, and agreeably, it was as busy as she had hoped it would be. She stood expectantly at the door, wearing a trench coat buttoned to her neck, the collar up around her throat, and the belt pulled as tightly as the need to breathe would allow. She registered Ella's father registering the turned heads, the hushed comments, and was satisfied.

He announced that he had to drop a book at his aunt's on the way out of town and off they went. Up in the old aunt's apartment, the heat was stifling, and the aunt repeatedly invited Ella's mother to remove her coat, and Ella's mother repeatedly refused. The aunt had set out cookies and tea, so they were obliged to stay for a time and be entertained. For half an hour, the aunt encouraged Ella's mother to take off her coat and for half an hour she declined, until sweat was forming on her upper lip and beginning to drip down from her carefully set hairstyle. Finally they left, and in the car, Ella's mother took off her coat, right there on their first date, revealing that she had on only her bra and underpants. Then she rolled down the window and fanned her forehead, checked her hair for signs of humidity in the rearview mirror.

"You see, back then, all the latest fashions were in the department stores in Detroit. You couldn't get them in Windsor. My mother thought she didn't have anything grand enough to wear to the theatre in Detroit," Ella said. "So she planned to go into the department store before lunch, buy a fancy new dress, and wear that."

Your father had come home from the conference halfway through her story, and stood in the doorway still holding his briefcase.

"It was a nicer time then, don't you think?" she asked. "You could take your coat off and let a boy see your bra and underwear and it wouldn't proceed to God knows what else. He wouldn't assume. That was probably the happiest time they ever had."

Your father set down his briefcase. "I thought we were against nostalgia."

"It's not nostalgia. It's just remembering," she said.

They went into the kitchen and left you staring at the Steinway grand.

Is it nostalgia or just remembering when you still play, twenty years later, *La fille aux cheveux de lin* without missing a note?

YOU NEVER DID FEEL that love enriched your life. Mostly all it did was remove the finer points of happiness.

Walking alone on a tree-lined, windy lane in the country. Floating on waves in Miller Lake, looking up at the cliff face. Lying in bed at night, preparing to sleep, preparing to stay awake.

There are experiences diminished by companionship.

It was your father who said this first, but it was a long time before you realized how true it was. He was going to the botanical gardens, and Ella wanted to go along. She hadn't been in years. He said she had to stay with you, you were too young to be left alone in a strange place.

"She'll be fine," Ella said. "She's not a child."

She looked at you gently, but regretfully, as if you alone were keeping her from something she very much wanted. They stepped into the next room, but you could still hear them.

"I prefer to see it alone." His voice made it clear that he had long since decided. You wondered if he had already moved on to the next one. Even then you understood that there is always someone ready to step into your place.

"We could experience it together," she offered.

"There are experiences diminished by companionship."

She came back into the room, looked at you, and delivered her expression, but sadly this time, without its usual bite.

"'Balls,' said the queen. 'If I had two, I'd be king.'" She rolled her eyes jokingly, but couldn't hide the sadness in them, in the downturn of her lips.

And even though she must have resented you, even just a bit, she was good to you when he left. She made iced tea and filled the glasses too full, so that when she dropped in ice cubes the liquid overflowed. She laughed as she mopped up the counters. You didn't blame her for wanting to go with him. Already, you understood how it must be to feel you'd give almost anything for half an hour alone with someone.

She took you to a park near her house. A small group of older Asian men and women was practising tai chi on the grass. At the far end was an area of thick trees, and she led you towards it.

"This part used to be all trees. Then they cut them down. Here, it used to feel like a forest in the middle of the city. They were so thick, you could stand in the middle and it would be dark. The sun didn't come through. There are trees in there great for climbing. I'll wait out here on the bench. Go have fun."

Through the darkness of the heavy shade, you could see a tree with solid branches low to the ground, moving up the trunk as close together as steps. This tree you climbed and sat on a branch with a U-shaped curve like a seat. The ground was carpeted in rust-coloured pine needles and the air was dark and cool. You leaned against the trunk and looked out at Ella sitting on the bench, gazing across the park at something you couldn't see. That morning, you had sat on the toilet while she had a bath. She soaked for half an hour, running more hot water in when the water cooled. When she was ready to get out, she pulled the plug and stayed in the tub, humming, while the water got lower and lower. From where you were sitting, it looked as if she was rising up to the surface of the water, floating there.

She gave you presents when you left New York. A collection of poems by e. e. cummings, a Bessie Smith record tied with a purple ribbon, a plastic heart pendant, a stuffed walrus. Your favourite: a tarnished silver comb, embedded with tiny coral and amber stones, a family heirloom.

When you married your husband, you wore it in your hair. Something borrowed.

THE *great*
ONE

There was a note involved, which helped set all this in motion:

> She is the finest painting ever to hang on his wall. She
> stands before him, her young supple breasts bursting
> from her white buttoned sweater. He will steal her virgin-
> ity, like virtue purloined from a nun. His loins are rag-
> ing. He tries to feign indifference. But how can he? He
> knows that he will be the one to deflower her. Her miles
> and miles of legs and curves will be his. He is waiting.
> P.S. Don't show this to your mum.

My mother's friend Carl handed me this note the week after my
nineteenth birthday. I had just decided that I wanted to be the kind
of person who was fundamentally interested in things, and I was
concerned at the prospect of existing forever as the opposite: someone interested in little more than getting through the day, someone for whom the world came alive only when injustice seemed
virulently, inexorably, directed at her. Since the beginning of my
first year at the University of Toronto, I had spoken to only two
people in my classes and every day I ate a lukewarm peanut butter sandwich in a corner carrel at the Laidlaw Library at University College. All I thought of were the students around me, and
whether they thought me appealing, possessed of a silent but cer-

tain intelligence; however, I was careful to appear as if they could scarcely be further from my mind. When I passed familiar faces in classrooms or hallways, I looked past them to an invisible point in the distance, as if I were sorting through complicated and impenetrable thoughts. Each person who sat next to me without striking up conversation made me steadier in my resolve to initiate nothing, to appear so indifferent to everything that the only conclusion anyone would be able to draw was that my life was so full I had no time for idle talking. In truth, I would spend days at school wishing someone would ask me even the most banal question about schoolwork. Most of all, what I hoped was that a man who seemed timid and serious, a man with a preoccupied voice and wavy brown hair, would see my face and perceive in me the insolent mystique that is a precursor to the purest, most elusive beauty.

The man who gave me the note was not this man. He was not twenty and careful with words. He was not slender and disarming. He was forty-five and he lived with my mother's friend Linda. Once, he had told me that he could judge what a woman would be like in bed by the expression on her face while she exercised. I had just gone for a jog around the track at the YMCA and he was in the weight room doing bicep curls. Sweat dripped down his nose in a line that cut his face in two, and he looked at me as though it would be years before I could know about myself all the things he knew about me already. Two years before, he had lost his job as a life insurance salesman because, according to Linda, every day for two months he had shown up for work reeking of scotch. Linda was a divorced teacher with a tendency to self-medicate who had once, in a pinch, taken her dog's prescription tranquilizers. After being married for twenty years to a horsy man with a legacy of family money and an inability to converse with people who didn't look well-bred, she chose Carl for his blue-collar flair and a sexuality so coarse and dogged that it seemed downright entrepreneurial.

Together, they ate Doritos for dinner, drank red wine until two
o'clock in the morning, and kept the television in the living room.
He called me the Great One.

He slipped the note into my hand while I sat in the back seat of
the Jeep and my mother was perched high in the front behind the
wheel, talking on her cellphone. He was wallpapering our hallway
for extra money, and we were dropping him off at the end of the
day at Linda's apartment. That morning in school, I had learned
the word *lugubrious*, and I asked him, didn't he think that sitting
in afternoon rush hour traffic engendered a lugubrious calm? He
turned in his seat and said, "Engender this lugubriousness." He
wiggled his tongue at me. "Save that highfalutin BS for someone
who'll be impressed." Then he said that university was making me
think I knew more than I actually knew. I replied that when he had
a real job, it was likely he would learn to appreciate the glories of
the English language. He glanced at my mother to see if she was
listening and said, "Oh, blow me get to know me, baby."

And it came to me that I might.

So it was that I found myself standing in the doorway of his
apartment on a warm Tuesday morning in March, determined to be
interested in all life had to offer, while Professor Albertson, using a
microphone headset, stood at the front of Convocation Hall lecturing my first-year psychology class about synaptic breakdowns.

When Carl opened the door, all he said was, "Well, if it isn't
the Great One."

I looked past his shoulder into the apartment. The living room
had the look of an invalid's lair, that dull morning darkness, the
healthy world rejected. From the front door, I could see that the
curtains were drawn against the daylight, the couch was pulled out
into a bed, and the sheets were tousled, as if someone had spent
a restless night there. The air inside the apartment was too warm
and smelled like dirty hair, which I supposed came from him,

standing a little too close to me, with that smirk on his thin upper
lip. I did not know at the moment that, for years, whenever I heard
the words *bedroom eyes*, I would think of a man with glazed blue
eyes, just a touch bloodshot, squinting down to my breasts, then
up to my mouth, as he licked his lips in a darting motion. I did not
know that associations such as these are sneaky and seldom truly
defeated. At that moment, taking in the smells, the heft of the air,
I felt prepared. I did not wonder why I had come. The man who
gave me the note was not, after all, a man who asked questions.

He stood back and motioned me inside, and when I crossed into
the vestibule, I was choked by a kind of excited morbidity, a sense
that had begun to creep up on me as I drove north in my mother's
Jeep on St. George, wound itself around my stomach as I made my
way across Bloor Street, then west, west to High Park, grew bold
and tight as I parked in the visitors' lot of his apartment building
and rose skyward in the elevator, and entangled me utterly as I
looked at his lined face and felt absolutely, defiantly certain that
what I was about to do was so inappropriate, so self-destructive,
that it was almost formidable, even prophetic. I had had sex with
no one. He had reportedly had sex with sixty-seven women. I
did not find him handsome, with his grey buzz cut and oily skin.
He failed even to have a ravaged kind of sex appeal, a worn-out,
smoky exhaustion that I might restore to its original vigour. But
I knew that he would ask no questions, and I knew that he would
deliver the thing that I wanted finally to be done with.

I did not know it, but at that moment Professor Albertson was
breaking my class down into groups of eight for the group projects
he had been promising all year.

"Do you want coffee?" Carl asked.

I never drank coffee, but it seemed the proper, adult prelude to
what was about to happen to me, so I nodded. He reached up to
the cupboard to get the coffee grounds, and with that movement

came the bitter stab of BO. The apartment was overheated, and I
could see by a damp circle on the back of his grey shirt that sweat
was pooling in the small of his back, and I was afraid that when he
turned around there would be pearls of sweat forming on his upper
lip. I reminded myself that when it was all over, I could go home
and eat Ben and Jerry's chocolate brownie ice cream, the reward I
had promised myself. He set a tall tin pot on a burner and sat down
across from me at the kitchen table.

"Now it just needs to percolate," he said. "Our coffee machine
broke last week, so we're using this old thing. It's out of date."

I had never heard the word *percolate* before, but I nodded appre-
ciatively, and thought that was the kind of thing he meant when he
said that I thought I knew more than I did.

"How was your birthday?" he asked.

"Amazing. Lots of fun."

I couldn't tell him that not one person outside my family had
called me all day, not any of my friends from high school, not
even one, and how my mother bought me four hundred dollars
worth of presents to make up for all the things she anticipated
I wouldn't be getting from other people, and how each present I
unwrapped before the audience of my parents and younger sister
made me sink a little further into myself. I didn't tell him about
how my former best friend Kate called from McGill three days
later and didn't mention my birthday but read aloud the notes written phonetically in baby talk that her boyfriend posted around her
residence room. I didn't mention how I had handled all of it with
very little grace, storming out of the dining room when my mother
marched out the birthday cake, trilling a "Happy Birthday" solo
in her high, atonal voice, and quite deliberately crying myself to
sleep while Cat Stevens's "Father and Son" played on repeat in my
dark room.

He leaned back in the plastic chair. "I remember I porked two
best friends on my nineteenth birthday. The morning comes, the

blonde leans over to the brunette and slaps her. 'You bitch,' she says. 'You sucked his dick for twice as long as we agreed.' She's all crying and still a little drunk. 'There were rules,' she sniffles. 'We made a contract.' So I porked her again later to keep her happy."

"Lovely," I said. The word *porking* made me think of farm animals wrestling in the mud: a riotous, rural earthiness.

"Well, she was no Great One, but I was nineteen. I'd put it in a snake if it would hold still long enough."

The coffee was ready, and he poured me a mug without adding milk or sugar. As I sipped slowly, I could feel it pooling in my stomach. He talked about how, when he was in high school, he and his friends used to brush their hands up against girls' breasts in the crowded hallways. There was a dot of gummy white spit on the centre of his lower lip that stayed put the whole time he talked. It stretched into a line when his lips parted, and sprung back into the perfect dot when his lips closed. I stared at it, thinking, what will come of that when it all starts. I felt all of what I considered necessary—the intimacy and the revulsion, the grandeur and the wreckage. I wanted in my body bacteria that were not my own.

He smiled, and I saw a black speck like a ground of coffee between his bottom front teeth.

In my psychology class, the students were collecting their knapsacks and gathering into their assigned groups on the field outside Convocation Hall. They were sitting in circles playing name games and jotting down phone numbers in their day planners.

I walked over to the sink and poured my coffee down the drain and filled the cup with water, took a gulp, swished it around in my mouth, and spat. I looked at Carl.

"I think it's possible that I might go through my entire life without having sex." I tried to sound reasonable, as if I had assessed alternatives and extracted the most sensible conclusion.

He let out a smoker's laugh and looked from my mouth to my breasts, then back to my mouth.

"It probably wasn't true when I said that you were the last person on earth I would willingly sleep with." I had said this to him months ago, before the note, before university.

He stood up, came towards me, and put a hand on my waist. I thought this was passion, doing things no one would ever expect you to do. Flares of unpredictability. No traceable line between the things you express and the way you behave. I was worried, though, because there was no sensation between my legs. It seemed that there had never been less sensation between my legs, and I had counted on my body to understand what my mind wanted. He buried his nose in my hair and pressed his groin into my thigh. Then he pulled his head back and looked at me hard, shaking his head slowly back and forth.

"Oh, Great One, what are you doing?"

I looked at his chin. "It's time," I said. "I kept that note you gave me."

"God, kid, I was drop-dead drunk when I gave that to you. It never occurred to me. It absolutely never occurred to me."

He groaned and pushed himself against me again, then nuzzled his nose into my cheek and started kissing me. He flicked his tongue in my mouth, then nipped my lower lip. The smell of hair was stronger now, so toasted and scalpy that I could almost taste it. My arms were crossed at my waist and he grinded himself against my thigh. The absence between my legs wouldn't recede.

"Oh, kid. What a beauty you are."

He grabbed my hand and led me through the kitchen to the living room. He paused in the doorway and leaned against it, pulling me into him. Then he motioned at the darkened living with one hand.

"'Come into my parlour, said the spider to the fly,'" he whispered.

I could hear a light rain against the window. Downtown, it was only cloudy at U of T outside Convocation Hall, with spots of sun, and girls were rolling up their pants and the sleeves of their shirts, leaning back in the patches of rough yellow grass as if they were sunbathing.

"Do you sleep out here?" I asked, pointing to the unmade pullout.

"Linda and I had a fight last night," he said. "I went to our neighbour's last week. She's this great big Jewish beauty. She wants me to pork her. In the end, we just necked a little. Her breasts had no meat. When her bra was off, I had to hold them up just to keep them at chest level. But God, she's a beauty, though, with her clothes on. So, anyway, she tells Linda about it, Linda gets pissed, I sleep on the couch."

While he said this, he walked me backwards towards the bed. With one arm wrapped around my waist and the other hand on my forehead, he pushed my head back so that the length of my neck was exposed. He moved his tongue down the bony back of my esophagus. Then he lowered me to the bed, running his tongue over my teeth, and he snaked his hand up under my shirt to my breast, then around the back to unhook my bra. He pulled my shirt over my head and sat up to look at me.

I had tried to prepare myself for this moment, since the week before when I had decided I would do it. As I would for a school test, I had thoroughly planned for this moment when I would be on a bed with the upper half of my body exposed and the lower half becoming insistently more and more numb. Nowhere was the kink in my stomach that came when I saw other people kiss, the flash that had surged again and again when I had watched *The Exorcist* in the summertime with Kate's older brother and he had stroked my palm with his index finger. Kate had given me a vibrator for a joke when we graduated from high school, and I had buried it at the back of a desk drawer so my mother wouldn't find it, but consciously, very consciously, not thrown it out. I had taken this vibrator out a week before in anticipation of this moment lying on the bed, and when I had turned it on, I worried the whole neighbourhood would hear its sound like a distant lawnmower. I used it over my underwear and forced myself to think about him and held it there and even began to rock it back and forth while I forced myself to think of him, and before long, I found that I could think of nothing but him. And there was degradation, even in my mind. And in my mind it had worked, it had helped, to know it all. His sour sweat, lukewarm on my face, trickling over the side of my lip, its taste like salt and wine. His breath, sharp and bacterial, with an undercoat of cigar smoke and a weedy sting. And I could think of nothing but him.

But I felt none of that internal rush now, none of that rushing all through me. None of it (as Professor Albertson walked from group to group asking for names).

I could feel his eyes on me even though my own eyes were closed. He touched his lips lightly to my eyelids and held my fingers up to his mouth. When I looked up, he was watching me sadly, as if he didn't want to go ahead but had no choice. I squirmed out of my pants and underwear, and he reached over to the window and drew back the curtain.

"I want to take in all of you," he said, pushing my arms out to my sides, his hands clasped around my wrists.

I lay like this while he turned his eyes over every part of my body. He passed his hand over my breast and rubbed his thumb in circles on my nipple. The sun had come out, and I could feel it all along the right side of my body while he looked and looked. And while he looked, his face seemed to get smaller and tighter, his eyes narrowed, and his lines deepened. His chin was clenched and resolute, as if he was perfectly matched in an arm wrestle, and determined not to be the first to relent. I had wanted pursuit, the smashing of propriety; I had counted on rough handling to be a respite from loneliness, but I hadn't anticipated looking, being looked at. I had been confident in my ability to forget the hard cyst on his back, his thin lips grabbing at my nipples, the inevitable pain. These things seemed the necessary tests I would have to withstand in order to become equal to something better.

What had never occurred to me was that my body would become a part of someone's memory.

He stood and removed his clothes slowly, as if trying to entice me with a striptease. I had never been, and have never since been, so aware of my breasts. Flabby and untidy, spilling everywhere. I crossed my arms over my chest. He straddled my lower stomach and uncrossed my arms.

"Even better than I imagined."

He brushed my hair back from my forehead in a restful rhythm and murmured softly words I couldn't hear.

"I'm ready now," I said. "You can do it now."

I think I looked at him not kindly.

"No, no," he said. "We'll take our time."

He stretched his legs out and lay on top of me, and started kissing my neck again, this time with a sluggish methodical tempo meant to prove that he knew how to be luxurious with time, that laziness and decadence were the same. He kept one hand on my neck, on top of my pulse, while he kissed the outline of my face, down to my chin, then over to my ear. I could smell his saliva on my face.

"I'm ready," I said again. "We can go ahead any time now."

He got up. "The condoms are in the bedroom. Back in a second."

He took another long look at me and shook his head, then turned away. I watched his naked body retreat down the hall. His wide torso and narrow bottom. His small white calves and broad back. His eager trot, tiptoeing with speed and stealth down the hall to Linda's bedroom.

That was the last time I ever really looked at him.

I suppose we came together with the relative ease of two people who are inappropriate together. I had wanted to be done with something and had no intention of leaving until it was accomplished, and I felt it fine to go about that in whatever manner was necessary. He returned with the condom and asked me to put it on him. He spoke of making love, words which did not conjure sex but made me imagine a potion being concocted in a lab, then formally presented on a cushion of crisp white linen while I stood by stiffly. He said the word *pussy* over and over, and I wanted to laugh because I couldn't hear it as anything other than an innocent, pink-ribboned word, though he growled it at me in a tone of passion and menace. The whole incident had been like that: every word or gesture made me think of something else. I did not know there was something there to hold on to.

I thought of the empty coffee mug in the next room. I thought about how I no longer had to picture myself at sixty-five with hair bleached to straw and cut short in a perm, tan pantyhose sagging on my thin, unused legs. I thought about how I had made the whole act remarkable. I thought it initiated me into the extraordinary, bestowed upon me a kind of damaged splendour that no other circumstances could produce. I did not think about the condom, its wet rubber slide against my thigh. I did not think about the man who wouldn't stop looking at me. I did not think about the drop of sweat trickling down my temple, the sweat that could have been his or mine.

As Professor Albertson stood on the steps of Convocation Hall with his hands on his hips, surveying the groups on the lawn like a worried father, my group made plans for coffee the next day.

Of course, I didn't know this at the time, as I tried my best to make my body pliable and careless. I pieced it all together the following week while a sorority girl named Marilyn told me what I had missed, sighing at the difficulty of fitting me in when the group had already broken down into comfortable pairs and the work had been evenly distributed. Nor did I know that Carl was sleeping on the couch because of unemployment, not Jewish beauties. I did not know that Linda had told him to get out and that he had pleaded with her, promised a complete turnaround, an earnest job search, university courses by night. I did not know that he had said, "There's nothing but you, I have nothing but you," and that he had stood naked before her, wedged between tears and fight, saying, "Look at me, I'm pathetic. You're the best thing of my life."

Nor did I know that ten years later, a week after I gave birth to my first child, I would see his picture in the newspaper and read of his body being found in a dumpster, asphyxiated by garbage, and that the fact of his death would become less real to me, and less appalling, than the moment just before death, that impotent fight as he clawed at nothing like a dog on its back, gasping for air, for the one thing that he had always taken for granted, before sinking back into tomato soup cans and orange juice cartons and bread scraps as he reached for what would never come again, for the air that would never be enough.

I did not know that for months and years before that, he would call me every three or four months, that he would confess to sitting on the steps of the Royal Ontario Museum all afternoon hoping I would walk by. I did not know that he would beg me not to hang up, that he would say, "I love you, kid, I'll love you for the rest of my life. You're the Great One," again and again until I would finally put down the phone, turn to my mother, and laugh and say, "He's just drunk again," as we stood in the kitchen on an autumn or summer afternoon.

I did not know any of this as he looked at me with fear and ambition. I was already in the bathroom scrubbing the smell of latex off my hands. I was already breathing the air outside, the damp cheer post-rain.

COCKNEY
sunday

Marriage is not for the women of Daphne's family. There is no end to the tales of wifely woe that Carol, Daphne's mother, parades before her. Even Daphne's grandmother would have preferred to remain single, if her traditional British parents had allowed it: she had a husband who would announce his desire for sex by returning from the bathroom at night and shutting all the curtains. Eyes closed, he would stand at the foot of the bed, his expression hungry and loathing and his back slightly arched, as if trying to transcend his body through his pelvis.

"Then he would climb aboard," Carol says.

Carol carries a bottle of lubricant in her purse, keeps a bottle in her night table, and another in the glove compartment of her car. She, at least, is prepared. Since beginning menopause, she has become increasingly preoccupied with vaginal health. She claims she is so dry that it plagues her even when she is just walking down the street. Once, when she and Daphne were shopping, Carol pretended she wanted to try on a blouse at Banana Republic so she could lubricate herself in the fitting room. She insists that thirty years of marriage have dried her up. Marriage is also to blame, she announced one year during Thanksgiving dinner, for her hypochondria. Just a week after the wedding, she became convinced she had breast cancer coming on. In the shower each morning, she cried as she rubbed soap over her breasts, kneading herself until her skin was red. She checked her body for lumps morning and night, commissioned a dermatologist to examine her back for melanomas at monthly appointments, called a neurologist she had met at a party to ask if two headaches in one week could be a symptom of something.

"It was marriage," she tells Daphne. "I never worried a day in my life until I got married."

Yvonne, Daphne's sister, believes the body's aversion to marriage is a generational curse and she is certain it started with her great-grandmother, whose much older husband sent her to finishing school in Switzerland for a year so she could achieve refinement and learn how to entertain properly. Responding to a contentious inner dialogue, Yvonne randomly remembers this injustice and starts to pace around the room, muttering to herself, "A wife is a partner, not an employee."

Yvonne is self-righteous about sex. "Pleasure is there for the taking," she suggests at opportune moments. She cannot tolerate sad-sacked women intent on depriving themselves of the ecstasies of the female body. In the gym of her old high school, she performs strident evening lectures on a woman's pleasure. These lectures involve detailed instructions on how to achieve orgasm, a process she calls Finding the Climax. Her tips are phrased as extended mountain-hiking analogies.

"You're trudging up there, huffing a little, moving real slow. You've got all the equipment. Why wouldn't you make it to the top?" Here, she holds up her right hand and licks her index finger, then moves it in the air in a circular motion. "If he can't take you there, use your own feet, ladies."

When Daphne characterized her sex life with Ashley as adequate, Yvonne offered her services as a coach, or at least as a consultant. Through semi-weekly e-mails, she requests updates. Sometimes, she calls Daphne at midnight, whispering earnestly, "I just had an epiphany about the relationship." Yvonne frequently has dreams and insights about Daphne's relationship, which she pronounces *reelationship*.

"I think you might be a lesbian," she tells Daphne. "It would explain your dissatisfaction in the reelationship."

Daphne, however, is determined to get married. Specifically, she is determined to marry Ashley. When she first met him two years ago, she thought he lacked something essential—a wry, confessional sadness in his eyes, that reserved lewdness and wandering smile. Where she had been hoping for witty cynicism, she got shrugging optimism. A constant dull glow where she wanted flashes of midnight and radiance. Ashley is padded with good cheer and never fails to be eminently supportive of himself. "Well, we're all human," is what he often says when he forgets to take out the garbage or when he misuses a word. In the end, though, what surprises Daphne is how pleased she is by his insufficiency. She immensely enjoys her clean deception—watching him sleep, her face doting and tender, glazed with affection, while her mind considers how much better she can do. She finds it far more invigorating than pursuing ideals, this foreboding sense that she is throwing herself away.

Still, the drudgery of dailiness can creep up, and in an effort to combat it, Daphne came up with the idea of accents. On Saturdays, they speak in Southern voices. Jolly twangs, slack and unrefined. Theirs are not the lilting voices of the genteel South, of debutantes and Tennessee Williams, but of marrying cousins and dropped *g*'s. In Daphne's mind is a good-natured South, a place of promiscuous greenery, a leafy resort for cheerful incest. Every time Ashley forgets to use his Southern tone, Daphne makes him put a dollar in a large Mason jar on the kitchen counter.

"Deposit," she says, her finger rigid and directive.

She used to spend Saturday nights feeling pitiable and discouraged, unproductive, as if she'd spent all day having sex and was surprised to discover she had nothing to show for it. Southern Saturdays have renewed her, as if she has uncovered debauchery in the middle of her kitchen. Ashley has taken to the change too, and returned recently from a business trip to England with an idea for Cockney Sundays, a day devoted to loopy accents and Benny Hill, to fish and chips and other food they never eat. At one point, Daphne considered making an appointment with a dialect coach so they could get their accents just right, but she realized, flipping through the Yellow Pages, that she wasn't looking for accuracy. She was looking for what she already had: zesty stereotypes, games that took themselves seriously, disinterest in her own incorrectness. She wanted different voices in her kitchen.

Her leg stretching across the kitchen table, she leans forward and rests her chin against her knee. "I hates these here hairy legs," she says. One unspoken rule on Southern Saturdays is that subjects and verbs must never agree.

Ashley assures her frequently that he prefers her legs unshaven. He also encourages her not to shave her underarms. Ashley is not a tree-planting, tofu-eating sort of man, but a Bay Street financial consultant who matches his socks to his ties and enjoys devising time-management strategies. Daphne suspects that he encourages her to let her body hair grow, not because he finds beauty in a woman's naturalness, but because he feels a secret charge, a prickly dance in his thighs, whenever he is confronted with things that revolt him.

"I like this new camera," Ashley says in his plain voice, snapping a picture of Daphne.

"Deposit," she says, jabbing her finger at the jar.

Daphne guesses that Ashley is worried, sometimes, by his desire to marry a woman given to such adamance, a woman with such a rule-bound sense of fun. For her part, Daphne worries frequently about the fact that she finds her future husband's voice sexy only when it's not his own.

FOR THE PAST THREE years, Daphne has worked as a high school economics teacher. What excites her most about her job is not explaining supply and demand or Keynesian ideology. She finds economics irredeemably dull, a discipline she fell into at the urging of her fiscally preoccupied father, but the minute she is faced with the disinterest of her students, everything changes. What she loves is the act of distortion, making things appear as the opposite of what they are. An unwilling audience is the best kind, providing the platform upon which she feels most powerful. She knows just how to distort the surface of the material so that economics seems worth learning, mysterious and flexible instead of stodgy and controlled. Her students' interest is incidental. It is the stylishness of trickery that matters: bending textbook material while appearing to maintain an almost forensic accuracy.

She first met Ashley in a psychic's waiting room. She had been sent there by Yvonne, who taught a seminar entitled "Lover, Know Thyself" that the psychic had attended. On the morning of her appointment, Yvonne instructed Daphne to appear receptive to insight and to use the phrase *intuitive reader* rather than psychic. Daphne had agreed to go because she lacked the energy to resist Yvonne—it seemed to her that passivity and compliance were subversive in their own satisfying ways—but she found the whole process distasteful. She had no patience for the messy, whispered predictions and revelatory moans of a psychic who managed to be simultaneously vague and emphatic. While she was still waiting for her appointment, Ashley had entered the room with a fleet of noises: extensive rustles while he hung up his coat on a creaky rack, several cosy sighs as he eased down into the vinyl chair, eager beeps at his cellphone, a comically impatient sigh when his coat fell off the rack and he replaced it, another stab at the cellphone, lint needing to be brushed off his pants, a punctuating throat clear when seated again, a final contented sigh. He began talking to Daphne straightaway. He confessed that he believed in the reader's powers wholeheartedly, if reluctantly.

"I'm half an hour early for my appointment," he said. "Intuition or what?" Then he winked.

He had worn a tailored charcoal suit, a royal blue shirt, and a matching, slightly iridescent, blue tie. She liked the way he kept burping noiselessly while they spoke. It seemed to her that each burp, a little swallow of air, punctuated a thought to which she couldn't have access. In many ways, he reminded her of the way Carol ordered coffee—"I'll have a medium medium." Height, weight, hair colour, complexion—all medium. She couldn't imagine what a person like this was all about, with his tidy business surface and his hope for the blessing of a psychic. His nose was long and serious, and there was a hapless downward turn at the corner of his lips. Nothing about him matched. The suit and the burps, the mouth and the nose. There was a kind of canine honesty in his eyes, but also a gentle worry around his lips that promised a half-swallowed sadness. Every few minutes, he looked at his watch with a sensible frown and said that he should really be getting back to the office, he had many clients depending on his constant surveillance of the stock market. Then he'd pull his cellphone from the clip at his waist and look at it, press a few buttons, and put it back. Things like this that would ordinarily have irritated Daphne flipped her into attraction. When the psychic finally emerged from the other room, Ashley stood up and gave a small bow. Then he asked her how she was feeling that day, each word tentative and cajoling, a voice for trying to trick a baby into a laugh.

"I'm sorry that I'm so early. I know I'm not until one thirty. Luckily, this lovely young lady has been gracious enough to entertain me." He gestured towards Daphne.

"You must be quiet while you're waiting for your appointment," said the psychic. "I cannot tolerate distractions when I'm with a new client."

"Of course." He nodded and stepped back with a small reverential burp.

The following day, they ran into each other on King Street, and Ashley asked for her phone number. He called her the next day, breathing asthmatically into the receiver for a moment before identifying himself.

"Did you enjoy being read?" he asked.

"Of course!" Daphne cried. "What a seer she is!" She had actually cut her appointment short and left through the back door. The psychic had fondled Daphne's leather glove for ten minutes, and then informed her that she had a vision of a tropical storm, a sure sign of a barren womb, and that she heard a children's choir, which meant that Daphne should be careful when crossing the street.

"You'll go again, then?"

"Certainly."

She did not feel that she was being unfair or dishonest. She felt that this was how things should begin, with relative truths and warm evasions. He suggested that they go to Il Fornello for dinner.

"Il Fornello?" she said, with an electric flick of laughter.

"A lot of people like Il Fornello," he replied, sounding wounded.

What an unlikely moment it was for her to divine that she might marry him. In that moment of certain disappointment, to be pleased. To spot in unsettling differences the very things that would settle her. And not just to divine, but to decide. For that is what she did.

Daphne remembers this moment with the strictest clarity—the moment she knew she would marry him. Such a union seemed appropriate. She had come to believe that marriage was the highest and most sophisticated form of distortion. As often as possible, she tried to use the phrase *the institution of marriage*. What, after all, could be more ordered, more unwaveringly accurate, than an institution? To give herself away, to be bound by moral rules as

well as clear legalities, while at the heart of it all was a love somewhat lacking—this struck her as thrillingly dishonest. It guaran-
teed that her life would always be shaped by a certain magic and
cunning, a sleight-of-hand artistry.

Single life had been formless, blatantly disorganized, and
how could she pretend otherwise, dating one man one weekend,
another the next? She had been embarrassed for herself as a single woman. Shortly after the dinner at Il Fornello, she had worried
that the downward turn of Ashley's lips was strictly physical, that
there was no beautiful distress lingering there. She suspected that
he might not want to trick and be tricked, that he might want to
sit on the edge of the bed pouring out his insecurities while she
massaged his shoulders, that he might be looking to discard propriety and live in a world of soulmates and coy romance. Then one
day, after their ballroom dancing class, she found in his study a
crumpled phone bill. It came to five hundred dollars, all owing to a
phone sex company in Burlington, Ontario. She put it back in the
garbage and patted the back of his chair. He was in.

She felt their purity of purpose, the knowing that held firm
beneath the labour of their distractions.

WHEN ASHLEY COMES home from work, Daphne is at their kitchen
table smoking for the first time. For weeks, she has been fantasiz-
ing about the inhale. At night, she dreams about smoke the way
some people dream about sex. In the dreams, in some inappropriate connection between nicotine and nature, she is usually standing
outdoors in the crisp October air, wearing her red fall coat with the
big hood, and she tips her head back and takes in the smoke, feels
its anaesthetic cool in her lungs. It's as palpable as a wet dream, the
smoke's restorative hold. She never exhales, but prolongs the act
of inhaling, drawing in again and again but never releasing. This
cigarette, her first while awake, misses the point entirely. The taste

is wrong. In her imaginings, smoke tastes the way she imagines warmed eucalyptus would taste. Instead, smoke tastes like smoke. Her first inhale is like an electric jolt in her throat. It catches, and it knocks her forward into a cough instead of rolling sweetly back.

"Oh, no," Ashley says as Daphne coughs hello. He picks up the pack of cigarettes and the lighter and stuffs them in his jacket pocket. "Oh, no. Smoking is bad for your health."

"Is that right?" she drawls. She is trying for a French accent, but lapses into the Southern.

"Oh, no," he states firmly. "I'm not living with any smoker."

She takes a deep inhale and coughs it out.

"I'm not having this," he says again. "There's a certain understanding when you plan to marry that what you seem to be getting into is, in fact, what you're getting into."

"Oh, yes."

She can tell that he takes her very seriously, that he is picturing life with an aging smoker, browning and lined. When they first met, she could see his inability to turn things like this into jokes, to turn anything into a joke. He liked it best when their dates were mellow and well planned. Energetic activities, such as hikes and squash games, had to be incorporated sparingly into their routine. Mostly, this pleases her; she has always welcomed the structure Ashley provides. But there are times when she has felt another need. She grew up in a loud house, a place where nothing could be done quietly, even whispering. When one of them had requested silence, the others would tiptoe across the creaky floors, telling each other to be quiet in stage whispers. Theirs was a house where all noise was held to a microphone, where dishes were constantly being washed and put away, where the dog barked if he was being ignored, where her mother screamed at the dog that if he didn't be quiet, she would put him in the basement. The low volume of her life with Ashley sometimes disarms Daphne, even though she believes she values the repose, the soft steady surfaces, of her coupling. One day, she woke him up by turning all the lights on full and belting out "New York, New York," slowing down dramatically at the end and ripping the covers off him by way of passionate finale.

"Jesus Christ," he'd said, pulling the covers back over his head. "Do you have to be so loud in the fucking morning?"

Ashley liked to wake up to his clock radio, to the voices of the CBC. He has always preferred an ordered approach: smoking when one is a troubled teenager, yelling when one is fighting, singing at celebratory occasions, or in choirs. She knows this. It is one of the reasons she has stayed with him for almost two years instead of her usual two months.

Waving smoke from the front of his face, Ashley holds up the pack of cigarettes, and says, "Look at me. I need you to look at me," and he drops the offending instruments loudly to the bottom of the garbage can.

"Did you see that? Are you with me?" He points to the cigarette in her hand. "That's your last one."

She wonders what it says about them that moments like this are far more disruptive than any major fight they could have.

"It's just one pack," she says.

"That's what they always say."

She is wearing a long necklace, which Ashley gave her on their fourth date. He scoops up the end of it with his index finger and twists it up to her chin. "Do we have an agreement?" he says, with a lopsided smile that makes her think of what his face looks like when he warbles Sinatra. The necklace is made up of small dark-blue spheres, each one imprinted with a gold flower swirling over its surface. It is a beautiful necklace, like none she has ever seen, and she always wonders when she looks at it how this man could have bought her the perfect thing.

"Swear," he says, nipping her lip.

She notices a smell beneath the fresh laundering of his suit, beneath the deodorant and apple shampoo, a smell like garden dirt, a hearty day spent in the outdoors. And for a moment she believes herself when she leans in and whispers, "Anything you say."

BREATH HAS A trajectory. Daphne turns her head as Ashley climbs into bed. She can smell his breath even though he's two feet away, and she can almost see it, the arc from his mouth to her nose. Buttery and tepid, a reminder of his body's humility.

"I want you," Ashley says, warming his hands on the back of her knees.

"I have to get up at six," she answers. She is wearing striped pajamas to ward off such advances.

She prefers feeling his desire to hearing his desire. She'd much rather he not express wanting so openly, with tender traps and flattery. If she could articulate what she wants, she would say that she'd like to be slammed down. He told her on their first date that he had only had one lover, a fifty-five-year-old woman named Celine. "Our relationship was really only about the sex," he said apologetically. Celine was highly instructive, composing lists of the ground she wanted him to cover each session. After sex, she often laid a chessboard across her naked stomach and he played chess with himself, as both the black and the white pieces; he seemed truly ashamed when he confessed to Daphne that he always secretly made better moves for the white pieces. Sitting squarely in a busy Il Fornello eating pasta primavera, Daphne found it puzzling that he so frankly disclosed things he considered private. Unlike Yvonne, whose life overtly revolved around sex, Daphne had always been fascinated by sex in an underground, heavy-hearted sort of way. As a child, she listened to her parents having sex at night. Occasionally, she invented reasons to go to the bathroom down the hall and pause outside their closed door. Whereas Yvonne invested in earplugs and hid under her covers, Daphne was drawn to their door as to the scene of a car accident. She would even try to picture what their bodies looked like, contorted and elastic, bent into positions that couldn't be natural.

Sometimes, she would search their room under the pretence of cleaning, and pillage their night table for evidence, condoms or a diaphragm, but the only thing that looked remotely suspicious was a large tub of Vaseline. After what she heard at night—pleading and gasping, furniture moving, a glass bottle hitting the hardwood floor—she was shocked by her parents' ordinary faces at the breakfast table the next morning as they drank their orange juice and exchanged sections of the newspaper. The whole situation repelled her, and she couldn't stop thinking about it.

When she first saw what a penis could do, at the age of fourteen, she became even more gripped by what went on in that room. A friend of her mother named Greg had been visiting, and Daphne had been giving him a fashion show of her new summer clothes while her mother went grocery shopping. After she tried on each outfit, she paused, making him assess what she looked like from each angle, then demanded to know whether she looked fat. "You look great," he had said again and again, as she fished for compliments and accused him of lying. After she paraded into the room dressed in her final outfit, a knee-length linen skirt and a green stretchy T-shirt, she had put her hands on her hips and demanded, "Do you swear I don't look fat?" At this, Greg had risen slowly from his chair and placed his hands slowly on his hips as he stood before her, looking down at the erection bulging from his pants. "Still think I'm lying?" he had asked matter-of-factly, as she looked away, tensely laughing. She'd heard of erections, but hadn't considered what they looked like. She'd known the penis became larger, but she hadn't realized it stood out, an insulting appendage

that demanded attention. It had seemed to her unnatural and incon-
siderate. She had wondered why anyone would want to come into
contact with an erection, why women moaned hungrily even when
they were just talking about sex.

Three years after seeing Greg's erection, Daphne had realized
that the only way around her fear of penises was to be fucked, and
fucked again. Not made love to—certainly not that. Fucked. So
she pursued this course of action until penises became a normal
part of life.

When she first had sex with Ashley, Daphne had been pleas-
antly surprised by his competence. He had kissed her with the mag-
netic pressure of determination. There had even been glimmers of
fierce wanting as he took off her clothes. Even though she has told
Yvonne that it is only adequate, she has in fact always enjoyed sex
with Ashley. Yvonne often says that there is nothing as intimate a
man can get as what a woman can, being penetrated. And Daphne
has begun to agree, she has come to see penetration as a necessary
invasion, something taken masquerading as something given. She
feels that sex in the context of a relationship is the sneakiest of vio-
lations. As the wedding comes closer, Daphne wants sex less, but
as Ashley nestles into her, his moist breath on her neck, she takes
him in a steady grip.

"You're a lovely man," she says, looking at his forehead.

And as he begins to rub himself in her hand, moaning "God, I
love you so much, I want to make love to you," she sees how her
parents drank their orange juice with the straightest faces each
morning. How sex can be all genital or all mind. She rests one arm
across Ashley's back and sees it there as if it is detached from her
body. She raises her knees, lets them fall out a little, feels their give,
their pliant flexibility. Ashley's weight has a way of settling into
her body. It has a heavy, unmoving quality, as if it belongs not to
a person, but to an inanimate object, like a lead X-ray vest. She

pictures her own body, caving to the pressure, and imagines that, when she stands up, there will be a long, deep indentation in her body from where he has been. She leans her head back and to the side, as if feebly submitting to a chain of events she has no power to stop, and she imagines how helpless and distressed she must look as she hooks her legs around his hips. The sensation of him working his way inside her, adjusting and readjusting for the most comfortable fit, is the most familiar feeling she has ever known. The way her body feels as if it is trying its hardest to lock him out, until the moment he is in, and her body clamps down upon him to keep him from retreating. There is a vigilant sameness about sex with Ashley, the simmering pressure, the cautious pacing. And yet each time feels somehow new. When she's not having sex, she can't think of what sex could possibly feel like. She loses the sense of it. It's not something she can summon, like the taste of a grapefruit, or the sting of a paper cut. Her pajama top twists and tightens as Ashley clutches its material in his hands behind her back, and she looks over his shoulder to her pajama bottoms, thrown to the bottom of the bed.

She thinks of orange juice and of her body, its faulty mechanics, the composition of fragments that won't quite join.

CAROL, YVONNE, AND Daphne convene for the fetching of the wedding dress. Yvonne is driving, and Daphne is in the back seat. She can see Yvonne's eyes darting from the road to Daphne's reflection in the rearview mirror. Carol taps Yvonne's knee, and Yvonne turns onto a side street, parks the car under an oak tree.

"Now," Carol says, bracing her arm against the dashboard.

"I have to tell you something," Yvonne says, making eye contact with Daphne through the mirror. "Ashley has been spotted with another woman."

"Ashley?" Daphne asks skeptically. "Are you sure?"

"Now this is not the end of the world. We all need to calm ourselves down." Carol starts in. "We just have to put our heads together."

"Ashley?" Daphne repeats.

Yvonne nods with solemnity.

"Who saw him with another woman?" Daphne asks.

"Now, I need you to keep an open mind."

"What was he doing? Who saw him?"

Yvonne turns around to face Daphne. "An open mind." She pauses. "Sylvia saw him."

"Sylvia?"

"Sylvia, the psychic." Yvonne pronounces *psychic* with a long *i*, so that it rhymes with *sidekick*.

"The psychic?" Daphne says. "Where did she see him?"

Carol and Yvonne look at each other.

"The other night," Yvonne begins, "Sylvia went home from one of my interactive seminars, and she fell asleep, obviously feeling very relaxed and open, and she dreamed that she was walking through a park with an ice cream cone and she saw Ashley having sex with another woman underneath a park bench."

Daphne looks at Carol, whose chin has receded into jowls of concern.

"In her mind?" Daphne says. "She saw Ashley with another woman in her mind?" She gets out of the car and slams the door. Carol gets out on the passenger side and closes her door gingerly, as if she's trying not to wake a baby.

"Be reasonable," Carol says.

"You be reasonable."

Yvonne gets out of the car. "All we ask," she says, "is that you go speak to Sylvia yourself."

Daphne feels strangely excited. She knows, of course, that Ashley is not having sex with someone else, but the suggestion of it, the brief twinkle of depravity that lights in the air just next to her tasteful engagement ring, is exhilarating. Undeniably so. Sometimes, during sex, she fantasizes about Ashley sleeping with other women, and the sex she imagines is vengeful and desperate. Along with the phone sex bill, these fantasies help her picture Ashley as a sexual person. If she opens her eyes during sex, all is ruined. What she sees there is loving and earnest, with the politeness Ashley feels is appropriate to love.

Carol and Yvonne are pacing nervously, hoping for tears. How, Daphne wonders, could anyone could go so far wrong in interpretation? She looks up, laughing, at the trees, their branches stretched like hands across the autumn sky.

ASHLEY IS FIXING the toilet, which is leaking from its base. So far, little progress has been made. It all started when the toilet began welling up with water every time it was flushed. After three days of intermittent plunging and holding his bladder until he got to work each morning, Ashley got fed up and decided to investigate by taking the toilet apart. Two hours after putting it back together and marvelling about how efficiently it flushed, he stepped into the bathroom to find great pools of cold water at the base of the toilet. Daphne is sitting in the kitchen when Ashley returns from the hardware store, makes straight for the bathroom, and closes the door with a tart, presidential authority. Shortly before going to the store, Ashley cross-examined her about what she knew of the toilet's ills.

"Have you been flushing Kleenex?" he asked suspiciously.

"No," she answered honestly, shaking her head.

"Tampon applicators?"

Another shake.

In fact, from the beginning, she has known exactly what is ailing the toilet: it is suffering from her reluctance to put her hand in a bowl full of urine. Though to be fair to herself, she thinks, Ashley is equally culpable, since it was he who failed to flush. Two nights before, when she was getting ready for bed, she reached up to the cabinet above the toilet for her jar of moisturizer, and she knocked a large plastic hair clip into the toilet. She had been bracing herself to plunge her hand into the cold septic water, when she noticed that the toilet was in fact full of urine. She now thinks it unfortunate that the toilet has become such an inconvenience, but she does not truly feel guilty about her choice. She flushed the toilet, hoping the clip would sit at the bottom, waiting for a cleaner retrieval, but the clip disappeared and was now, she assumed, lodged in a pipe. She knows not to divulge this information to Ashley, who has been complaining all day about how much he hates wet feet.

A minute after Ashley closes himself in the bathroom, Daphne hears a big bang, the sound of Ashley's toolbox hitting the floor, then the metallic scatter of tools across the tile. The bang is followed by silence, then a torrent of Italian swearing. Ashley only swears in Italian—a language he neither speaks nor understands—as if his inner angry soul is ethnic and unkempt, unrestrained by the niceties of Canadian culture. She walks to the bathroom, knocks lightly on the door.

"Is everything okay?" she asks.

She gets no answer, so she opens the door slowly and peers in. Ashley is on his hands and knees, gathering his tools into a circle in the centre of the bathroom. The toilet has been disassembled, and its parts are laid in an intricate webbing across the bathroom floor.

"Ashley," she says in alarm. "What if I have to go to the bathroom?"

He sits up on his knees suddenly and whips his head around.

"Never disturb a handyman!"

"I'm not trying to bother you," she says, "but I'm just wondering how long you're planning to take. I might have to go to the bathroom at some point."

He stands up and steps towards her. In his face is a dry, self-righteous anger, the chafed fretfulness of someone who is brought to the brink many times, but always denied the explosion.

"Never disturb a handyman!" he shouts in a turbulent voice, leaning into the plunger as if it were a cane. "A handyman is under a great deal of stress!"

Daphne closes the door. She doesn't know what to think of the indignant clarity in Ashley's voice, of his sudden interest in manual labour and its accompanying impatience. When they first moved in together, he had tolerated question upon question, demand upon demand. The bathroom had been full of gnats, and she found their dead bodies on her toothbrush, embedded in the hair of her comb, swimming in water around the drain. It was the middle of the winter, and they came out of nowhere, but Ashley had willingly tried to kill them all when she asked.

She stands in the hall for a moment, listening to Ashley mutter to himself in the bathroom as he plunges the toilet; then she goes to the living room and takes a pile of books from the bookcase, returns to the bathroom door and sits.

"I'm going to read to you," she says to the closed door. "To help the time pass."

"I can do without."

"Don't worry," she says, as if he's dismissing her for her own sake. "I'm fine."

She chooses randomly, starting with Chekhov's "The Lady with the Pet Dog." She reads slowly, lingering over each word, pausing at the end of each paragraph, and when she is finished, she reaches for Coleridge and reads on. Ashley is still banging away inside, and she can't tell whether he's listening, whether he can even hear her over the clang of metal on porcelain. She reads "Christabel," moving now at a less leisurely pace because she is afraid he will tell her she has to stop. She grabs Theodore Roethke's *Collected Poems* when she comes to the final word of "Christabel," and flips through the pages, starting near the end and moving back and forth through the collection.

When she comes to the end of "My Papa's Waltz," Ashley says, "I plagiarized that poem when I was in grade ten."

Daphne puts down the book and stares at the closed door. Her mouth is sticky and dry from the reading, and she has trouble swallowing.

"I'd forgotten all about that. I won my school's poetry competition. I plagiarized and no one knew, at least not at first. Not one teacher in my whole school recognized it. They thought I was a prodigy."

"How did they find out?" Daphne asks, sitting cross-legged in the dim hallway, the books resting in the sliver of light along the bottom of the bathroom door.

"It wasn't until much later," he says. "I got to read the poem out in front of the whole school before they found out. I even loved it. I didn't feel guilty at all. The night before I got to read to the school, I practised in front of my bedroom mirror. I tried raising my voice and lowering it. I was trying to find the perfect pitch. Sad and kind of troubled. Like things had happened to me. Real things. Stuff they couldn't understand. And it worked too. I even cried a bit during the last verse. It was almost eerie after that too. People acted as though they were scared to talk to me, even teachers, as if I was too good for them. I really enjoyed myself. I can't explain, but I felt deserving of the whole thing. I think I convinced myself I really had written the poem."

Daphne hears the toilet lid drop to the seat.

"They even sent me to Ottawa," he continues, "as the school's representative at the provincial competition. I'd never been to Ottawa. Even though I was only going for a week, my dad bought me new luggage, one of those little suitcases with the wheels. I took four or five hours to pack the night before. I wasn't usually that careful about things. I wasn't much of a planner as a kid, but I enjoyed packing for that trip. I wanted to be sure I had enough clean socks. I remember being concerned about that, running out of clean socks. I really liked that suitcase. It was almost the best part of the whole thing."

The shadows change under the door, and Daphne can tell that he is moving around the bathroom, lingering behind the door, where she hears him rearranging the towels on the racks, then retreating to the middle of the room. He returns to the toilet, where he sits with a thud, and claps his hands on his knees.

Daphne asks what happened in Ottawa.

"Nothing much," he says, unconcerned, back to himself. "They found out on the first day, and they sent me home. That was it. No lectures or punishment. They just sent me home. The principal of my school made me apologize in the gym in front of the school. I told them I plagiarized the poem. And I pronounced Roethke as *Roask*. My English teacher corrected me afterwards."

Daphne pictures him at fifteen, skinny and entitled, with legs so spindly it seemed they could never hold him up, standing in front of a tall microphone before his entire school. She pictures him at home after school, crying and crying in his bedroom.

"How terrible," she says.

"Well, it wasn't that bad," he answers. "Everyone forgot about it a week later."

"That was it?"

"Things went back to normal. That's what happens." His shadow retreats again, and she hears him open the shower curtain and rest his toolbox on the rim of the bathtub. Then he starts to plunge the toilet, with power that makes the water rock against the sides of the bowl.

She wishes she could be this way, that she could have this same ability to forget about things, that resilient knack for freeing herself from the burden of too much memory. She wonders if this is a fundamental difference between men and women, boys and girls: their conception of embarrassment, the ability to get over things. When she was in grade eleven, a teacher made her spit her gum into his hand, then write line after line on the board, "I will not chew gum like a cow in Mr. Erickson's history class," and she had been humiliated by the thought of this incident well into university.

As she opens her book, she feels shocked, less by Ashley's story than by his seamless forgetting, by the prospect of sleep untroubled by thoughts of how things might have gone differently. And as she starts to read Yeats to the closed bathroom door, she thinks that this might be something to strive for. The perfect pitch of forgetting. She listens to the plunging of the toilet, to Ashley's grunts as he goes faster and faster, and she listens to the sound of her own reading voice, to the sound of Yeats, to "Leda and the Swan."

ONE COCKNEY SUNDAY, a night two weeks before the wedding, Daphne meticulously cleans the apartment while Ashley goes grocery shopping. She feels she can't get married unless her apartment, her car, and her classroom are freshly scrubbed and vacuumed. While she is cleaning Ashley's study, Carol calls and leaves lengthy marital advice on the answering machine, lecturing Daphne about her neighbour, who has a son with Down's syndrome.

"I'm just saying," she warns for the third time. "You're almost thirty. The risk just increases with age. Marie was only thirty-two. You should just see her. The whole time we're talking, he's insisting I give him a kiss on the lips. 'No,' I say, 'on the cheek.' '*Sur la bouche!*' he yells. '*Sur la bouche!*' You kids just shouldn't waste time."

When Carol begins to describe the boy's heart surgeries, Daphne deletes the message and dusts the empty spaces in the back of the filing cabinet, and re-alphabetizes Ashley's books. Then she spots the wicker garbage can, empty except for a few dirty Kleenexes and a crumpled piece of paper. She removes the paper and opens it up, expecting another bill from a phone sex company. It's a letter in Ashley's handwriting dated three days before, addressed to her:

> Daphne. I have thought about things a good deal. Over the past several months, I've become extremely concerned by the discrepancy between the future I envision for myself and the future I seem to be pursuing. I don't know what to do. It seems too late for all this. But should one swallow one's doubts and behave with rectitude or should one follow one's instinct, however scorpion-like it might be? What I mean is this: I have been plagued by the question of whether it is better to hurt you now, or whether it is better to damage you by subjecting you to my performance as a sub-standard husband.
>
> Do not misunderstand me. You are mainly a wonderful person. It would be inaccurate, however, for me to state that I do not have grave doubts. My mind has been pondering the following questions. Are Daphne and I a good fit? Does she slip into my life as a foot into a shoe? Is she destined to be the mother of my children? Is it wrong to want more?
>
> These, I think, are reasonable questions. Occasionally, I look at my life six months from now, and I can't see you there. I certainly have a sizable amount of affection for you. But where do we go from here? How much love is enough?

The letter is signed, simply, A. Daphne stands in the middle of the dim study, Windex in one hand, the letter in another. For a minute, she wonders if it is indeed Ashley who has written the letter, it sounds so cool and matter-of-fact, and Ashley usually has so much trouble getting down serious thoughts. But the arches and spaces are all in order; she can even see where he has paused, an awkward writing habit, before each *s*, a large printed letter in the midst of tight cursive. Even the opening—just, Daphne—seems an announcement that the letter is not for her. Around the apartment, he leaves her notes about dinner plans and grocery lists, and he addresses them differently each time, in a way she thinks of as typically Ashley—earnest even in his attempts at eccentricity. *Dearest D. To Daphne, bearer of freshly squeezed orange juice. Hello goddess of Rice Krispies, ally in intuition.* She feels her forehead, damp under the bandana she's wearing for cleaning. It is as if the air has thinned, like the air of higher altitudes. She can't quite get a proper breath. She sees her wedding dress, hanging unsteadily in the doorway, and notices a small spot of blue along the hem, a spray of Windex on the white silk. *Hola, Daphners, partner in crime.* Although she knows she has just discovered something distressing, terrible even, still she cannot gather sadness for the letter and its intent. All she can think is that this letter, with its formality and its petered-out woefulness, cannot be for her. *To Daphne, about whom I have grave doubts.*

How can it be she who went so far wrong in interpretation?

She doesn't want to be home when Ashley arrives with groceries, to unpack Cheerios and raspberry yogurt and bananas with him, wondering whether, in the plan of his world, they are getting married in two weeks. To be around such domestic things and pretend to be concerned about them. *Did you remember my milk? Is this peanut butter all natural?*

So she leaves in the car. She simply drives. Because she steers without forethought, without the barest notion of how to get from one destination to another, she drives around the city streets, moving from her apartment, through the weekend rush of College Street, the martini-drenched dress-up, into the deeper downtown streets with their crowds of taxis. Past Nathan Phillips Square and the

Eaton Centre, she drives slowly, signalling her left and right turns well ahead of time, easing into them with geriatric care. In fact, she has no idea where she is going as she makes her way north.

To Daphne, whom I do not love.

She drives and drives. And her mind fills with a single thought: all she would like is to drive home and find the apartment dark and quiet, to see Ashley lying in bed already asleep, his mouth slightly open like a child's, and to slip into bed without waking him and lie quite still there, so she can hear the wispiness of each breath in the air, the way sleep seems to lift him a little from the bed, as if he bears no burden of adulthood. She would give anything to hear it now, that level of noise just above silence, the airborne rhythm that barely identifies itself as sound. Is she allowed to wish for this? She thinks not. She is beginning to know that there are no wishes to be had any more because she never even knew how to wish properly, or even improperly. More fitting than marriage is that she should be left with the captive life of retrospect, the wheel in her hands.

Looking at the dashboard clock, she realizes how late it is, ten o'clock, and she has no idea where she is. Without pulling over, one hand gripped on the wheel, she reaches over to the glove compartment to retrieve her Perly's road guide.

There is no noise, at first, when it happens. She is wrapped, still, in this altered calm, her conviction that there are no decisions, no confrontations to be made. A moth flies along the length of the windshield and lands on the dashboard just above the steering wheel. She monitors its movement, glancing back and forth between the road and the moth. As she turns a corner onto a softly lit side street that has already descended into a midnight sleepiness, she looks down for the moth, and it is gone. Then she feels a brush at her cheek, a feathery kiss, followed by the moth's panicky flutter across her ear and into her hair and back again to her cheek. Letting go of the wheel, she slaps at her cheek with both hands and slams on what she thinks is the brakes. There is a moment of delay before she feels the bumps. A moment before her mind registers what she hears. Then it all comes at once.

A series of high-pitched, clipped yelps. The front wheels over a small bump, a moment, the back wheels over a small bump. She slams on the brakes and sits, waiting for something more, yelling or instant sirens, something dramatic like a flood of gunshots. But the street is quiet. She opens the car door. The yelps are trailing off into low groans, faint whimpers broken by pinpricks of sound, then another single yelp. Daphne can't fit the yelps and the groans and the bumps together to form an understanding of what's happened. The noises, the bumps in the car, seem isolated, as if they are outtakes of different events that can't connect. She wanders, feeling vacant and baffled, to the back of the car, and her eyes follow the road. "Oh," she says, "Oh, God," and her voice has a brittle, collapsed quality she finds unfamiliar, a formlessness that is barely verbal, as she falls to her knees, realizing what she has done.

There is a dog, a little terrier, lying behind her car, one of his hind legs stretched back behind his body. As she pulls the leg back into place, the dog yelps again, weakly. Its breaths are shallow pants, and it groans in a far-off, unreachable way. Its eyes are glazed over, aimed at a distant spot in the night sky.

It seems impossible to her that there are not ambulances streaming down the street to help her out of this.

Leaning over the dog, she runs a hand across its blond fur, so soft, like the wisps of a baby's hair. It doesn't respond to her touch, doesn't move its head or twitch its skin. She looks up and down the quiet street, at the houses, all of them dark, even the houses with two cars in the driveway. Carefully, she slides both hands under the dog's side, feels its ribs, some still intact, some cracked at their centres. Then she crouches and slides her hands farther in until she has the dog cradled in the crook of her elbows. As she lifts and stands, the dog moans faintly. It is limp in her arms, still staring at the spot in the sky.

The dog seems too heavy, so much weight in so little an animal. She feels as if she is standing at the bottom of a cold river, as if the water above is pressing her into the sticky bottom, and someone has just told her she has to travel from one shore to the other. Her movements are thick, muddied, each step requiring strength she doesn't have. She wades her way across the sidewalk.

She walks up the path to a house and rings the doorbell twice. She waits a minute, then rings the doorbell again four times.

"Hello?" she calls, trying to sound like a sane person. "Please answer."

She cradles the dog, waiting for someone to answer the door, for surely someone must answer. Someone must answer at a time when her arms have never seemed so inadequate. The neighbouring house is also dark, but she cuts across the lawn and up to the door. She rings the doorbell, but doesn't hear its noise reverberating back to her from within. Then she thinks she hears noise from inside, a television or a radio, and she rings the doorbell again, and presses her ear to the door's cold wood. Then, with all her strength, she kicks the door. She stands on the top step for another minute, then steps back, looks at the black windows, and rings the doorbell again, willing someone to come to the door, picturing a correct resolution with all her ability to desire. When still no one comes, she hardens her body and kicks the door again and again.

"You have to help me," she shouts at the white door.

The dog gasps and lets out a long low moan. She bangs on the door with her foot. Her shoes leave black smudges on the shiny paint.

The dog groans again and shudders. It turns its head from the sky and rests its cold muzzle on the inside of her arm. It lets out a long breath and licks, with the tip of its cool tongue, the centre spot on her wrist where her arm meets her hand. She kicks the door again and again. She is certain now that she hears the organized laughter of a television show.

"Come!" she shouts. "You're in there!"

How could there be no one, when she has come to do the right thing? She turns and looks up and down the street at all the houses, at the rows of black windows, the emissaries of all the people living in the backs of their homes.

CRUSADE

Your new boyfriend is not welcome in your house. Your mother declares that his curly red hair is an assault on her senses and that she doesn't understand how any girl in her right mind could be attracted to him, not with that shiny Christian face. You argue without conviction. Tell her that she's a reverse bigot. That it's not a crime to go to church three times a week. That she worships at the altar of sexual charisma like a teenager. You slam the door twice leaving the room. Your father emerges from the basement.

"Who's slamming doors?" he shouts.

Your mother holds up her hands. "It isn't me."

"I'm not fixing any more doors," he calls out to you.

On an impulse, you invite your boyfriend to dinner even though you and your mother have been fighting steadily. His Holiness, she calls him. Certain revelations about the degree of his Christianity do, in fact, trouble you, but ever since you've been confronted with your mother's aversion, you have become his most strident defender. During dinner, he holds forth. Your mother is perched on the edge of her chair, her tight smile stitched to perfection. Every time he refers to his group, Campus Crusade for Christ, she lays down her fork. She seems to oscillate between shocked remove and direct terror, on her face the wondering assessment of a woman watching news coverage of a tornado or a hurricane, natural phenomena far from home but nonetheless alarming. Your father nods approvingly every time His Holiness refers to God as "my Saviour." The faces of your two younger sisters are contorted with the effort of choking back laughter. Every time they kick each other under the table, a bubble rumbles noisily to the top of the water cooler. Your older sister is in her last year of university and is just discovering her affection for impugning the values of men she views as misogynists.

"But surely you can see that the Christian church is mired in patriarchal institutions that inhibit a woman's freedom to think," she says helplessly, beginning to understand his affable smile as a wall of steam you can't see through.

You eat quietly, listening as he answers your family's questions, nodding, Yes, he does believe premarital sex is wrong, shaking his head, No, he does not believe God is infringing on his right to live his life. He tells anecdotes about his church, the youth group he headed as a teenager, the Bible retreats, the fundraisers and clothing drives, the Christian camaraderie, the good works—all related with such cheerful piety, such absence of self-protectiveness, that you fear for him. When your mother tells him about a friend's illness, he suggests a prayer chain.

"My younger sister had meningitis a few years back," he says. "Our reverend, who's just the coolest guy you could ever hope to meet, got all the churches across Ontario banded together to pray at the exact same time each week. We hand-picked several older, more experienced churchgoers to pray every night. My sister's recovery was so fast that even the doctors granted that there was likely something in that prayer chain. Even the doctors."

Your mother clears her throat, a compulsive habit.

"I see that frown," he says, smiling at her. "But there's power in everything. Never say never."

After dinner, you walk him to his car. It's almost the beginning of spring, and almost the end of your first year in university. The air is still wintry. You draw your finger along the warm underside of his mouth, notice its solemnity curving into kindness. Standing so close to him, you feel calm for the first time all day. With a light deliberation, he places one finger on the pout of your lower lip, as if blessing your mouth.

"I sensed a tension," he says.

"In my family, you're the kind of boy I can't bring home."

"Hang in there," he says. "We all have our crosses to bear." He gives you a stiff-handed pat on your bottom.

When you return, your mother and sisters are assembled in the front hall.

"Why on earth are you dating a born-again Christian?" your mother asks before you even close the door. When she pronounces the word *Christian*, she rolls her eyes slightly and lets her shoulders slump, as if reluctantly granting you a point in an argument.

"I'm not. He's just a regular Christian," you say. "Like you used to be."

When you spot opportunities to remind her of the minor shames of her past, you seize them with the speed of a hand drawn back from a hot stove.

YOUR MOTHER TELLS you she hates you almost daily. You can see the catharsis these words provide, the way they set calm on her face like a restorative breath. The littlest things set her off. Your spoon clicking your teeth when you eat cereal. The way you shorten the word *the* before vowel sounds. The way you knock over chairs to get to the ringing phone. Sometimes she throws things. The wooden fish-shaped flute. The Beatrix Potter bowl you ate applesauce from as a child. Her keys. Lately, you've begun to chart her explosions with a scientific interest, plotting in mental graphs the arc of her anger—like a mountain, its confident ascent, its tired slope downwards and out. You are amazed by its triangular containment, its pointed insistence. You discover that there are countless mathematical ways of understanding anger, its origins and results. Each time her eyes tighten and her voice compresses, you lapse into algebraic wonder. If z is the outburst and x is your deliberate mispronunciation of the word February, what is y? You begin to call her Mother. Talk with your mouth full. Cut your hair too short. She throws the toaster.

"You push me," she protests. "You know I have a temper."

You shrug. "You're supposed to be an adult."

In the morning, she stands at the kitchen counter slicing grapefruit for your breakfast. She stops a moment to draw a white terrycloth bathrobe over the black lace slip she wears to bed. Moving slowly around the kitchen, from the cupboard to the refrigerator to the toaster, she tells you her dreams.

"You were kidnapped by a heroin addict and I was searching for you everywhere. Then someone told me that you were at the bottom of the lake so I dove down to find you, but I couldn't swim because the water was thick and sticky like toffee." She turns to you expectantly, like someone waiting for her sentence to be finished. "What do you think it means?" She hands you half a red grapefruit.

"Mother," you say. "I neither know nor care. Now let me be."

"Then I dreamed I was running in a marathon and it was the best run of my life, but then I was driving in the car and I was in Italy. Then I was having sex with a taxi driver."

"How odd," you say, reading the paper with a great show of focus. "A thirty-five-year-old woman is fighting for the right to keep a python as her pet. She claims he is quite affectionate."

She spreads butter on your toast, hands it to you, and leaves the room. As you eat, you let your crumbs fall on the table, and when you are finished, you leave your dirty dishes on the counter. It seems easier to stop trying for peace. Recently, you have taken to angling your phrases with a formal, almost British flair. You request that she not take the Lord's name in vain. All this annoys her, which motivates you to continue. "That's just my fancy," has become your favourite way of punctuating your ideas and observations. You think it sounds aristocratic and self-deprecating. She tells you she cannot bear your new affectations. When you wake up, you throw your pajamas on the floor, forget to make your bed before you go to class. When you come home, you leave your keys in the front door. What appears as rebellion is really just laziness. You have begun to see anger on the flip side of everything. At night, you dream a different mother. One who wears aprons and knows the ratio of eggs to flour in baking. One who gardens wearing a straw hat and attends Sunday mass with a rosy enthusiasm. One who sleeps in a flowered flannel nightgown and greets each morning with a cheery stretch, who laughs off life's disappointments and dreams a landscape of shimmering domesticity.

THE ONLY PERSON who approves of the boy's faith is your father.

"It's the only good sense I've seen in her for years," he tells your mother.

"You don't know what you're talking about," she says. "If you knew her at all, you'd know he's not her type."

Your father approves of a young man with sound Christian values, the sort of boy who goes camping with his family, who knows how to erect a tent and hook a fish for dinner, a boy with God on his mind instead of sex. A boy who can strum "Blowin' in the Wind" by night and lead the hymns come Sunday morning. Your new boy is not this outdoorsy type of Christian, but you can't be bothered to explain this to your father. His mind is already bent with problems he can't find explanations for. He can't understand how the female side of his family has gone so wrong, supporting abortion and arguing the dangers of religiosity. Your older sister pins newspaper articles about church corruption on the refrigerator, highlights sections about Catholic priests molesting young boys. Your mother stopped taking you to church when you were ten. Her sole explanation was that she had had enough of hypocrisy. She cited your father as the first fool in the parade of hypocrites and insisted she would not subject her children to the litany of lies to which she had been subjected. Your father sleeps in the guest room and goes to church every Sunday morning.

You don't care what either parent thinks of your boyfriend. You dismiss your father's approval of your good sense, ignore your mother's insistence that dating a Christian is a form of post-adolescent rebellion. It seems to you that God has laid Christianity not just in your boy's heart, but on his skin, a glaze that can almost be mistaken for sexuality. It is true, as your mother reminds you, that his bright red hair is a little too flaming, but what she doesn't see is the way his professed sexlessness careens into sensuality. He expresses only positive thoughts and enjoys holding hands. In an effort to shock him, you pretend to be more cynical than you are, claiming to be a resolute atheist, arguing that his love of God is only motivated by fear of hell.

"I think you're an agnostic, at worst," he tells you. "You just haven't found the right church."

"I'm not a good person," you warn him. "I sometimes hurt people intentionally."

He squeezes your hand. "You just haven't found someone who brings out the best in you."

As your dates begin to unfold in these battles for your eternal soul, you worry that he views dating you as the ultimate good work, your conversion as the triumph that will secure his seat in heaven. And when you offer your cheek for a goodnight kiss, you feel in his lips the fleshy diffidence of wholesomeness, the purity that courts, even demands, corruption. Secretly, you have determined to wheedle his virginity out of him. You whistle as he drives away.

YOU HAVE BEEN SEDUCED many times, but have no idea how to
seduce. With pencil and paper, you sit at your desk to dissect past
seductions, chart patterns and map goals, pinpoint techniques and
calculate probability. Resolved to master the tricks of past lovers,
you clear your desk of schoolwork and compile a list of the boys
you have slept with. The number comes to seven, and you feel
strangely panicked, simultaneously corrupted and inept. That's
almost two for every year since you started having sex at fifteen.

You cross the first few off your list with black marker. You can
learn nothing from these first boys. They seduced you with self-
pity, sadly confessing their romantic failures. One announced that
you were the shining speck in his rusted life, settling unattrac-
tively in your arms like dead weight. More successful were the later
boys. They seduced you quickly, like a band-aid removed pain-
lessly in one swipe. They drew you in with specific flattery and
vague cajoling. Targeting your weakest areas—your hated inner
thighs, your tender lower lip—they placed themselves outside the
action. These boys noticed the shape of your hands, the soft skin
just below your navel. They took you in by inches, seemed to bow
before your naked body with such concentrated reverence, such
well-rehearsed appreciation. They told you that you were beautiful and intelligent and fun and knew that it would be enough to
carry you through. You were seduced with your own ego and left
empty-handed.

You are not confident that you have it in you to be this cunning, but you are willing to try. His Holiness's desire for you, so
sweetly dispassionate, so unencumbered by lust, fills you with a
sense of purpose. Standing at your bedroom mirror, you take off
your shirt and stare at your breasts, imagining your body as a net
in which you will catch his affection. When you were getting to
know him, he told you about when his parents fell in love. They
sent each other notes using the words of the Bible, the verses of
psalms. They were shy, he explained, and it was the only way

they knew to express their feelings. "I love the house where you live, the place where your glory makes its home," his father had scrawled in his mother's datebook. She left a reply in his hymn book: "I have treasured the words from your lips; in the path prescribed walking deliberately in your footsteps, so that my feet do not slip." You wondered how these religious fanatics managed to hold down jobs where they had to speak without the aid of God's Word.

"Are you allowed to do that?" you asked. "Use stuff from the Bible as your own words?"

"If you're doing it for the right reasons," he said. "Faithful you are with the faithful, blameless with the blameless, pure with the one who is pure."

Thinking of his parents, you decide to put your own spin on romantic communication. You write him a little poem, hinting at depths of feeling, avoiding anything overtly sexual:

> you bending over me:
> it is like
> standing still
> in the heart of a hurricane
> a shiver of sorrow
> rippling forever

When he tells you he thinks it is sweet, you write another, leaving it on his knapsack after class:

> your taste sparks
> tea with honey
> darjeeling fantasies
> words get lost
> in this brew of hope

You don't care if he thinks the poems are silly. You know how to let yourself be wanted, but are just learning how to want.

LATELY YOU'VE BEEN possessed by the suspicion that everyone is having a good time except you. During lunch at school, you read the work for afternoon classes while everyone else sits in small groups talking; food fights seem to erupt with unusual frequency. Even though you are almost at the end of first year, you feel you have learned nothing. You are biding your time, waiting for your ignorance to be revealed. Every time you hand in an essay, you fear you'll be found out. Sometimes you feel that if you put as much effort into learning as you do into pretending to learn, the world would be taken by storm. Instead, you take long naps in the afternoon.

His Holiness invites you on a Bible retreat. At first, you plan to decline. You cannot imagine being trapped north of the city with a group of people determined to preach God's word. At night, you're kept awake by the thought of his slender back. Just when you're almost asleep, you're awakened by the sound of your father, moving down the hall to your mother's room. His footfall vibrates the whole house. The door closes and the movement stops as you hear his voice, less audible than a murmur. Silence follows, and you hear his voice more loudly this time. Her voice starts out of nowhere, exhausted and alarmed. The voices grow louder. Stillness flattens the air each time one voice becomes clear enough for you to hear the words. A moment later, your father closes her bedroom door and heads down the stairs. You get up, open the curtains, and return to bed. The streetlight reflects the glare from patches of March snow. You burrow under the wintry brightness of the night.

The next morning you awaken to the sound of fighting in the kitchen.

"If you think you can afford it, think again," your father is saying. "I doubt if you'd be happy in a one-room apartment without the girls."

"The girls would come with me," she says. "You could never get the girls to go with you."

"I doubt they'll want to live in a tiny apartment." He intimidates by not shouting. "In any case, they won't be living at home for much longer."

She yells, suddenly, "You're such a fat bastard!" Her voice is loose and crazy. "I'd get the house. The girls would stay with me."

"You're wrong about that," he tells her. "I've been doing my research and you wouldn't get the house. I have an ace in the hole."

"You don't know what you're talking about," she says. "What's your ace in the hole?"

"A good card player never gives away his ace in the hole." You can tell he is smiling.

Closing your bedroom door, you find a radio station playing rap and turn up the volume. You shut your eyes and lie down and for a moment feel soothed by the music's metallic certainty, that repetitive hammer of noise. Your father listens only to classical music and Leonard Cohen. You decide that a weekend of preaching is better than a weekend of fighting and imagine how happy His Holiness will be when you tell him. Just the thought of calling him comforts you.

FOR LUNCH, he eats tofu with noodles while you have a hamburger.

"I love the way you eat," you tell him. "It's so polite. You even make tofu look good."

You are captivated by the smallest things. He seems amused and pleased by your hyperbolic fascination. You're amazed by his restraint, a quality you have never encountered in a man. When he first saw you in the junior common room of University College, he approached tentatively and invited you to attend a night of murder mystery organized by Campus Crusade for Christ. You told him rudely you weren't interested and didn't believe in God. He apologized, lingered for a moment before walking away. The next day, you spotted him in your Romantic poetry class. When you sat down, he came and sat next to you. He spoke with quiet certainty and told you he was sorry for bothering you, he knew people's attitudes towards Campus Crusade for Christ.

"The word *crusade* is unfortunate," he said, laughing. "We're not trying to recruit unwilling people to Christianity."

You liked his deferential manner, his lightly freckled skin. After class, you agreed to coffee. Sitting next to him was like holding an orange in your hand, feeling its perfect weight. In your memory of this day, he is wearing red velvet pants, though you know this cannot be so. You often argue this way with your memories, moments that are vivid but seem unlikely. You remember him telling you he loved you in the pause between rainstorms. Sitting in the car after a movie with the rain coming down so hard you couldn't hear each other speak. In a quiet moment, the rain dripping like a metronome, he said, "I love you," and you were too embarrassed to answer. When you really think about it, you know that this is not how it was. There was no rain, and you were the one who spoke the words, but your mind will not accept this as the reality. All you can do is back away from the real memories, and let the false ones stand.

While he eats his tofu, he watches you with curiosity. You can't think of anything to say, so you sit in silence. Ordinary moments like this stay in your head with cinematic accuracy.

"You know Jack, the teaching assistant in our Romantic poetry class?" you ask him. "He accused me of plagiarizing."

"Does he have evidence?"

"Of course he doesn't have evidence," you say. "I didn't plagiarize. He said the writing style differs from the style of my other papers." You worry that you've told him so many times you're a bad person that he won't believe you now, that he classifies unchristian, wicked, and dishonest as qualities that cannot exist separately.

"Jack's a good guy. It seems to me that if you tell him you're not guilty, he'll believe you." His solution is appallingly swift and innocent. He returns to his tofu. "At work a few years ago, my mom was accused of embezzling company funds. She didn't know what to do so she marched into a board meeting with her Bible and swore on it that she hadn't committed any such crime."

You pause, choosing carefully from among potential responses. "Are you suggesting that I produce a Bible and swear to Jack that I didn't plagiarize? That this will solve my problem?"

"You never know until you try."

You slump in your chair, arms crossed like a child refusing to yield a point. "I hate Jack," you say.

"Come on now, let's not use the word *hate*. Jack's a good guy. I would even risk my life for him."

"Are you serious?" You didn't see this much goodness coming, although conversations with him do tend to go this way, with random announcements that you used to think he came up with expressly to unsettle you.

"Of course," he says. "He's a solid person. He's taught me a lot and has always been fair to me. I couldn't see him in danger and not help."

"But you're not even friends with him."

"It doesn't matter," he says. "I couldn't stand by and not help him."

You can see the strain this places on him, having to explain pure instincts, virtue for its own sake, to a woman in a sulk. Analyzing his conviction does no good here. Disarmed, you stare in confusion and resolve. Such selflessness is foreign to you. You cannot trace its origins or map its consequences. He is sitting by the window, and you imagine, as his hair appears to light with sun, that goodness is contagious. You settle your chair closer to his, placing yourself within the perimeter of righteousness. Just righteousness, without the prefix of self. And you think it might actually be working. Goodness might be landing on your fingers, finding its way to you through the gateway of your eyes, because you feel sure as you listen to his calm assurance that you would risk your life for him, would gamble all you have to keep him in this world.

YOU WALK AROUND your house slowly, moving in and out of a consciousness of Christianity, as you pack for the retreat. Your mother sits on your bed.

"Do you really want to go?" she asks. "Is he making you feel obligated?"

"No, Mother," you say. "I'm tired of being here. I need to get away for the weekend."

"Don't go on any snowmobiles." She presses your hand. "I don't think you realize how dangerous they are."

"Mother, nobody is going on snowmobiles. This is a Bible retreat."

"Well, you never know what they might try to get you to do." She gets up to leave. "Watch out for those Christians. They're not as good as they appear. If you want to come home early, call me. I'll pick you up."

"Yes, Mother, I know," you say, closing your suitcase as the doorbell rings.

"That'll be His Holiness," she says, standing with her hands on her hips, surveying you with concern and frustration, as if she's measuring the space between your eyes.

You grab your suitcase and she follows closely. She doesn't wave as the two of you drive away.

"I think she's afraid I'm going to become a born-again Christian and marry you," you say to him, laughing. "And that you're going to turn out like my father."

"Your father seems like a great guy," he says.

The day after their wedding, your father said to your mother, "I know you wanted me to tell you I loved you yesterday, so of course I couldn't." You considered telling His Holiness this, but you are beginning to see that he might be immune to such stories. You simply say, "He wasn't at all nice to my mother on their wedding day."

"Well, sometimes brides are a real handful. I can especially see your mother being a handful." He turns on the radio and stops at a station playing Bob Dylan. He hums along for a minute, then starts singing in his off-key tenor, changing the words and mixing songs. "Hey Mistress Tambourine Girl, play a song for me. Don't think twice, it's all right." He taps your knee in rhythm to the music.

When you arrive at the camp two hours later, it's almost dark. He turns to you expectantly, as if your face will be lit differently in Christian surroundings, shaded by pine trees, reflected through the lake's mirror. He takes your bag and leads you to your cabin, explaining that you'll be rooming with a prayer buddy.

"We do group prayers after each meal," he says. "But we find that sometimes you get your most intense praying done with just one other person."

After introducing you to your cabin mate, Janine, he kisses you on the cheek and tells you he'll meet you at the main hall before dinner. You turn to Janine, whose eyes are thickly lined with black shadow, lips coated with dark purple lipstick. She turns to you with a teacherly sigh.

"We've been brought together because I was like you once. I know what it is not to know the way of the Lord. I'm glad God brought you here, and I think you will be too by the time this weekend is over." She has your hand firmly sandwiched between both of hers. "I want you to know that you can talk to me."

"I'm starving," you say, "Let's go to dinner." You can't bear the drama of drawing your hand away.

You break away from her in the cafeteria when you catch a flash of red hair across the room. He's arguing quietly with a man wearing a yellow T-shirt bearing the words GOD'S WAY OR THE HIGHWAY.

"What's going on?" you ask him.

"My cabin mate couldn't come because he has the flu, so now I don't have a prayer buddy."

You gesture towards Janine. "You can pray with us."

He forces a tolerant smile. "It doesn't work that way. Three in a group upsets the balance. I'll just pray by myself."

The fluorescent lights flash on and off. The man in the yellow T-shirt moves to the front of the room and raises his hand.

"People, can we have some silence? John and I would like to address the group." The room falls quiet. "Before everyone eats, we would like to introduce ourselves and tell you a bit about the activities we have planned for this weekend. John, want to take over?"

John, in a matching yellow T-shirt, picks up his clipboard. "Thanks, Pete. It's great to see all these familiar faces. And especially exciting to see some newcomers." He winks at you.

"Pete and myself are in charge of the activities this weekend, your camp counsellors, as it were. For those of you who might not already know, let me tell you a little bit about myself. I first started hanging with the folks in Campus Crusade for Christ in my first year at U of T. I started going to the meetings because nobody else at school was friendly." He approaches and kneels before your chair, rests a hand on your knee, projecting to the group, but looking at you.

"But then I realized these folks had something to say that I needed to hear, that I'd been waiting to hear. I've been active ever since, and I think these retreats are a great way of regrouping. We can share our feelings about God and discuss any Bible passages that might have us puzzled. I don't know about you guys, but I always return to the city with a renewed sense of the Lord in my life." He stands. "If there's anything you need, feel free to find Pete or myself. We're the dudes in these yellow T-shirts. It looks like dinner's ready now, so if you're ready for some grub, head on up and help yourself."

After all the people at your table have gathered their dinner, they encourage you to stand and lead them in grace. Panicked, you search for words of gratitude, but cannot summon thankfulness. You pretend the honour is too much for you to accept. "I couldn't possibly," you say, looking down, and they don't push you.

You eat tentatively, listening to the stories. One girl is a former cocaine addict who discovered God when she was lying naked in an alleyway, confused about where she was and how she got there. Another boy is a former compulsive shoplifter. When he tried to make the transition to grand theft auto, he got arrested and took it as a sign from God. Most of the people, though, have been raised in sound Christian families, lifelong followers of the Word. People finish eating and slowly filter out of the room, making their way towards the bonfire that John is starting by the lake.

"I'm going to head down to my cabin for a quick nap before we start the evening activities," says His Holiness, standing up. His face is flushed, the redness absorbing his freckles.

You look around as if you've forgotten where you are. "I guess I'll meet you at the bonfire then."

You sit a moment longer, then decide to find Janine. Even though the Christians are friendly, you feel uncomfortable alone. When you reach your cabin, you find Janine arguing with Pete about Romans, chapter 8. A Bible is open on the bed.

"Pete," she says, her voice rising, "I'm not saying that your primary interests shouldn't be spiritual. I'm just saying that you can have unspiritual interests too. The Bible says the unspiritual are interested only in what is unspiritual, but it doesn't say that the spiritual must be interested only in the spiritual."

"You're missing the point," Pete responds calmly, lifting the Bible.

You close the door. Genesis is the only part of the Bible you've read, research for a high school essay. Wandering along the path from your cabin, you decide to find His Holiness, to wake him to keep you company. You come to his cabin and open the door quietly. When you step inside, you are disoriented by the completeness of the dark, the northern night to which your eyes haven't yet adjusted. You see the outline of his body on a low cot and you step lightly, afraid to wake him suddenly. You kneel at the side of his bed, watching as the darkness lifts and his face comes into focus.

It occurs to you that he is better than you in every way one person can be better than another.

The floor creaks under your shifting weight, and he simply opens his eyes calmly as if he had only been pretending to sleep. He doesn't start when he sees you there and he looks hardly awake, but he takes your cold hand and places it on his chest, beneath the wool blanket. You say a silent prayer for virtue, hoping there is no one to hear it, no one to grant you in this moment what you've never had. Closing your eyes, you lean over and kiss him gently, in a way you doubt he has ever been kissed. With purpose. You are surprised that he doesn't pull away, stunned when he pulls you towards him, then onto him. It seems to you that he is the one removing the clothes, the one saying, "I've never wanted anyone the way I want you." It seems to you that even in a moment of triumph and desire, even in a moment when desire is greater than triumph, you wouldn't say such a thing. But you can't now see the difference between his hands and your hands, between what he wants and what you want.

His naked body seems so long, much longer than when he's clothed. You feel his face, and it is hot, almost feverish. Your eyes skim the shape of his body, imagining his outline against yours. It seems that maybe this is all that matters, the outline of what's happening. The details—where you're touching him, the expression on his face, whether you wrap your legs around his body—seem unimportant. The most seductive part of the moment is knowing that he is your lover. The official sound of the title *lover*. It sounds almost evangelical, saturated with desire. You say it over and over to yourself.

Afterwards, you watch the laboured rise and shaky fall of his chest, listen to his loud, wakeful breathing.

"It's okay," you say. "I'm on the Pill."

Standing, he wraps his bathrobe around himself. "I'm going to take a shower."

When he leaves, you lie in bed worrying, hoping no one is around. You imagine getting expelled from the Bible retreat. You imagine black T-shirts: FORNICATION. JUST SAY NO. When he hasn't returned half an hour later, you get dressed and go looking for him. Opening the door to the showers, you hear water running quietly, with weak pressure. It runs evenly, with little variation, as if there is no body beneath the spray. You move from stall to stall and find him in the last one. He is sitting on the concrete floor, his knees to his chest. He faces the wall, folded into himself.

"Are you okay?"

His shoulders twitch at the sound of your voice. He turns to you. "What are you doing here?"

"I came to see if you were okay," you say, shaking. You had anticipated gratitude.

His voice is cold and hard and there are goosebumps on his skin. "Leave me alone."

You know you should be quiet, but you have too much to say. "It's just sex. I told you that you have nothing to worry about. I'm on the Pill. I can't imagine why you're acting this way."

"Just sex," he repeats. "You would say that."

"I should have just let you be," he says, pressing his forehead into his knees.

"What are you saying?" you ask. "I can't hear you."

"I should have known," he says, but not to you. "Faithful you are with the faithful, blameless with the blameless, pure with the one who is pure."

"I didn't force you, if that's what you're saying." You no longer want to go to him.

He looks up at you briefly. "I met your family. I knew what you would be." He turns from you again, beneath the weak water.

You step from the steam into the lakeside chill and follow a thin path through the trees to the main lodge, where the phone is. As you wander, you grab a narrow branch covered in pine needles, and you pull them off one at a time, thinking, He knows me. He knows me not. Who knows me?

WHAT YOU

said you WANTED

A man once told Tasha, "Sleeping next to a skinny woman is like lying next to a piece of Styrofoam."

She held on to that for a long time, even past the time when she needed to hear such things just to get her clothes off. When the man said that to her, she called her mother and told her right away. She still needed to pass on such comments. It seemed she would never stop.

"That's fine for him," Isabel had said. "But don't go using that as an excuse."

An excuse for what?

"For portliness."

For Isabel, *portly* was one of the merriest, most benevolent descriptors in the English language. The world it conjured—the ripe medieval feasts, pewter goblets and game hens, bawdy laughter—mitigated the message, and she believed that if she applied this word to Tasha's body, she would avoid inflicting the psychological damage associated with words such as *hefty* and *overweight*. *Chubby* was meant to deliver this conviviality but was simply without character: a bland, featureless word that contained none of the Falstaffian plenitude of *portly*. She could say it again and again. It was transporting. Not to mention functional.

Isabel was still living in the big family house, though her husband, Ron, had left five years before. Isabel's friend Rita had recently moved in, and although Rita seemed to occupy a separate bedroom, Tasha spent much time trying to figure out the nature of this friendship. Tasha visited Isabel almost every day, not out of an obligation to Isabel but out of some obligation to herself, a resolve to be the kind of person who would choose duty over fun.

Not much had changed in the house since Tasha's family had first started living there when Tasha was ten. The house was her father's inheritance from his parents, and although it was tall and imposing, with a gloomy, forsaken beauty, no owner had put any confidence in its grandeur. Tasha's parents—her father was a high school math teacher, her mother a drama teacher—were not well off enough to bother. They also thought renovations ruined a house's character. Although the house seemed impressive from the outside, with three floors and a small turret, the interior was dim and smelled stale. As a girl, Tasha often thought the smell, mil-dewy and medicinal, resistant to detergent, had attached itself to her clothes. There were long, deep cracks like lightning strikes in the plaster on her bedroom walls, and the old oak floorboards were creaky and uneven. The ceilings were spotted with water stains. All the rooms, even the kitchen, were painted a decades-old dingy beige and Isabel and Ron had left up most of her grandparents' art-work, so the walls were covered in paintings of empty rural land-scapes, winter gardens, and sloping farm fields with a single horse grazing.

Tasha's bedroom was in the turret, and every year or so, she would go back and live there for several months while she changed jobs or men. On the walls still hung her childhood posters of golden puppies, an Impressionist-style painting of a shepherd boy playing a flute to his sheep, a watercolour of a pearly white uni-corn under a blooming rainbow. Modernizing the room would have meant admitting it was still hers, that she would be back for it, and she wasn't prepared to do that. At the same time, she felt a childish proprietary greed when Isabel suggested new posters. Returning to her girlhood room was somehow the consummation of all the bad luck she'd had out in the world, the proper conclusion.

As a girl, Tasha had wished her home could be like the houses of her friends, everything pretty and cheerful, packed with lively clutter, the overflow of full lives. Her house had a different kind of disorder, not of abundance but of objects misplaced and never found, of dust balls lurking under all the beds and in all the corners. If she wanted to know where her clean clothes were, where her schoolbooks had been left, she had to keep on top of these things herself. Isabel's meticulousness was not of that kind. Tasha's friends had often envied the privacy of her turret bedroom, but unlike them, Tasha did not want her life to play out in private space. She wanted noisier complications, boisterous messes. She wanted to bicker with siblings, she wanted nosiness and door slamming, she wanted to eavesdrop and be eavesdropped on. She often wished for life to feel more crowded. In the blue evenings, she had liked to sit in her window seat and look down at the street, imagining that she was a princess, confined and abandoned in a turret, wrenched from the glory of her former life.

Tasha went by Isabel's house one evening before her second date with a new man. She brought two outfits to get her mother's opinion about which looked better. The house had no full-length mirrors, so she had to stand on the bed in the master bedroom to get a view of herself in the mirror above the dresser. She was standing under the overhead light, a familiar position, with her head cranked to one side so she could see her reflection. One outfit was a long black dress, skimming her body, but not tight, then flaring out in an A-line just above her calves. The other outfit was a white blouse with ruffles along the front and a silky blue skirt that fell to her knees. The black dress was new, and it was supposed to make her look elegant and unreachable, lithe and cruel. She preferred the white blouse and blue skirt, which perhaps made her look innocent but seemed a more honest outfit.

"The black dress," said Isabel, down in the kitchen. "The blouse makes you look like a schoolmarm."

"This is a trendy blouse," Tasha said. "I saw a blouse just like this in a magazine. I got it on Queen Street. I don't think schoolmarms shop on Queen Street."

Schoolmarm was another of Isabel's favourite words.

"You go out on a date in that white schoolmarm blouse, and I guarantee you—I guarantee—this man will not be falling all over you at the end of the night. What's more, the black dress is slimming."

Tasha started gathering up her things loudly. She was opening cupboard doors and banging them shut, looking for her water bottle, although part of her remembered she had left that upstairs.

"You break the hinges, you're fixing them," Isabel pointed out.

"Your fashion sense is outdated," Tasha said.

"You asked me what I thought. I'm giving you my objective opinion. Who can be honest with you if not your own mother?"

Tasha had no sibling to commiserate with her. What she had was her mother.

LATER, TASHA TOLD Isabel about the date anyway. She told her about how the man—his name was Alan—had a double chin even though he wasn't fat and how a remnant of Parmesan cheese had taken up residence on his bottom lip and stayed there all through dinner. She knew Isabel would like that. Isabel kept saying, "So it just wouldn't come off?" and she double-checked different scenarios, as if she couldn't believe Tasha hadn't made up this story expressly to please her.

"Didn't he take a drink? Didn't it come off then?"

No, it stayed.

"He never used his napkin?"

"He never licked his lips?"

Tasha delivered the best part: that he went to the bathroom, and when he returned, the piece of cheese was still sitting there.

What Tasha didn't deliver was the news that she went back to his apartment anyway. She had continually been afraid, since she started having sex in university, that she might never find another man inclined to have sex with her. She was terribly undiscriminating, and as a result, somewhat promiscuous. This was one thing her mother did not know. Isabel had approved of the fact that, at the age of sixteen, Tasha had still not kissed a boy. She applauded Tasha's decision not to get mixed up with boys because participation meant submission, and submission meant the disabling of one's own mind. How many people respected you—not how many people liked you—was Isabel's measure of how well you had done in the world. In fact, she thought respect and liking were incompatible. The truth was that the only reason Tasha hadn't kissed a boy by the age of sixteen was that no boy had tried. She had attempted, on several dates, to look pitiable and open, but no boy had shown willingness. Sex, to her then, was a world of ribaldry and optimism, a place to which she would have paid, if she could, to gain entry. She had envied men the seeming ease with which they could buy prostitutes. Fifteen years later, Tasha was having sex, but her essential position hadn't changed. She didn't care about being respected; she cared supremely and only about being liked.

Isabel had presented sex as an initiation into worriedly counting calendar days, a leaky place full of openings and fluids. Tears, discharge, semen? What was the difference? All would combine to haunt you once you experienced that elevated back arch, the spread and manipulation of legs, the digit that couldn't possibly be a finger poking you in the back in the morning. This was a situation into which no bright girl would willingly put herself. Isabel warned that you never knew what kind of penis you were going to encounter. It might be circumcised or not. It might be alarmingly large or alarmingly small. It might fork. She reported that she had once seen in a French movie a penis that was covered in a large brown birthmark shaped like a beluga whale.

So Tasha didn't tell her mother that she had been in the man's bed all night. Isabel asked her what ended up happening with the cheese. Tasha had lost track of it somewhere between the restaurant and the car.

"I wonder if it fell off or if he ate it," Isabel said.

This man Alan had a voice that made her do unlikely things. It was strong and tenacious, like a heavy oar through choppy waves. It cut through things. "Lift your leg." "Turn over." He wanted her to describe in detail how certain things felt. "Be specific," he ordered. Saying, "It feels good," wasn't enough for him. He wanted *staggering and explosive*. He willed *illuminating and haunting. Like a thousand angels are fluttering their wings in my vagina.*

"He probably ate it," Isabel concluded.

Then she asked if he wanted to see Tasha again, and Tasha said that he did.

"There you go," Isabel said. "I guess he agreed with me that the black dress was slimming."

ISABEL WANTED HER to lose weight. Did Tasha want this for herself? She couldn't tell.

She did compare herself unfavourably to other women, a habit that was not as common as people seemed to think. A good number of the women she knew believed they were much prettier than they were. They didn't suffer from fits of great ill will towards their faces, as she did. They complimented themselves without restraint, and they passed on compliments other people had given them. Her friend Patricia, especially, was enchanted by her own unobjectionable but ordinary looks. She had tested out the word *beautiful* many times around Tasha, put it in the mouths of numerous strangers and acquaintances. Reports had come in from all across the city, apparently, alleging her resemblance to a number of movie stars. If Patricia didn't approve of the movie star, she became offended. She pretended to prefer Tasha's coarse, frizzy hair to her own flat blonde hair. "My hair looks the same all the time," she cried once when they had sought refuge in a bar during a rainstorm. Tasha was trying to tame her hair in the bathroom. "Your hair has so much body. You can work with the weather to find different styles. It must be so exciting never to know how your hair will look!" Tasha hadn't spoken to her in several months.

Tasha mostly felt friendly towards her own looks, unless someone was looking at her. When she was alone with herself in front of the mirror, she liked her full, pale lips, her round, milky cheeks. She thought that her mess of curly reddish-brown hair made her look interesting. But she could access that satisfaction only when she was alone. For four years after university, she had half-heartedly tried to become an actress, and she had finally abandoned it when she realized how much she hated the way she looked after every audition. No matter how cheerful and obliging the auditioners seemed, she felt herself growing to beastly proportions before their eyes. She became lumbering and dowdy, and she suspected that her attempts to look more attractive had the opposite outcome. On one of her last auditions, for a minor part in an obscure show at a poor downtown theatre, she had attempted glamour by applying red lipstick and by playing up the wild shrub of her hair. The effect was garish and aging, almost deranged. She knew it. On the bus later, the other passengers gave her a wide berth, especially when she began swearing quietly as she realized she had lost her directions. After that, she stopped trying. In high school, she had been pacified by the idea that she was persecuted and misunderstood. At twenty-eight, she no longer saw the romance in being reviled.

If she had known how, she would have dressed to look deliberately ugly, stylishly ugly, and darkly, splendidly lit with contempt. Because she didn't, her everyday clothes had an unflattering shapelessness about them, and as Isabel pointed out, they made her look possibly larger than she was. She wasn't so very large. She was five feet, five inches, and she weighed 152 pounds. The trouble was a lack of division between waist and hips, sturdy farm stock legs. There was insipidness in the bulk of her, a matronly complacence that Isabel felt she encouraged by dressing unwisely. After she quit acting, Tasha had decided to consider herself pleasant-looking, like a good neighbour. Isabel often told her she looked sulky.

"Let's be objective" had always been Isabel's rallying cry. Accordingly, she tried to provide an example of objectivity. Isabel was not one of those women who give birth to beautiful babies. Tasha had been an ugly baby, and Isabel said so. For all Tasha's life, it was important to Isabel that people should understand that, no matter what, she was still objective, that her judgement had not been made common by doting. In the delivery room, when the doctor passed her the baby, Isabel had looked at her from a sensible emotional distance and said to the nurses and to Ron, "Isn't she ugly?"— because she was, after all. Bruised and red, with wrinkled, simian fingers, Tasha gave no aesthetic pleasure to her gazers, and Isabel wanted everyone to understand that she could recognize that.

She had wanted a boy, but because she was superstitious, she had tried reverse psychology on her body and wished for a girl. When she and Tasha fought, she often expressed regret that she hadn't had more confidence in her magical abilities. This, she believed, was her single concession to self-delusion: her ability to consider herself improbably possessed of the power to bring key desires, and key fears, into reality through her focus on them. To compensate for this lapse of objectivity, she widely acknowledged her awareness of it—to be led by irrational ideas and subjective opinions was only truly harmful when one did not realize what was happening.

Isabel felt her objectivity was most marvellously put on display when Tasha was a baby. Her favourite story told of one afternoon when Tasha was about a year old. Tasha's nap dependably
lasted three hours, and she had been sleeping for just an hour.
Heaps of laundry cluttered the narrow hallway and dirty dishes
were piled around the house. It occurred to Isabel that she hadn't
had sex in eight weeks—she knew this because she marked each
encounter with a red dot on the calendar. She stood at the calendar with two food-encrusted sleepers in her hand and stared at that
expanse of weeks, the absence of red dots on two consecutive pages
of the calendar, then promptly dropped the sleepers on a mound of
other dirty baby clothes and headed for her room, realizing that
she could do for herself what her husband was failing to do.

She left the curtains open as the afternoon light streamed
through the wide windows, and she stripped, kicking her shorts
joyfully off the tip of her toe. The sun, the open windows, the full
nudity—these elements combined to make her feel decadent and
young. They renewed her sense of daring, which had suffered
badly since Tasha's birth. She felt that she was doing something
wrong, possibly in full view of a neighbour sitting innocently in
a window seat looking out at the trees. Even more, she realized
that she was not in the mood for hasty satisfaction, that she meant
to take her time. She nestled down under the covers and enjoyed
the coolness of the sheets. Then, just as she was beginning, Tasha
awoke two hours ahead of schedule and started screaming. In the
privacy of her mind, Isabel cursed Tasha and cursed her life, then
stretched one arm out to the nightstand and turned the radio on
and the volume up. She proceeded to enjoy herself for the next
twenty minutes until she was filled with benevolent mirth, so that
when she finally fetched Tasha, she felt only the most minor twinge
of guilt when she saw the baby's drenched red face and her hands
twisted up in her curls.

As a teenager and as an adult, Tasha had begged her mother not to tell this story to her friends, lest they think she shared her mother's masturbatory gusto, but Isabel loved to be unpredictable. She told the story because it highlighted the things she most enjoyed about herself: her capricious sexuality, her resolve in the face of opposition, her maternal irreverence. She would no more stop telling that story than she would wake up at six o'clock in the morning to bake fresh blueberry muffins. When Tasha had been quite young, Isabel would be full of fiery maternal impulses at one moment, and at the next, cool withdrawal. She might fall into a fever of stifling affection, reading Tasha her favourite fairy tales, "Snow White and Rose Red," "Rumpelstiltskin," and "The Princess and the Pea," and she often read Tasha the original Grimm's fairy tales because they had more literary merit (another instance of objectivity triumphing over maternal coddling). Just half an hour after reading fondly to Tasha, she might be preparing a peanut butter and jelly sandwich for Tasha's lunch in a fit of resentment and boredom. She felt it was all part of her return to objectivity.

"Be objective," Isabel said to Tasha one day when Tasha stopped by after an audition. "Don't you think you'd like to wear short skirts?"

"Yes, yes," Tasha would say. "Yes, yes."

She had perfected her yeses: the string of them, round and simple and same, like a string of pearls, ending at the same place they had begun. Really, she preferred to be soft on herself. It seemed to her that, as in sex, a certain amount of subjectivity could facilitate a life. Certainly, it made things more pleasant.

"AS A YOUNG MAN," Isabel said, presenting Tasha with an exercise regime, "your father dated a woman named Shelley who loved French fries. Loved them like even you could never imagine. She ate them every day at lunch and dinner. Both meals, if you can believe that. Well, her arteries hardened, of course, as arteries will when you treat them like that, and one day your father let himself into her apartment and she was dead on the floor in front of the television. Dead at twenty-three. Dead on the floor with ketchup on her chin. Is that how you want to end up? If you don't lose the weight, you'll attract a chubby chaser like your father and you'll sit at home eating fried foods until you both have coronaries. Objectively speaking, I think that's the future you have to look forward to if you don't get the weight off as soon as possible."

Isabel never felt more useful than when she was able to exercise someone. She had done it to Ron at the beginning of their courtship. He had been chubby and had liked his women chubby until Isabel came along and exercised him to a fifteen-pound loss. In old photograph albums were picture upon picture of Ron with a mop of curly hair and an agreeable roundness everywhere, especially his stomach, where he tended to rest his arms. The plump, smiling amiability of Ron seemed to contradict Isabel's report of Ron as a fat unhappy teenager, a chubby chaser whose idea of a perfect date was a shared banana split at an ice cream parlour. It was plain with the turn of one album page: Ron's transformation from portly good-times guy to strict measurer of portion size and butter intake, Ron the strategic eater, the stamp of Isabel on his life. Isabel looked much the same then as she did now: dark, ironed hair and long, muscular limbs, hawkish but pretty, severe and elegant, with a surprise glint in her eye that signalled her streak of rowdiness, that impulse towards upheaval.

Tasha's small apartment near Harbord Street was not far from Isabel's house in the Annex, and Isabel began arriving at Tasha's at half past six in the morning to rouse her for exercise. She opened Tasha's curtains and turned on the overhead light. (When Isabel was twenty-one, she had quit smoking cold turkey and she scorned people unable to do the same, people who wallowed in comfort zones and couldn't get to the business of being honest with themselves. Other than her fondness for the word *portly*, she had no inclination for euphemisms of any kind.)

The light allowed for no euphemisms anyway. Because she didn't trust Tasha not to turn out the light and climb back into bed, Isabel stood at the door with her back turned while Tasha got dressed. Tasha moaned and complained, but she allowed it. At half past six, she would have needed more strength not to allow it. Under the thorough glare of the overhead, its brightness made stronger by the dark grey sky of the autumn morning, Tasha was offered a view of her body that she would rather have done without. This pleased Isabel. She felt Tasha would be spurred to action.

The first morning of the new regime, Isabel arrived with Rita. Rita usually worked out by herself at a gym, and Tasha suspected that Rita had been brought along as a motivating force. Overweight for most of her life, Rita had been known to pillage many a fridge until she was thirty-five and started counting all her calories, including quarters of apples and bites of cookies and the half-spoon of sugar in her tea. For ten years, she had exercised vigilantly and kept off the weight. Isabel presented her proudly as a good example. Rita was wearing a red one-piece leotard and bright white running shoes, and her blonde hair was tied back into a tight bun that accentuated her long, slender nose and her prim mouth. Tasha wore an extra-large grey sweatshirt and black sweatpants.

As they walked to the track, Isabel called out, "Let's make it a race. Let's make it a walking race." When they arrived at the high school, they set up camp in the bleachers. Isabel came well supplied, with bottles of water, which everyone drank, and towels, which were also ostensibly for everyone but were understood to be for Tasha since she was the only one who sweated.

"Where will you work out when the cold weather comes?" Rita asked. "Do you plan to join a gym and really tackle this thing at full force?"

"By winter I won't need to jog," Tasha said. "I'll get off the weight by then."

She did not really believe this was true. She didn't see herself as very likely to experience a revolution of body and mind, that coveted leap from portly to svelte. *Svelte*, not *thin*, was the word Isabel used to describe Tasha's desired state. She loved its curt, smooth sound.

Isabel frowned at the track as if trying to see through fog. "That's not the talk of a convert. In fact, that's the talk of a quitter. A portly quitter. That's a pretty bad attitude. Look at Rita. She only weighs 110, and see how keen she is. Isn't that what you want? You've said as much before."

As they warmed up, Tasha thought that she might already be sweating, and as their jog hit full speed, she tried to delay the drips threatening to stream down her face by holding her arm across her forehead. Isabel wouldn't have it.

"If you'd wear a leotard like Rita, you'd be much, much cooler!" she said.

Tasha let her arm drop from her forehead, and she began pumping both arms half-heartedly.

"That's it," Isabel called, several paces ahead. "Sweat it out."

Each salty trickle seemed to confirm Rita's 110 pounds, and Isabel's 117, and her own burbling, resplendent 152. Isabel jogged with Rita and Tasha, but in front by a foot or two, glancing back and lifting her knees high as if to spur them to greater cardiovascular heights. Sometimes she jogged backwards a few paces like an army drill sergeant. She sang while she ran them. At thirty-three, she had discovered Led Zeppelin, and it had been the main music of Tasha's childhood.

"Hey, hey, mama, said the way you MOVE, gonna make you SWEAT, gonna make you GROOVE," she sang, jerking her hand in the air like she was whipping a horse.

The song invigorated Rita, who took a deep breath and stepped up her speed. Isabel pointed to Tasha and held up her stopwatch.

"Oh, oh, child, way you shake that thing, gonna make you BURN, gonna make you STING."

When she sang the word *burn*, she pumped her arms and grimaced. She turned frontwards again and jogged in silence for several paces before turning around again.

"I don't know but I've been told, a BIG-LEGGED woman ain't got no SOUL."

Tasha was certain that here Isabel and Rita were both looking directly at her legs, and she thought that one of Isabel's hand gestures might have been encouraging them all to take in her thighs, which brushed together.

They jogged in silence for some time, and just when Tasha thought she was getting used to the morning air in her throat, her pounding pulse, and the stickiness on her tongue, she felt a palpitation between her breasts, a flutter that felt like a muscle twitch. Instead of slowing down, she began to sprint, as if she could outrun it. She pounded her legs so vigorously that she felt barely in control of them.

"There you go," Isabel shouted. "Way to go!"

Tasha ran faster and faster until her awareness of place slid out from under her. She didn't hear her mother cheering, but ran until she couldn't feel her legs, until her head fell back as if her neck were too weak to support it. The trees encircling the track were hazy in her sightline, and above them, the sky looked blanched and runny. She tried to signal to Isabel, but her hands and arms seemed caught in the motion of running and she couldn't break from the mould. She imagined the paramedics arriving, the attempts at revival, the heads shaking sombrely, then the funeral arrangements, the sparse turnout, the tart maternal eulogy. Finally she stopped running and doubled over with her hands on her knees. She closed her eyes and thought, Please let it come quickly.

"Why did you stop?" Isabel asked. "These things take perseverance."

When Tasha opened her eyes again, the trees had clear outlines, the sky was a solid morning grey.

"Leave me alone, Mother."

"Don't call me that."

Tasha straightened and started walking away from the track.

"I can't imagine what your problem is," Isabel said, walking after her. "Exercise is supposed to put you in a good mood. Every cell of your brain should be engorged with endorphins right now."

Rita looked longingly back at the track, then slowly gathered up the towels and water bottles and trailed Tasha and Isabel at a polite distance.

"Well, now everyone is disappointed," Isabel said. "This behaviour isn't fair to Rita. We all came here to exercise, but look at that—only fifteen minutes and you're ready to quit. No one is impressed."

They walked in a line back to the apartment, Tasha leading the way. Isabel followed in her version of silence: stretches of quiet punctuated with sighs and mutterings to herself. Tasha felt that she had been caught in the scene of a gross impropriety, such as picking her nose. It was the same way she had always felt, especially when it came to her mother. The year she was fifteen, she had been terrified of dying in humiliating circumstances. She had been concerned about sudden heart attacks and massive cerebral accidents, strokes, aneurysms, anything that would cause her to drop dead without warning. She was convinced that it was not only possible, but likely: her body might simply shut down, one normal function derailed, and the whole system would explode silently and magnificently. In the frantic theatre of imagination, she was always involved in something private and embarrassing when this occurred, such as one of her morning naps. On Saturday mornings before she started her homework, she used to lie down, still naked, to nap after a hot shower. Then, just when she was waking up, she felt a gasp in her head, an unwillingness to wake up, and she foresaw the end of her ability to breathe. She pictured them finding her: the cigar-drenched old coroner, repelled and fascinated by her naked body; the aerobic Isabel, wishing she had done more sit-ups; Ron, quiet as ever but clearly disappointed. Conclusions would be drawn. Gathered around her bed, they would hypothesize about the reasons for her nakedness. They would all agree, sadly, upon the same reality. The coroner's report: "Young subject died of a massive stroke while engaged in the act of masturbation." Tasha would watch this from heaven. "No!" she would cry, unheard. "I wasn't! I was napping!" People would be brought in to photograph the angles of her body for the files. *Click:* The head-to-toe overview. *Click:* The subject's hand laid suspiciously over her thigh.

Aside from dying during a nap, Tasha had also imagined dying when she had just gotten out of the bath, or simply while she was changing clothes, her underwear still around her ankles—something tragic, something extraordinary, would come about while she was in some state of undress. Of this she was certain. Dying in such a way would remove all the dignity of untimely death. No one would remember the joy of her in life. The final view—the evidence of overeating and underexercising, the unbecoming flabbiness of an inanimate body—would be all. How sadly people would contemplate her pervertedness. Before long, they would be reassured that her passing was perhaps for the best.

As she walked five paces ahead of her mother, she thought about this. Where did it come from, this constant feeling of having been caught out in an unspeakable idiocy, in a flustered, cataclysmic moment of dishonour? Where did it come from, this belief that her disgraces would speak for her more strongly than anything good she might have done in her life, such as volunteering weekly at a food bank, or walking the dog of her elderly neighbour? To be fair, she had to admit to herself that she hadn't actually done these humanitarian things. But she might. She just might. And she knew that even if she had done these things, even if she lived altruistically, committed good deeds, and thought of others first, she would still feel it came to nothing. Exposure was forever imminent. Exposure and contempt.

The more she ate, the more careful she was to eat in seclusion. And when she lived with Isabel, she resorted to tricks, though they were hardly clever and sophisticated. She knew how to take just enough from all her favourite foods so that nothing initially appeared to be missing. She skimmed a layer of ice cream evenly off the top. She dug under each row of cookies to get to the one beneath. She tried to leave things exactly as they had looked before she got to them so that there could be no immediate discovery of what she had eaten, or at least so that the discoverer of the missing row of cookies would be puzzled about what had happened, would conclude that perhaps mistakes had been made in the packaging process. She was resourceful. She would say to Isabel, "I just looked at the bag of jelly beans, and it was strange how many were gone. Who ate them all?"

Isabel knew what was going on anyway. Ron knew. Rita knew. How could they not know? She didn't want them to think that she ate a lot and was piggish. But what was the alternative? That she couldn't help being portly. She didn't consider how their opinion of her would likely be worse, their disappointment and derision that much stronger, if she put on weight just by looking at food.

How could one live this way, with even fears of death framing themselves around the terror of being caught at something?

One could eat cupcakes, which was what Tasha did when she got home.

WHEN SHE FETCHED her mail in the evening, she noticed a strange letter on top. On the envelope were the words, *Opening this letter may change your life!* She sat at her little kitchen table and stared at the envelope, then threw it out without opening it.

The following day was garbage day, so she emptied her waste-baskets and stuffed her green bags into the communal bins at the back of her building, then went to work. Off and on for the past year, she had been giving Shakespeare workshops to drama classes at high schools around Toronto. She enjoyed the work—it barely felt like work—though she had no passion for it. In a lot of ways, she wished she liked the work less. The presence in her life of enjoyable work was unsettling in a way that tiresome work was not. It made her aware that, even in the absence of reasons to complain, she felt no passion. She doubted that there was ever a time she had felt passion for anything. The high school students made her more sensitive to this. They arrived at drama class feeling lunatic and lighthearted, willing to try anything, to humiliate themselves in the name of fun, so relieved were they to escape the real work of school, the tedious obligations of their core classes. Where was her own passionate lunacy? Where was her willingness to be startled and consumed?

"It's the strangest thing," she told a colleague over lunch, "I can't stop thinking about this stupid, useless letter I got yesterday."

Opening this letter may change your life!

The exclamation point seemed an assault of optimism. Insidious, its pretending at generosity for the sake of a marketing ploy. Worse was its smarmy and ingratiating peddling of false hope. And that knowing smirk underlying it all. She felt that there was yet another person who knew something about her, knew that her life must be unremarkable, that it must need changing.

The colleague, a scrappy and combative woman, said, "That's reading in. The letter wasn't addressed to *you*. Hundreds of people, at least, got that letter. Likely it was a contest you didn't win."

Tasha nodded. More yeses. She had thought of all this.

What bothered her most—this she didn't tell the colleague— was that she hadn't opened the letter before throwing it out. She hadn't failed to open the letter by accident, or because she couldn't spare time to read about a contest she wouldn't win. She had thrown out the letter quite consciously. All day at school, she kept asking herself, Why not open it, then throw it out? She did not want to think that she was disallowing the possibility of changing her life.

She tried to dig it up out of the garbage when she got home, but then she remembered the day was garbage day. The letter was gone.

SHE DIDN'T WANT to be out in the world, and she didn't want to be alone, so she invited the man with the cheese on his lip, Alan, to her apartment. She wanted to be around someone who didn't know all her secrets.

She had decided that she was too submissive the last time they had been out. Too accommodating, too smiling and chirpy, too willing to bend any which way. A bachelor uncle had told her when she was fifteen, "Guys like to date girls who don't talk much and just want to make out." She had taken this advice, perhaps, too lit-erally—and not when she was fifteen, when the advice might actu-ally have helped her, but when she was twenty-five and beyond. Lately, she had begun to feel that she had gone too far in dredging up mindless enthusiasm, a certain required perkiness. She knew that such poses eliminated sultriness. At the end of their last date,

dinner at a small Italian restaurant near the university, she and
Alan had gone back to his apartment, which was a small loft in a
building on Queen Street West. The loft felt wonderfully expansive and smart, with its high ceilings and exposed brick wall and
the kitchen equipped with gleaming appliances, a spotless stainless
steel blender, a toaster free of old crumbs. Her own kitchen was
cheap and stained in various places, filled with hand-me-downs
from her parents and her friends who had moved on to marriage, to
ownership. She had realized, looking around Alan's kitchen, that
she hadn't bought a single thing in her kitchen, not even a knife
or fork. More than anything in her life, it was Alan's loft, the pur-
poseful splendour of it, that reflected her real age back to her. The
morning after their date, and in the week since, she had wished that
she had been less ready to say, *Like fireworks, like a comet streaking
across the night sky, like a meteor.*

Looking around her living room at the time Alan was due to
arrive, she felt dreadfully embarrassed by her apartment. By invit-
ing him there, she had undermined her own plan, for she surely
couldn't act graceful and withdrawn when she was running
around trying to prepare a well-balanced meal while he sat on her
saggy couch. At the last minute, she lit too many candles and
placed them around the living room and dining room, draped a
red throw blanket over the couch, set up a cloudy old mirror from
the basement on the mantel, and arranged more candles inside the
alcove of the unrestored fireplace. She hoped he might think her
charmingly haphazard, her apartment romantic in a casual, bohe-
mian way.

She wondered, as she made these adjustments, whether she
even liked him.

Alan arrived, apologizing, with a dog he had adopted from a
shelter the day before. The dog, which looked like a silky black
German shepherd, had begun to yowl when he left, he explained,

which was not surprising, considering that she became distraught even when he left one room to go to another. He said that what the dog liked best was to sit at his feet, panting. The shelter staff had named the dog Fanny, but he was thinking of Smudge, the name of his childhood dog. Tasha thought it rather morbid to name a new dog after a dead dog, and this dog looked as little like a Smudge as it did like a Fanny.

Alan hovered nervously over the dog and kept opening his mouth and looking at Tasha as if he were about to say something. The boldness of his bed voice was gone. There was no more issuing of instructions, no further soliciting of more imaginative descriptions. He even looked different than he had looked lying next to her in bed. He seemed paler and thinner, his chin that much more recessive. So concerned was he that Tasha might object to the dog that he offered to tie her under the kitchen table. He thought the dog wouldn't mind that, as long as she could see him.

Tasha had worried that she couldn't handle seeing him again. Something too revelatory had taken place when they were in bed together. Too much, it seemed like their true, needful characters had been exposed, and somehow without their consent. Luckily, he had now reverted to the man with the cheese on his lip, but without the cheese.

"They didn't know her past, the shelter people," he said. "She was collected as a stray. But they loved her there. They absolutely assured me that she had shown no aggression, not to dogs or to people."

He seemed to think that Tasha was afraid of the dog, though she had done nothing to indicate this. Every time the dog moved in Tasha's direction, Alan was on the edge of his seat making kissing noises, coaxing her back to him. There was something of a paternal reprimand in the way he would call the dog back when Tasha reached out to the dog to give pats. Tasha resented it, and was reassured by it. She perceived that she had regained some advantage.

"We had a dog that ran away when I was a kid. My family did," he said.

"That's unusual," Tasha said, coming in from the kitchen with two glasses of wine. "Dogs don't tend to run away, do they?"

She felt light and casual now, feeling his tension, her advantage.

"Well, the circumstances were exceptional," he said. "There was a lot going on. I think the dog was confused about various things. We kept waiting for her to come back."

"When I was a girl, I had a friend whose family moved to Toronto from Prince Edward County, out in the country near Picton. They left their dog with another family who had lived near them on a farm, a family that had lots of dogs roaming around in and out of the house and the barn all the time. They seemed happy, the dogs, but they couldn't have gotten much attention. My friend's family's dog loved to run and run, and they were afraid that she would be miserable in the city. They were convinced that she would be happier on the farm. My mother was very judgemental about this. We never had a dog, but my mother believed that once you got a dog, that was it, you kept it no matter what. She even stopped speaking to my friend's mother, who was an old friend of hers, because she gave the dog away. But anyway, the dog ran away, back to its old house—which was miles and miles away—and lay on the porch, waiting and waiting for the family to come back. The new family living there eventually took it in because my friend's mother wouldn't budge. She kept insisting that the dog would be miserable in Toronto. My mother had a mammoth fight on the phone with her once. 'We have dogs in Toronto!' she screamed. 'Toronto families have been known to keep dogs.' What was my point though? Oh, yes, that dogs don't usually run away from their families. They run to them."

"Yes, well, as I said, our circumstances were unusual," he said somewhat defensively, then got up to go stand by the window.

Tasha thought, Only I could lose my advantage so quickly.

"It's awfully hot in here," he said. "Do you mind if I open the window? I think Fanny, Smudge, needs air."

An image had stuck in Tasha's mind, of her mother on the phone in the kitchen, yelling at her friend over giving the dog away, and of herself standing in the doorway, trying to figure out some way she could smooth things over between them. How was it that she remembered that sinking feeling so well, the despair of knowing that if the mothers were at odds, her own friendship would be over too? That heady despair, the wretchedness of having no control over her own life, the melancholy and moodiness. When her mother hung up the phone, she felt that her life was over. The finality of a hung-up phone, Isabel's righteous cool, her unwillingness to seem the least bit sorry. But everything wasn't final. Isabel's friend had kept calling, trying to explain her position, reasoning with Isabel, and pleading for some understanding. Isabel was rigid, but eventually gave way in small, grudging increments. Whenever the phone rang, Isabel made Tasha answer it. "Oh, God, is it her again?" she would moan. Isabel never lost her advantages. How was this?

"That goddamn dog," she had said at last, giving in. "All this over a dog."

Tasha couldn't figure out whether Isabel truly loved dogs, or generally found them convenient to use as leverage when she had a point to make. When Tasha was fifteen, Isabel had promised to buy her a dog if she lost ten pounds. This was the first time Isabel had tried to exercise Tasha, to get the weight off. She had pointed out that Tasha's baby fat was blossoming into full-fledged adult flab. She had consulted with Tasha's pediatrician, Dr. Solomon, behind closed doors, then returned with a weight-loss plan, a 1,200-calorie-a-day diet. This was also the first time Tasha ever realized that people were looking at her, that they were seeing something different from what she saw when she looked at herself. Her body had become the subject of medical scrutiny. Even then, Tasha had been reluctant to follow her mother's orders, though she

was equally inefficient at outright rebellion. Her way was to follow along, sort of. To do what she liked, sort of. It was difficult to
respect yourself when you lived along such margins.

Isabel had come upon the dog bribe when six months had
passed and Tasha had lost only two pounds. Isabel couldn't get
to the bottom of Tasha's eating strategies. "I know you're cheating," she would say. "I don't know how, but I will crack this." Her
will was formidable, but her logic skills were, for some unaccount-
able reason, quite clumsy. "How are you cheating? How?" she
kept asking. It escaped her that she was dealing with an expert.
Isabel called around to various dog breeders, took copious notes,
and told Tasha that if she lost just ten pounds, the puppy she had
been begging for since she was five would be hers. But much as
Tasha wanted it—and she did want it very badly—she came to a
stop at six pounds. The more vehemently she told herself that she
was almost at the goal and that she mustn't, mustn't eat badly, the
less able she was to control her cravings. She had taken to sneak-
ing down to the kitchen after her parents were in bed and pouring
herself a bowl of Cheerios sprinkled with brown sugar, then washing the bowl and putting it back in the cupboard so no one could
guess what had happened. At one Saturday morning weigh in, she
had not lost a pound, but gained two. Isabel held up the dog maga-
zines and information packages from breeders and dumped them
ceremoniously in the garbage.

"We never had a dog," Tasha said to Alan, "but I did want
one—desperately, in fact. You were very lucky, to have had one
for a time."

Alan returned to the couch. "She was a good dog. She was very
loyal, although I'm sure it doesn't sound that way."

"What do I know about dogs? I've never had one, after all."

She had put out an appetizer plate of raw vegetables, a suggestion made by Isabel, who had been shocked to hear that Tasha could
want to see Alan again, after the cheese situation. She gave Tasha

menu suggestions, which Tasha took in spite of herself. When she
ate in front of men, she always restricted herself to healthy food.
She had in the oven a roast chicken and root vegetables.

While they ate, the dog lay at Tasha's feet. (Alan had finally,
after much coaxing, let the dog be and allowed it to wander where
it wanted.) He was immensely appreciative of the chicken, which
was overcooked, and he claimed it tò be the best roast chicken he
had ever tasted. He insisted that he preferred chicken a little bit dry,
a quirk left over from childhood. Relaxing, he also admitted that,
when he was a child, he wouldn't eat egg salad with mayonnaise
but loved egg salad made with water. He and his mother and sister
would go on picnics at a conservation area not too far from where
they lived, and his mother would produce from a wicker basket
two separate versions of egg salad sandwiches, as well as frozen
peas, chocolate chip cookies without the chocolate chips, and
watered-down milk. He and his sister would go tearing around her
in circles, whooping in excitement.

"If you like your food with water," Tasha said, "then it stands to
reason that you wouldn't like your chicken dry."

"What can I say? I was a weird kid. I also made my mother
wring out my steaks so they were good and dry too."

He was the kind of adult who was difficult to picture as a
child—unlike herself, whom she imagined to be still very close
to that apple-cheeked, frizzy-hair girl who liked her egg salad
with as much mayonnaise as possible. She had altogether forgotten that she had slept with this man, that they had lain naked
together (naked, but expertly arranged under a sheet) in his roomy
king-sized bed. There was a distance, not uncomfortable, between
them. It was a kind distance, warm, the benevolent distance that
exists when discovery lies ahead. She had forgotten the cheese on
his lip. He had eaten every mouthful of dinner with deliberation, a
kind of cautious relish, as if he were eating a rich dessert. He was

methodical and calm, concentrating, and watching him filled her with an affection and gratitude. He was very much unlike her, and she liked him very much.

She told him about her job teaching Shakespeare workshops, and he was impressed that she had tried to be an actor. He believed it was brave, so she didn't tell him that it was the opposite, that she couldn't figure out what to do with her life, and that acting felt less like work than any other job she could come up with. Of the workshops, she told him, "I worry. Should they let me near the kids when sometimes all I want to do is say to them, 'Do you have any idea how stupid you are? Do you know that you might be the stupidest person I've ever met in my life?' I would never say that, of course, but I fantasize." She told stories of how noisy and disobedient the students were, how they disrupted the class by making bird noises or giggling maliciously, although as she spoke, she felt guilty that she was unable to represent anything as it was, that in telling stories she always misplaced the truth of them. So she told him about how she worried sometimes that she had never had a passion for any work she had done.

He said, "You're still young. You have so much time to find out what you have passion for."

"Nevertheless," she said. "Well, no, not nevertheless. I'm not so young. If I had passion for something, I'd surely have a sense of that by the age of thirty."

"If you had no passion in you, you wouldn't worry about that." He reached across the table and touched the hair at her temple.

The dog started paddling at the door.

"She needs to go out. Smudge-Fanny," he called, holding out the leash, "Fanny-Smudge, come. She doesn't really look like a Smudge. I don't know if this name is going to take."

"I have to be honest," Tasha said. "I don't understand why you want to name this dog after a dog who ran away from you and who, presumably, died doing so." She was laughing. She thought it could be funny, if she got her tone right.

He took the dog out, to the small park across the street, and she watched him from the window. When he returned (to her relief—she had imagined him walking on, into the darkness beyond the trees), he sat down in the middle of the couch and said, "I don't know why I'm bent on naming this dog Smudge. It was a name we all came up with together, my family. We absolutely loved that dog. Especially my mother. We didn't neglect her. It was that my sister died. We thought that was why she ran away. Or that had something to do with it, somehow."

She did like ferreting out information when she suspected secrets were being held. She had been pushing for something, a story, though certainly not this one.

He told her that his sister had died when she was ten and he was thirteen. She had been killed in a snowmobile accident at a friend's winter chalet in northern Ontario. The girls were taking turns riding on an inner tube behind a snowmobile driven by the friend's older brother. On his sister's ride, the brother made a sharp turn on a plain of ice, sending her flying off and directly through a line of flimsy young trees that had been planted just that fall. He said that they had been travelling at such speed that the force of his sister's body had been so strong as to bend the fledgling tree trunks back into perfect arches to the ground. Uncooperative and fighting for breath, she was flown by helicopter to Sick Children's Hospital, and she died from her injuries several hours later.

The dog had run away a month or two later. Some people speculated that it went looking for her, and some people thought it couldn't bear the sorrow in the house.

His mother had been a tall, Nordic type, fair-skinned and hearty and sensible. She lost twenty pounds in the months that followed, and she spent all her time reading novels in her bedroom.

The only time she refused to be in the bedroom was at night. For two years, she slept in a rocking chair in the kitchen. Alan had heard his parents arguing about this. One night when he was fifteen, he came home late to find her there, curled up in the rocker with the engravings from the back of the chair pressed into her cheek like pillow creases. When he touched her, she tried to pretend that she had fallen asleep there by accident while reading. This was her nature, he said.

"I suppose it doesn't make sense that I would want to name the dog Smudge," Alan said. "Considering."

"No," Tasha said. "But then, maybe yes."

"My mother still spends all her time reading novels," he said. "I know this because I've caught her. But if you were to arrive at her house, you would never guess. You would think she was the happiest person you'd ever met."

In Tasha's favourite stories and novels, mothers often spent all their time reading. These mothers were contented and self-contained, nurturing independent inner lives. They were marvellously and benignly neglectful, and Tasha had spent most of her life wishing her own mother were like this. She had thought of maternal escape as a delightful thing, an assertion of freedom, the quiet battle with indomitable children won. It hadn't occurred to her that such mothers might be hiding for other reasons—not a shirking of duty, but duty's purest expression, protecting their children from themselves.

Alan told her that his mother made him dozens of plastic containers filled with food. He did not say that such a thing could be a burden, but it was there, in his voice.

She told him then about the exercising. "My mother prefers to take my food away," she said, laughing just a little.

By then, they were sitting close on the couch. He didn't say, "A curvy body can be an asset if you dress it properly." He didn't say,

"I prefer a woman with meat on her bones." He didn't say, "I think fashion models are disgusting."

What he said, softly, was "You have a laugh that could move mountains."

She closed her eyes and thought she might cry.

Funny, the things that could get through.

YEARS LATER, Tasha still sometimes thinks of this night. It has taken on great meaning, not because she expected to end up with Alan at the end of it, but because she didn't expect it. They had lain awake all night with the dog sleeping soundly at their feet. He had paid much attention to the soft-skinned underside of her arms. But she would never have guessed. She hadn't prepared for good fortune. It continues to amaze her how her life could change course so abruptly and so quietly, without her own jubilant, terrified readiness.

Isabel called Tasha at ten o'clock the following morning. She and Alan were just eating the breakfast he had prepared, pancakes with fresh blueberries and real maple syrup.

"Did you enjoy sleeping in?" Isabel asked. "I'm assuming you did, without me banging down your door."

Tasha said that she had.

"Well, I'm happy to tell you that you can get used to it," said Isabel. "From now on, I'm going to exercise with Rita. I know I should let you be. I will let you be."

How suddenly Tasha's burdens had lifted then. How surprising, what settled in their place. Not joy, crazy release, a glimpse of her coveted independence, but something else altogether—disorienting calm, a freedom that felt remarkably like sadness.

ACKNOWLEDGEMENTS

I am grateful to the many people who have supported me along the way: Jill Bridge, Edward Bridge, Philippa Bridge-Cook, and Jeremy Bridge-Cook; John Maxwell, Mark Rogers, and Ken Hunt for being the best first readers and most caring critics I could have imagined; the Toronto Arts Council and my understanding employers at Humber College; and especially Elisabeth Harvor, whose brilliance and encouragement, quite simply, changed my life.

Versions of these stories first appeared in *Toronto Life*, *Descant*, PRISM *international*, *Prairie Fire*, *The Journey Prize Anthology 17*, and *05: Best Canadian Stories*. Thanks to the editors of these publications, and in particular to Camilla Gibb.

Thanks to my editor, Jennifer Glossop, and to my agent, Anne McDermid.

And most of all, with gratitude beyond words, to Peter Wambera, for being extraordinary.